Passage from Home

To
Vasiliki Georgia Sarantakis

Passage from Home

by

Isaac Rosenfeld

with a new foreword by
Mark Shechner
State University of New York at Buffalo

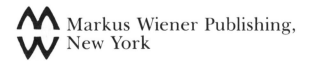 Markus Wiener Publishing,
New York

*MASTERWORKS OF MODERN JEWISH WRITING SERIES is
issued in conjunction with the Center for the Study of The American
Jewish Experience, Hebrew Union College—Jewish Institute for
Religion, Cincinnati.*

First Markus Wiener Publishing Edition 1988

© Copyright 1988 for the introduction by Mark Shechner
© Copyright 1946 for Passage from Home by Vasiliki
Rosenfeld

For information write to:
Markus Wiener Publishing, Inc.
2901 Broadway, New York, NY 10025

Cover design, Cheryl Mirkin
Cover photo courtesy of Barbara Rubin

Library of Congress Cataloging-in-Publication Data

Rosenfeld, Isaac, 1918–1956.
    Passage from home.

    (Masterworks of modern Jewish writing series)
    Reprint. Originally published: Cleveland, Ohio :
Work Pub. Co., 1946.
    I. Title.   II. Series.
PS3535.07138P37   1988   813'.54   87-40105
ISBN 0-910129-75-4

Printed in the United States of America.

Introduction

Every age has its theme words, its verbal icons and semantic beacons that footnote its history, highlight its conflicts, and trace, however hazily, the stream of its consciousness. In the 1940s, words that gained favor among a small but influential group of intellectuals were "crisis," "transition," and "alienation," this last of which was virtually a cult term among those homeless radicals who saw life "without dogma and without hope" as their fate and, making a virtue of necessity, their refuge as well.

Unlike key words of more militant eras, "exploitation," "struggle," and "masses" in the thirties, or "self-determination" and "participatory democracy" in the sixties, alienation was anything but a call to action. Though it came in many packages, of various Marxist, existentialist, and psychiatric origin, alienation came into common use as a term of negation, signalling a dual rejection of American life and the orchestrated insurgency and partisan dogmatism of the revolutionary left. By and large it was the password of the post-Marxist fraternity that had migrated from faction and dogma to homelessness and indecision, pronouncing as it went its standing antipathy to a bureaucratic and materialistic America and its born-again immunity to party and line. One version of the alienated's creed was that of the Daniel Bell, at the time a young sociologist and an editor at, of all places, *Fortune* magazine, who had been scarred by the faction fights of the left and disillusioned by the *cul de sac* into which revolutionary Marxism had led him. In 1946 he would broadcast his estrangement in this fashion:

> " . . . The intellectual knows too well the ambiguities of motives and interests which dictate

individual and institutional action. He cannot surrender himself wholly to any movement. Nor can he make those completely invidious or utopian judgments regarding the nature and needs of man which the cynic and romantic make. He can only live without dogma and without hope. He can only, as an intellectual, realize his destiny—and by consciously accepting it, rework it—through seeing the world, in Friedrich Schiller's phrase, as disenchanted."

Bell is a prime witness here, since this credo of alienation came at the end of a review of Isaac Rosenfeld's *Passage from Home,* which Bell read as a parable of post-Marxist nausea *and* Jewish uprootedness: a summary of "the phylogeny of a race in its search for moral independence. . . ." However, in taking Rosenfeld for a troubadour of alienation, Bell was doing little more than taking cues from Rosenfeld himself, who placed in the mouth of his hero, the fourteen-year-old Bernard Miller, avowals of desolation that rang with the lonely metaphysics of the decade.

"I had come to know a certain homelessness in the world, and took it for granted as a part of nature: had seen in the family, and myself acquired, a sense of sadness from which both assurance and violence had forever vanished. We had accepted it unconsciously and without self pity, as one might accept a sentence that had been passed generations ago, whose terms were still binding though its occasion had long been forgotten. The world is not entirely yours; and our reply is: very well then, not entirely."

"The world is not entirely yours; and our reply is: very well then, not entirely." Behind such spiritual-heroic renunciations as this—and they were legion—lay the bitter experience of the Marxist Fall of the thirties (Spain, the Moscow Trials, the Stalin-Hitler pact) and knowledge of the Holocaust, of which Rosenfeld was painfully aware but his teenage hero innocent. Because of that, *Passage from Home* is both more than the vision of intellectual home-lessness that Bell would claim it to be and less. It is more in the sense that as the story of a specifically Jewish childhood in pre-war Chicago it possesses the savor and grit of a particular ethnic milieu that no metaphysics of alienation can possibly account for. But it is less inasmuch as the shocks and disenchantments registered in its language have not yet descended upon its characters; the great public unmasking of Stalin, which was a profound event for Jews of radical temperament, was still around the corner, and the death camps were still up the road. Fourteen years old some time in the early 1930s—the year in *Passage from Home* is not precisely given—Bernard Miller knows only the agonies of his own childhood, not the horrors of his generation. It is the book's singular weakness that its author bears the sorrows of Judea in his heart while his main character knows only the sorrows of the young Miller.

Passage from Home tells the story of a summer in the life of Bernard Miller, who at fourteen flees his father's house in a quest for adventure and knowledge, which he hopes to find in the company of his Aunt Minna, whose Bohemian life gives tantalizing promise of thrilling, possibly sexual, adventures. On visits to her apartment, where he frequently turns up unannounced, he makes amorous advances to his aunt which she peremptorily rejects. At last, in order to gain entry to Minna's life, Bernard stages an introduction to "cousin" Willy, a hillbilly and migrant from the South who had been married to his cousin Martha, who had died three years before. Bernard's motives are murky, though they seem to involve an erotic attachment to Minna as well as a need to escape the house of his father, a fussy, sour autocrat.

The introduction, awkward and comical at the outset, is a success, and it is not long before the unemployed Willy moves in with Minna to form precisely what Bernard, playing teenage *shadkhen,* has been angling for: an alternative household for himself. A family quarrel, instigated by Minna's unexpected appearance at his father's birthday party, gives Bernard the opportunity to storm out of the house in Minna's wake and attach himself, unbidden, to her and Willy. With its books, its records, its casual untidiness and simple utilitarian furnishings, Minna's apartment is everything his home is not, seeming at first blush to offer the passion and freedom that his young manhood demands.

> The pictures on the wall, their wild, broken colors and unrecognizable forms, took on meaning and welcomed me. Here dwelt that spirit which we barred from our lives, and in its freedom it was friendly, not raging, and not destructive, but liberal. This was its natural home.

The romance of Bohemia starts to sour, however, as Bernard takes up residence on a cot between the table and the sink, amid the dirty dishes and the cockroaches. Art, freedom, and eros have sunk their roots in disorder, and Bernard's delicate senses, schooled in fastidiousness, are repelled by the untidiness of this emancipation. "I went to the sink to wash under the tap, but saw a roach scurrying across the drainboard and drew back, nauseated. The moment of nausea was in the nature of a perception and the kitchen suddenly became for me a room of utter disorder, the paint flaking over the sink, the wall behind the stove streaked with dirt and grease." As for the erotic, there are quarrels in the dark and the fearsome sounds of drunken coupling—alcohol!—from behind closed doors.

Bernard's escapade with Minna turns out to be a training in disillusionment, as one by one the veils of romance peel away from Minna's life like paint from a tenement wall. Bernard looks upon Minna and Willy naked and sees only nakedness, not revelation. His cot is lousy with bedbugs that commute nightly across his body. The lovers quarrel. The odd menage is finally shattered when Minna and Willy separate, as Willy turns out to be a freeloader who has been using Minna for a meal ticket, and Minna herself proves to be married to another man, a Jewish cabaret owner named Fred Mason with whom, for secret reasons, she cannot live. And the separation is effected cruelly, at a party that Minna and Mason throw for the purpose of humiliating Willy and driving him away.

Summer over, his options closed, Bernard boards the streetcar and heads ruefully home, to his stepmother's cleanliness and order, his father's silence and disapproval. " 'So you're back,' " is all his father can muster as he enters. "In my embarrassment I avoided him, keeping my eyes averted to the floor, and while I still expected him to speak to me, it seemed to me that he, too, was staring at the floor. I saw him turn and leave and go to the front room. There, I knew, he would stand at the window, looking out." Avoiding the "cliché of the resolved mood," as Rosenfeld once called it, the novel leaves its themes unresolved: Willy fades away, Minna's history with the family remains unexplained, father and son are no closer at the end than they had been at the beginning. The novel is as untidy as Minna's kitchen. The passage from home leads only back

[v]

home, but to what? To vexation and bewilderment, to a father at the window looking self-consciously out, to a son at the door peering self-consciously in.

This is admittedly a thin plot, poignant at moments of separation and return but no more so than a hundred novels of domestic travail before and since. What summons us back to this novel, however, is not its plot but the ambience in which it is carried out: a Jewish world in crisis in which the conflicts of father and son, more than just household spats, are symbols of a revolution in culture and belief that was changing American Jewry from a transplanted old world culture to something distinctly new and American. The mood of the book and its historical moment transcend the story and transform it into something more capacious than a mere record of Bernard Miller's experiences.

Passage from Home is a litany of the woes that were festering in Isaac Rosenfeld's heart as he wrote it, and with the solemnity of David at psalms he wrote about his childhood as if by incantations of regret he could exalt the miseries of a Chicago boyhood into world-historical rites of passage. That was not so vain an ambition, since the conflict between Bernard and his father is, in one sense, just a summer stock rendition of the same drama that was being played out everywhere in Jewish life: the drama of culture and family in crisis. As documentary, *Passage from Home* takes its place as a fairly typical novel of Jewish life as we have come to know it since vernacular Jewish fiction began to be written a century ago. From Mendele Mocher Sforim's *The Travels of Benjamin III*, in which Benjamin deserts his wife to go off in search of the Ten Tribes, to the novels of Saul Bellow and Philip Roth, where the family is already a museum piece and the Jewish man is usually found casting off his first (or second or third) shikse amid much wailing and gnashing of teeth, the decline of the Jewish family under the impact of modern conditions seems to be the most hackneyed of Jewish themes.

The Jewish family *in extremis,* then, was already a cliche by the time Rosenfeld got around to it, and indeed some of the bitterest portrayals of it are to be found in the domestic storm and stress literature of the 1920s and 1930s: in the explosive battles of father and daughter in Anzia Yezierska's *Bread Givers;* in the blows visited by father upon son in Henry Roth's *Call It Sleep;* in the omnibus bickerings and betrayals that mark Clifford Odets' *Awake and Sing.* In such company, *Passage from Home* seems to be a routine dramatization of Jewish civilization and its discontents, the son longing to take flight from the father, the father distant and inscrutable, given to sudden rages and bursts of rejection. But in *Passage from Home,* a book published twenty-one years, and thus a generation, after Yezierska's account of a young woman's bid for liberation from the family, the father's world is already a threadbare remnant of the Jewish tradition. In *Bread Givers,* at least, the father is a student of Torah, his iron dominion over his daughters sanctioned by his role as the keeper of law and preserver of memory. It is not an appealing picture of the Jewish tradition, since the father's immersion in study appears to be a mask for self-interest, but it is one in which the traditional elements of the family are initially in place, even if they must be shattered for the next generation to breathe freely. By contrast, the Jewish world in *Passage from Home* is already a decomposed one in which the father's tyranny has been divorced from any semblance of religious authority. He has inherited the Hebraic strictness of conscience but nothing of its piety and harmony. An American, Chicago born, he knows—to borrow a formula from Abraham Joshua Heschel—the danger and gloom of this world but not the infinite beauty of heaven or the holy mysteries of piety. Where Yezierska's father sat wrapped in phylacteries, Rosenfeld's sits wrapped only in sadness, and the son's revolt is infused with pity for the father and a nostalgia for a past with which he has no contact except through the grandfather.

It is precisely in this that *A Passage from Home* departs from the routines of Jewish revolt literature, for it is not toward the shabby avant-gardism of Minna's walkup that Bernard is finally impelled, though he does not understand this at once. The zone of enchantment, rather, is in the past, which has been there all along. Sent to his grandparents for a refresher course in "the Jewish spirit," Bernard does a tour of the old neighborhood with his grandfather. In his daily life, the grandfather is a petty man, a maestro of grievance and vanity, and as he leads Bernard through the streets of the old Jewish section, descanting on this one's fortunes and that one's bankruptcies, Bernard is repelled by this "poor, overdone figure of an old man, [with] his endless complaints and ironies, his arrogance, wit, familiarity, his pinchings and pettings, angers and cranks, his constant, unalleviated *shlepperei.*"

Yet on these walks, as nowhere else, Bernard's sense are stirred and the novel vibrates with the color and vividness of those teeming streets in which the Jews first settled upon their arrival in America. The return to the old neighborhood calls to mind the grandfather's old grocery store, a sad kennel of a shop that had gone bankrupt and has since been spruced up and made profitable by a new owner.

> Flat tins of sardines he had in profusion—little
> oval cans, key attached, wrapped in wax paper

with red labels pasted on, bearing the portrait of a Norwegian king. A tub of butter stood in the window of the ice box, tilted toward the customers. Eggs lay in a trough behind the counter and in unopened crates on the floor. The ice box leaked, and the scattered sawdust always turned damp and gave off a sour odor.

A little epiphany of old world defeat amid new world abundance, it was more a state of mind than a business, a piece of stirring, history-laden *shlepperei*, like the grandfather himself. Eventually, this *Spatziergang* leads to the home of Reb Feldman, an aging *melamed* at whose house a small band of Hasidim gathers to drink tea, play chess, kibbitz, and trade theses and conundrums from Talmud and Torah, while in the corner, propped on a divan, lies the *melamed*, a man with a puffy face, a black beard, and rings on his fingers. Like the grandfather's ancient store, this apartment, reeking of age and decay also throbs with passion. Here, amid the shabbiness and the pilpul, the chess and the tea, the stained fingers and the earlocks, something quite magical is taking place, the transubstantiation of Jewish law into sacred music. Without any visible cues from Reb Feldman, the gray room begins to ring with divinity.

In a corner of the room sat two men playing chess. I had not noticed them when I came in. Their light was poor and, as they bent over the board, they themselves seemed like nothing so much as chessmen, knights with narrow, pendulant faces, carved out of bone to which skin and hair still clung. They did not speak to each other, but occasionally one struck up a melody in which his partner joined, humming and intoning the syllables, "aie, dai, dai, dai dai—yam, bim, bom." Together they would nod over the melody, sharing and extending it, turning their hands in and out at the wrist, their elbows planted before them on the table. During pauses in the discussion one could hear them, and the melody also seemed to be issuing in an undertone from the remote and ponderous Feldman, as well as the men at our table, a slight weaving rhythm catching their heads.

What Bernard hears is the niggun, the little melody that underlies every Jewish prayer, suddenly arise in a wave of song and fill the room. Here, off to the corner of the novel, is its center, a sanctuary of light within Judaism in which the young man experiences the joy and the community he fails to find at home. Here is the living heart of ecstatic Judaism in exile, playing out its last days as an ancient, minor cult in the houses of Chicago.

Seeing the light among these men, Bernard vows to seek it in himself:

> For, as at Feldman's house, when I had seen a moment of understanding pass before a group of old men and had felt that this represented what was best in their lives and in Jewish life, so I now felt that possession of such understanding would be the very best of my own life, and knowing the truth, itself a kind of ecstasy.

But this is an ecstasy from which Bernard is locked out, the keys to it having been lost by his father. His own sundering from his father, indeed, is a replica of his father's sundering from his roots, and it is his artist's birthright: "tradition as discontinuity," to take a phrase from Irving Howe. Bernard's fate lies no more with Reb Feldman than it does with Aunt Minna. For better or for worse, he is sentenced to America and alienation.

Rosenfeld didn't set out to write a parable for his age. He wrote rather to soothe his own lacerated heart and purge it of its poisons. In so doing, however, he drew a profile of contemporary Jewish life in which the decomposition of his own family took on a certain collective meaning. The passage from home was the standard experience of Jewish boys of his generation, a collective emigration of the spirit away from the uncertain Judaism of their parents, which was especially agonizing for having to be undertaken alone. Like other adolescents of his time, Bernard Miller has two Bar Mitzvahs: the ceremony in which he takes his place as a man in the Jewish community and the trial by ordeal that initiates him into the actual terms of his life: the strangeness of his relation to Jewish tradition, the pain of his relation to the world, the hardness of his transactions with himself.

Moreover, as a typical post war world-disenchantment book, *Passage from Home* shared the climate of diffuse indolence that was endemic to books of the age, from Bellow's *Dangling Man* (1944) and *The Victim* (1947), to Lionel Trilling's *The Middle of the Journey* (1947), Delmore Schwartz's *The World is a Wedding* (1948), and Arthur Miller's *Death of a Salesman* (1949), to name just a few. In all these, excepting Trilling's novel, in which the politics are in the foreground, the critical events usually transpire in the parlor or the kitchen where the explicit drama is a domestic one. But in all too, the nimbus of history looms just beyond the horizon of consciousness, unremarked by the characters, but casting a shadow of menace over them all, like a motion picture soundtrack. "This is the experience of the generation that has come to maturity during the depression," wrote Delmore Schwartz in 1944, "the sanguine period of the New Deal, the days of the Popular Front and the days of Munich and the slow, loud, ticking imminence of a new war." Schwartz was speaking of *Dangling Man*, but he might have said the same of any of these books that, written in the 1940s, testify to the agonies of recent history.

Brilliant as its moment was, however, alienation would probably have left a dimmer trace had it not found embodiment in a style through which it gained a kind of embalmed second life. The alienation of the Jewish intellectuals was a distinctly literary affair, something like the romantic despair of eighteenth-century Germany when *Werther* was the rage and young men in blue coats and yellow vests went around reading *Ossian* in tribute to the century's first martyr to bourgeois normality. To Rosenfeld and a few others, most notably his high school friend and literary comrade-in-arms, Saul Bellow, alienation meant Dostoevsky, and *Passage from Home* is as much the Dostoevskian novel in American garb as were Bellow's novels of that era: *Dangling Man* and *The Victim*. For both Bellow and Rosenfeld, who were children of Russian Jews, Dostoevsky called up the romantic strangeness of a world they knew only through legend and literature but could feel in the strained atmospherics of their own homes. For both too, the pre-revolutionary Dostoevsky came to be a symbol of their own post-revolutionary malaise. By pointing the way to levels of the problematic beyond the agit-prop commonplaces of the 1930s and by being the prophet, as they saw it, of the decline of the Russian revolution into Stalinism, Dostoevsky became the muse of their apostasy from politics. Rosenfeld and Bellow were even known in New York as "the Chicago Dostoevskians" for the somber and "Russian" mood they sought to capture in their early writing and for their heroes, inhabiting imaginary Saint Petersburgs and acting out mute and desperate yearnings in their searches for redemption through self-abasement. In his journals, Rosenfeld touted Dostoevsky's underground man as his "patron saint," declaiming, "I hold to the conviction—it amounts to something of a theory—that embarrassment represents the true state of affairs, and the sooner we strike shame, the sooner we draw blood."

The libretto of *Passage from Home* was set to Dostoevskian melodies, as Rosenfeld set about striking shame in the hope of drawing blood. The character of Bernard is a clear bid to plumb the emotions to their root in order to expose the illness that in his Dostoevskian days he would see as shame but in a later, Reichian, moment would think of as a sexual plague. Stalking his Aunt Minna in the streets, placing his ear to her door, walking in on a naked, sleeping Willy and Minna, Bernard compulsively places himself in humiliating positions as though exposure and shame were precisely what he was seeking. His relations with his father especially are exchanges of embarrassment and guilt, the father tormenting the son out of impotent love, the son denying the father, whose love he can approach only through torment. " . . . I felt guilt not only in my own behalf; it was for his guilt, too, that I was being punished. I bore his guilt as I bore the equal burden of his love. I was his son, and bound to suffer." In such families, natural expressions of human affection are prohibited, and love comes only in the form of stratagems.

Bernard is not the book's lone undergroundling. There is also Fred Mason, Minna's secret husband, whose appetite for humiliation is so voracious as to mark him as a virtual distillate of the underground character. Unpredictable, self-mocking, wounded to the core by Minna's refusal to live with him and yet ready to do her bidding on an instant's notice, he is a neurotic whose Jewish identity, cut off from ritual, belief, and community, expresses itself only in symptoms. In such a dead-end Judaism, the Jewish character is robbed of all that is distinctive and positive and reduced to being little more than a breed of disablement. Bernard sees Mason as a mystic who "spelled out the invisible truth from the letters of the invisible world. (In his own fashion, I suppose, one might call him a mystic—a mystic who elevated not holiness but vulgarity to a fantastic principle.)" And it is precisely in his extremity, in the perfection of his alienation, that Mason takes on meaning, for he is Bernard's own mirror on the wall, the man in whom the distortions of the heart that are just incubating in Bernard have grown florid and monstrous.

Passage from Home was an auspicious debut for a young writer; just 28 years old in 1946, Rosenfeld had a bright career before him. Two years earlier he had published a striking first story, "The Hand that Fed Me," in *Partisan Review,* and a year later had won a *Partisan Review* award with his second story, "The Colony." With *Passage from Home,* he would appear to have been launched upon a major career, and by some measure he was. At the time of his death of a heart attack in 1956, just ten years after *Passage,* he had published some twenty short stories* and well over one hundred essays and reviews. Though not so dramatic a success as Bellow, who by 1956 had *Dangling Man, The Victim, The Adventures of Augie March,* and *Seize the Day* under his belt and was well on his way to becoming

*There are several selections of Rosenfeld's essays and stories. For essays and reviews, see Isaac Rosenfeld, *An Age of Enormity: Life and Writing in the Forties and Fifties,* edited and introduced by Theodore Solotaroff. Cleveland: The World Publishing Company, 1962. A selection of Rosenfeld's best stories can be found in *Alpha and Omega: Stories by Isaac Rosenfeld.* New York: The Viking Press, 1966. A recent collection combining some of both with selections from Rosenfeld's journals is *Preserving the Hunger: An Isaac Rosenfeld Reader,* edited and introduced by Mark Shechner. Detroit: Wayne State University Press, 1987.

America's leading novelist, Rosenfeld was a writer to be reckoned with, a regular presence in the pages of the *Partisan* and *Kenyon* reviews and, especially, *The New Republic*, where for a while he was an associate editor.

However, though Rosenfeld would later write a clutch of brilliant stories, his promise as a fiction writer was never fulfilled, and it is the reviewer and critic in Rosenfeld—the New York intellectual—who is now most commonly remembered. Much of his subsequent fiction lacked either the immediacy of "The Hand that Fed Me" or the sustained tension of *Passage;* it is abstract and allegorical, modeled more on Kafka than on Dostoevsky, and conscious of making a metaphysical statement. His second novel, *The Enemy,* was to prove unpublishable, and an Indian novel, *The Empire,* was abandoned after years of work. He outlined at least two other novels, set respectively in Russia and Greenwich Village, but neither went beyond the stage of notes. As the 1940s drew to a close, Rosenfeld came to believe that his talent was biologically frozen and that to continue writing he would first have to free it up and restore its flow. His immersion in Wilhelm Reich's theories of the "orgonomic" basis of life persuaded him that his writer's block signified a sexual inhibition, and he spent much of the late forties locked in protracted combat with the more rigid and prohibitive sectors of his own character.

For Rosenfeld, who trusted only latent contents, what lay beneath the American dream of individual fulfillment was the life of quiet desperation, and he set his face implacably against it, abominating it in his Reichian fashion as the emotional plague. In the struggle between civilization and instinct, he aligned himself with instinct, and set out in quest of remote inner landscapes where the beleaguered ego could luxuriate among the flowers of the libido in a state of grace. He bet everything on his chances for self-renewal, on breaking through to his animal nature. "A scientist experimenting on his own sexual possibilities for lack of someone else," remembers Alfred Kazin, "Isaac drove himself wild trying to make his body respond with the prodigality promised by theory." And yet this Sybaritism was always concept-ridden, more postulate than practice, and over time his failure to transform his life into the image of his principles damaged him.

Unlike other Jewish intellectuals of his generation, Rosenfeld never made his peace with America. Rather, he followed a code of personal conduct that looked like unswerving downward mobility, recoiling from the icy touch of success that lurked everywhere around him in the late 1940s. In 1949, after a dispiriting visit to the offices of *Commentary,* where his work was no longer held in esteem (in part because of a brilliant and scandalous essay, "Adam and Eve on Delancey Street," which almost cost editor Elliot Cohen his job), and where, as he saw it, his contemporaries—Nathan Glazer, Irving Kristol, and Robert Warshow—had already taken the decisive turn toward accommodation with the middle-class, he lamented, "Alas, alas. Youth is fleeting. The young men locked in office, locked in stale marriages and growing quietly, desperately ill."

In time his Bohemianism resolved itself in asceticism, as he took up forms of marginal existence that bore the stamp of the ghetto. Long before the 1960s made a sacrament of elective poverty, Rosenfeld became a *Luftmensch* by design. "He did not follow the fat gods," Saul Bellow said of him after his death. "I think he liked the miserable failures in the Village better than the miserable successes Uptown, but I believe he understood that the failures had not failed enough but were fairly well satisfied with the mild form of social revolt which their incomplete ruin represented." Under a self-imposed injunction to simplify in order to purify, he jettisoned the excess baggage of the conventional life: steady work, a profession, and in the long run, even his family and his fiction.

In the early fifties, Rosenfeld withdrew from the nexus of modernist literature and post-revolutionary politics that prevailed at *Partisan Review* and moved away from New York, first to a teaching post at the University of Minnesota and three years later to the University of Chicago. In Chicago, recalls Bellow, "the disorder had ended by becoming a discipline."

> In the intricate warren of rooms called the Casbah and on Hudson Street it was simply grim. Toward the end of his life, on Woodlawn Avenue in Chicago, he settled in a hideous cellar room at Petrofsky's where he had lived as a student. The sympathetic glamour of the thirties was entirely gone; there was only a squalid stink of toilets and coal bins here. Isaac felt that this was the way he must live.

And yet, there are signs that in the final months Rosenfeld experienced a breakthrough of sorts or at very least a remission of conflict that showed up in his writing as a relaxed and genial manner, a mellow *adagio* in his rhythms. One of his best stories, "King Solomon," was written during this period as was the draft of an essay, "Life in Chicago." Rosenfeld's King Solomon is a foppish old Jew, an overweight, cigar-smoking, pinochle-playing monarch who can barely recall his former wisdom but is still beloved by young girls who come from all over Judea—or is it Brooklyn?—to lie beside him and place their hands upon his breast. At the age of sixty he is courted fiercely by an overblown, bejeweled Queen of Sheba who cannot arouse him from his pinochle. But there is little tension in this: Solomon's pain is only a wistful, geriatric melancholy. In both, Rosenfeld's themes are familiar but his agitation is gone. "King Solomon" is tender and ironic, and the Chicago essay is cool, urban sociology. We cannot say from the writing alone what brought these changes about or what engines of creativity were set throbbing by the new mood, though this writing gives evidence that Rosenfeld's lyric gifts were very much intact. The last entry in his journal, written, perhaps, within days of his death, is poignantly affirmative, a call to life.

> This is what I have forgotten about the creative process, & am only now beginning to remember—that time spent is time fixed. One creates a work to outlive one—only art does this—& the source of creativity is the desire to reach over one's own death. Maybe now, if I want to create again, I want once more to live; & before I wanted, I suppose, to die.

Rosenfeld's heart attack cut short this affirmation and froze his career into its final shape—the brutal, downward curve of depression.

There was another side to Rosenfeld—the irrepressible humorist and man of spontaneous warmth. Rosenfeld—we should call him Isaac, as all did who knew him—touched people to the quick and was remembered tenderly for his humor, his passionate nature, and for, I believe above all else, the nakedness and innocence of his passage through the world. In a memorial eulogy, Bell spoke up for this other side, the side that did comic impressions of Dostoevskian characters and once wrote a Yiddish sendup of T. S. Eliot's *The Love Song of J. Alfred Prufrock* featuring such unforgettable lines as "Ich ver alt, ich ver alt, un der pupik vert mir kalt," (I grow old, I grow old, and my navel is growing cold).

> His great gift was for laughter, for joke-telling and fun, tempered always by the slight self-mockery so characteristic of Jewish wit. . . . He was boyish, prankish, yet never mean or narrow-spirited. People liked him instinctively, drawn by the open, engaging manner, recognizing his willingness to share rather than dominate.

By the turn of the decade, alienation had pretty much run out of rhetorical credit. In 1952, *Partisan Review* would run the symposium "Our Country and Our Culture," in which writers and intellectuals would queue up to testify, with a fair amount of uniformity, that a reaffirmation of America was under way and that "the American artist and intellectual no longer feels 'disinherited' as Henry James did, or 'astray' as Ezra Pound did in 1913." Saul Bellow would celebrate the moment in *The Adventures of Augie March,* which begins with the rousing "I am an American, Chicago born," and builds its case for the American century from there. And Bell, in *The End of Ideology,* his summary of his political hegira of the Fifties, would cease to speak of alienation as a force, as anything more memorable indeed than a footnote to Marxist philosophy.

Rosenfeld alone held firm to Bernard Miller's vision of the "empty space, which one might never hope to fill, stretched between person and person, between ignorance and knowledge, between one hand and the other," as he held firm to Bernard's cadenza of defiance: "The world is not entirely yours; and our reply is: very well then, not entirely." By the Fifties, however, there was virtually no one left to pledge these renunciations with him. And yet, isolated though he was during these grim years, his death was a shock to those who had been touched by his wit and his charm, his fervor and his intensity, his warmth and humor, which was the cosmic humor of a man who had pondered long the absurdities of being. "Reflecting on his own death," Bell observed in his eulogy, "he might have said, *'C'est la vie,'* and added wryly, 'And you call this a *vie?'* "

Mark Shechner
State University
of New York, Buffalo
November 1987

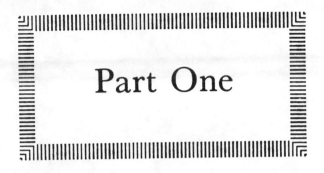

Part One

Chapter 1

I remember the year in which I first felt respect for human intelligence. I was fourteen, a precocious child, as sensitive as a burn. Human intelligence meant my own. Without growing more than an inch, I had suddenly shot up—that is, in my own estimation—and it seemed to me that I towered over life. Life meant the family.

We had a large family. Marriage and death have since reduced it, but in those days we were all together, as closely knit as one of my grandmother's flowered scarfs. Most of us lived in Chicago. It is hard to give the exact number of our tribe, which trailed off at the edges where the blood ran thin into distant cousins and nominal relationships, but there were always a good two dozen who would gather, of a Sunday, at my father's house or at the home of my grandparents. We would sit around the table drinking tea and eating honeycakes and all of us would be talking at once. The children would run up and down the house, disregarding the cries, "Stop that now, people live downstairs!" A baby or two might be squalling; or, suppose some youngster would trip over the carpet and come up screaming, with a lump the size of an egg on his forehead—then there was always a commotion and a chorus of sighs, the women clucking in sympathy and the men snorting their admonitions, while someone would press the blade of a table knife against the young one's bruise to bring down the swelling. We loved noise, loved the banging of doors, the sound of dishes in the kitchen, the swirling of water in the bathroom. But we also had a capacity for silence, a quiet feeling and respect for the family's presence which would show itself, some time after supper, during one of the last rounds of tea, when

[3]

everyone would be sitting, heavy, drowsy and contented around the big table in the dining room, with the lights lowered, and a few might be singing softly, the rest humming —and then not even the babies would cry.

The men, especially, had a great love for these silent, meditative hours in which, they felt, the whole heart of the family lay. Once, during such a session, my grandfather, who was sitting next to me, embraced me, drew me from my chair and tried to sit me on his knee. I fought him off, pushed away from his prickling, tea-stained beard. I felt I was almost committing a sin by doing so—but goodness, I was too old for that!

These gatherings were very well attended. But my mother's sister Minna, who surely should have had access to the family's inner circle, never appeared. Minna was my favorite —though the warmer women of the family, the sweet voluble aunts and cousins, would have thought me an ingrate for my preference. Her very distance made me feel close to her. Minna had no patience with children, which is why I loved her. For in showing that she had little use for me she would always, unconsciously, treat me as an adult. Whenever—rarely—I forced myself upon her (she was the only member of the family whom I would deliberately seek out), her coldness would delight me. She would ask none of the usual questions: How are the folks, how is school, what marks did you get? And she would make none of the usual observations: My how you've grown! or, you could use a new suit, or, your nails are dirty. Minna would put me off by talking solely about herself and about concerts and art exhibits, books which were too deep for me, people I had never met and whom, her tone gave me to understand, I never would meet. All of which, naturally, was precisely what I wanted to hear.

[4]

Surreptitiously I entered her world and moved about in it. I loved that world, loved Minna, patterned myself after her. I would go home practicing her aloofness and archness. For weeks afterward I would speak in her weary and rather nasal tone of voice, even mispronouncing a few choice words. I would raise an eyebrow and shrug my shoulders as I had seen Minna do, or run the tip of my tongue over my teeth and lips—a gesture so becoming to her that, I thought, it would surely lend some of her charm to me. Furthermore, I drew only those books from the library which I had seen upon her shelves, and played the radio solely for the purpose of hearing the jazz records she would occasionally condescend to play for me.

The family always knew when I had been to see her. They would meet my coldness with an unspoken censure, never mentioning her name, saying no more than, "It's fine tricks you're learning." Until my father, in an unwarranted rage, would cry, "Why are you keeping to yourself? Don't you have any friends? Go out, for God's sake, go out with the boys, go out with girls! Since when have you become too good for the world?"

I did not know how many of Minna's ways could be attributed to spite of the family. She had certain obvious traits, such as my grandfather would call *"Moisha kapoir,"* meaning, "Morris upside down," or, spitefulness and stubborn caprice. Thus, the family lived on the West side, Minna lived North; they were all fairly stout people, Minna, as if by choice, was thin; none of the women would think of smoking, Minna smoked, and drank, too—I know, for if there were any bottles standing about when I came she would not take the trouble to hide them. And, in general, Minna had her life, and we had ours.

I am not sure that Minna understood me, or sensed my

[5]

love for her. When she spoke of her strange existence, she was undoubtedly taunting the family in my own person. It was always as a Miller that she put me off. But how was it that she, occasionally, welcomed me in? I can't say whether she relented, perceiving my love for her, whether she accepted me only for the sake of a none too powerful flattery, or because of a genuine, however faded, remnant of family feeling which she, as my mother's surviving sister, could not withhold from me. And perhaps she was sincerely touched by my devotion, finding in it not only a small, selfish comfort but also a sign of my own worth. Nevertheless, when Minna spoke with me, it was basically with herself that she was speaking—reassuring herself, finding dignity and value in her own life. I had my recompense. For whenever she grew animated with self-satisfaction she would produce a certain warmth—more precious, for being rarer, than the family's quick kindling—a little of which would overflow in gratitude to myself. I served as the occasion, the means of assuring her that she had lost nothing in breaking with the family.

But even from the beginning, Minna to my mind was inseparable from Willy. It was at the time of which I am speaking that my Cousin Willy, who was really no cousin at all, re-entered our lives. Since the death, some three years before, of his wife, my cousin Martha, he had completely disappeared.

Willy was not only no cousin—he was no Jew. Strictly speaking, he was a hillbilly; born in the Tennessee hills, he had lived South, lived West, been a miner, a newspaperman, a sailor, and had seen the world. I really do not know what he was doing among us.

A fourteen-year-old, compared with a man three times

his age, is the merest child. Clap ten years onto both of them and the interval has narrowed. Between the middle twenties and the early fifties there's no longer such a leap; why, the younger man, if he has his wits about him, can even claim the advantage of a greater experience. He is closer to his own life by the immediacy of being plunged in it. The fifty-year-old has cooled—those gray hairs are ashes on a fuddled head, and all that wisdom and that slowness, the measurement he gives to each word, are but a subterfuge, a pause, a rest to enable him with each breath to recoup his losses. But not so with myself and Willy. My ten years were of no account to me; I thought I should always feel myself a child where he was concerned. The sense of growing older, the knowledge that I must overtake and surpass him was a source of guilt to me, as if I had willed his destruction.

I know that what I felt for Willy involved me so deeply, it were almost better not to delve for it. Who knows to what need our emptiness responds when it fills itself out with emotion? I suspect that what I gave him so generously, I withheld from another—from my father. I was forever disappointed in my father, just as, I know, he was disappointed in me. As far back as I can remember, I was always denying him. Let Willy be the proof of my ability to give!

But returning to him. Willy came to us a day before Passover when the house was undergoing the annual cleaning in preparation for the feast. I was home from school; my stepmother was putting away the dishes which we used every day and which would be forbidden to us during the holiday. In came Willy; and when the greetings were over— the screams, the kisses, the reiterated questions—and when Willy was done feeling my muscles and pinching me, he rolled up his sleeves (exposing the sailor's tattoo on his left forearm) and got to work. Putting away the chair my step-

[7]

mother had been standing on, he piled the dishes and utensils on the top pantry shelf and covered them with cloths. Then he wrested the broom out of her hands and did the carpets, poking into all corners, under couches and chairs and radiators and several times nearly upsetting the marble statuette of Psyche and Eros which stood on the center table. Next, Willy got pail and mop and swabbed down the floors, humming all the while he worked, and intermittently admonishing my stepmother, Go lie down, don't get in my way, leave it to you and you'd never get done.

He stayed for supper. It was the last meal of leavened bread. Tomorrow night we would go to my grandfather's for the Seder.

My father was not a gracious man, and it seems to me I observed an antipathy on his part toward cousin Willy. He was unusually quiet at the table, ate more rapidly than ever, pushed his plate aside when he was through with a course and did not linger on after the meal to play, as he often did when in a good mood, with chunks of bread, rolling them into balls and piling them up in mounds like gunshot. My father rose, leaving his dessert unfinished, and, without a word, left the room. An even more uncomfortable silence fell over us. I was embarrassed. My stepmother, who always took everything upon herself, looked guilty. She interceded for my father, explaining that he worked very hard these days. And immediately, to avert further attention from her husband's abruptness, she began showering Willy with questions, many of which she had asked when he first came in. Willy understood everything, said nothing to the point, and smiled as if to indicate that she need make no effort on his behalf. Before we left the table my stepmother said, "You're coming tomorrow to the Seder? We're expecting you." And added, to reassure him, "It will be at grandfather's house."

We found my father at the parlor window peering out. It was dark outside, there was nothing to see. Willy stood beside him for a while, also looking out; then, putting his hand on father's shoulder, he asked, "What's the matter, Harry?"

My father lit a cigarette—he did not offer one to Willy—and seemed at a loss for an answer. "Nothing, nothing. I'm just tired, that's all," he said angrily.

"Anything troubling you?"

My father gave me a severe look. He wanted me to leave the room—for no reason except that he disliked Willy. I stayed.

"No, I'm just sad," he replied, not knowing what else to say.

"Why are you sad?" Willy was all smiles and indulgences. He was humoring my father.

"Life is sad . . ." replied my father. "When I saw you I began to think about poor cousin Martha. You should be sad, too."

I saw Willy grow angry, and I understood that he resented my father's mentioning her name. The death of his wife was Willy's sorrow; what right had my father to put it to his own use as a pretext for sulking?

Willy left soon afterward, saying good-bye only to my stepmother.

"Why did he run away?" she asked, coming into the room with a dishtowel in her hands. "Harry, did you say something to him?"

"Never. I only mentioned Martha. I don't know why he ran away."

"What did you say about her?"

"What did I say? I only said I felt sad."

"Why did you have to say it? You know how he feels."

[9]

"So did I do him any harm?"

"But why all of a sudden Martha? You weren't thinking about her."

"Maybe you would stop bothering me!" he said to my stepmother. And to me, "What are you hanging around for?"

"Now what is he doing to you? You stay right here!" she declared. "Everybody bothers him! Harry, that's such a mean thing. Whenever you're blue you always have to take it out on someone else. Now tell me, what have you got against Willy?"

"I've got nothing against him. He's a wonderful man. Simply wonderful!"

"Harry! You ought to be ashamed of yourself! At a time like this, before a holiday?"

"A holiday! What's so wonderful about a holiday?"

I believe my stepmother knew all along what was troubling him. Through what little feeling I had for unspoken trans-actions, for hinted motives, I could sense that above all it was the approaching holiday which was making my father ungenerous. Evidently, he realized that my stepmother had invited Willy to the Seder. Now Passover is traditionally the hospitable feast, the day on which there is no greater pity than for a man to be alone and, accordingly, the day when all are welcome. And my father, just as he had used Willy's sorrow for his own purposes, suspected Willy of using our holiday for his own ends—for a meal, for company, for an opportunity to express himself gaily in that broad human manner which gatherings of my family always encouraged. And as I made out from my stepmother's attitude while she argued with my father, her understanding communicating itself to me, it was this which he resented most. He was jealous of his own humanity, perhaps because he had so

[10]

small a store of it, and he envied Willy his larger endowment. So large was this endowment that Willy, though he was practically a stranger and a Gentile at that, could nevertheless constitute a threat to my father, threaten to outdo him, outshine him, outwarm him at the warmest of Jewish feasts.

All this I gathered from my stepmother's insistence upon the extraordinary importance of the holiday and my father's equally vehement insistence that one holiday was like another and they all meant nothing to him. Presently, my father's unexpressed motive came a little nearer the surface when he said, "Understand me, I have no objection to Willy. If the Seder were here in my house I would have invited him myself. But how do you know the old folks will like it? They don't know him, after all. And then, all of a sudden you bring to their house . . . a goy." Whenever my father protested his considerateness of others, I knew he was thinking only of himself.

My suspicions confirmed, I stayed to hear no more of the argument. I knew that my stepmother would win, since my father, as was so frequently the case with him, was quarreling only to conceal his wishes. I left the room, more than ever disappointed in my father, who had grown even smaller in my eyes.

Grandfather was an improvident man who lived like a king. He had wasted his productive years, and was now spending his remaining days reaping the rewards of idleness. He was supported by the various members of the family, each contributing a tithe in accordance with his degree of kinship, his ability to give, and his inability to resist exploitation. The house which grandfather had thereby furnished for himself attested to a manifold and inconsistent charity. Thus, in one room lay a fading, cast-off Oriental rug, and in another a modern, figureless, solid green carpet. On one wall hung a copy of a small cubist painting; on another, a reproduction of justice in a white robe, blindfolded, scales held aloft, while a third showed a forest fire raging. Of furniture there was a similar abundance and variety. In fact, so well stocked was the house that an overstuffed armchair with a patch on one of its arms that always reminded me of cousin Willy's tattoo was obliged to stand in a corner of the kitchen, under a coffee mill and next to a sewing machine.

All this splendor was wasted on my grandmother, a plain and severe woman who wore high laced shoes that reached nearly to her knees. She could never bring herself to regard this house and its furnishings as her own. Only her small and original property—several knitted table scarfs, the silverware, some bedding and chairs—had value for her. The rest was an accumulation of shame. She perpetually wore a humiliated expression which read, "It is a bitter thing for an old woman to come to this."

Grandfather, however, had no sense of shame. He was proud of his house—his, all his—and he felt that he had earned it. And he had his way of accumulating more. Thus he once said to his niece Deena, "What a shame that you went to so much trouble to teach your children piano, and now the piano stands in your house and nobody touches it!" What would my grandfather want with a piano? Ah, you don't know him.

When we arrived for the Passover, bringing Willy with us, my grandfather had already returned from the synagogue and he was standing at the door, his beard combed and clean, most of the tea-stains washed out of it. A new, stiff, black and shiny silk skullcap was on his head, a pair of embroidered velvet carpet slippers on his feet. (He always wore carpet slippers in the house, as if to show how thoroughly at home he felt. In this he was the opposite of my grandmother, whose boots one would have reason to wear only in a snowstorm.)

The old man drew my father aside as we came in, and I could hear father begin to apologize, speaking Yiddish in a low voice, for having brought Willy along. But grandfather interrupted him; there was a more important matter at hand.

"Where is the wine?" he asked.

"What wine?"

"You mean you didn't bring any wine?"

"But just last week we brought you two gallons of wine."

"But there are so many people! Just look, the whole world's here. Do you expect me to use my own wine? Aie, a fine son you are. You should see what Chiah Gitel brought—a whole kitchen full of matzoh!"

Passover has always been my favorite holiday, although, even when I was a child and nearer my period of religious instruction, it never had more than an almost perversely romantic significance. It was, above all, the only occasion on which I was permitted to drink wine—and it was to wine, rather than the history of my people, that I owed my sense of reverence. The wine would stand throughout the long ceremony in its special Passover decanter, surrounded by the Passover goblets. It was touched only four times—twice before, and twice after the supper which came in the middle of the service. My attention, much as it might wander from one member of the family to another, from my grandfather who raced ahead over the Hebrew words in a loud slurring singsong to my grandmother who would always fall several pages behind in her reading of the *Haggadah*—my attention would always return to the wine and remain riveted there. I gazed at the decanter and the goblets which were of a single pattern, fashioned of a brownish-rose glass and blown with clusters of grape, vine, stem, leaves and all. In the center of each grape stood a point of light, reflected from the chandelier overhead, stained with the color of the glass and the color of the wine within, and shooting off rays of beaded green and red and purple in all directions. These danced before my eyes, twinkled and winked. They were the original Egypt, colored and revived, the parting of the waters, the Red Sea agape, the journey through the desert. They merged with the sinuous melodic Hebrew droning at the table and blended with the smeared black prints of the *Haggadah*— Pharaoh's daughter at the bulrushes, Moses striking dead the Egyptian overseer, the scenes of plague, the sky dark with locusts, the ground crawling with frogs. Even the advertisements inserted among the religious prints by the matzoh manufacturer who distributed the *Haggadah* in pamphlet form, were overlaid, for me, with a perfect appropriateness, a sense of final testimony to the accomplishment of Moses.

Our Seder progressed without incident. My little cousin Bobby asked the "four questions"—years ago I had done the same when I was the youngest literate in the family. There was the usual racing by the men, and the usual faltering— interspersed with whispers and giggles—by the women, and my grandmother's inevitable complaint, as she bore down after the pack, several pages behind, "Morris, where's the fire?"

The first of the "four questions" asks why this night of Passover differs from all other nights of the year—purely a rhetorical question to which the *Haggadah* furnishes its lengthy answer. But how did this Passover differ from all other Passovers of all other years? There was nothing to mark it off. All previous sessions ran together in my mind, un- rolling like the scroll from which our pamphlets were

[14]

printed. Not even Willy's presence—he sat with a grin on his face, flipping the pages of his *Haggadah*, swaying, occasionally, as the other men swayed, exchanging smiles with everyone and winking at the children—not even Willy was sufficient to make this night different from all other nights which celebrated our deliverance from the bondage of Egypt.

Scripture speaks of the ten deadly plagues that were visited upon the Egyptians; and the head of the family, in illustration thereof, inclines his cup of wine to let ten drops fall into a saucer. Here my grandfather's hand trembled and the wine spilled out of the raised cup, splattered the saucer and left a wide, spreading stain on the tablecloth to distinguish this Passover.

"If you weren't in such a hurry, Morris, maybe you'd see what you were doing," said my grandmother.

"Ahha, she's here! Who sent for you?" cried my grandfather. "We'll get along without you. Thanks!" And went on muttering stormily, "So, so, nu, so!" while the women mopped up around him with their napkins.

Grandfather seemed not in the least concerned over the trembling of his hand which, with grandmother's help, he had converted into an occasion for a quarrel, thereby obscuring its significance. But the rest of us were shocked as by a reference to age and death. We kept our eyes averted from the stain at the head of the table.

I had already had two cups of wine, and during the meal Willy sneaked me a third. I am sure my father saw him, for he stiffened, reddening slightly, and it seemed to me he must even have taken a certain satisfaction in what he had seen, for it enabled him further to justify his hostility toward Willy with the belief that my cousin was a bad influence on me.

But I was rapidly slipping beyond all influence of anything but wine. Three cups were all I could safely drink. No one had acknowledged my illicit third cup; tradition itself vouchsafed me another two. I was in my element. My head began to spin and my glossy tongue to slide. And then, whether it was because of the wine itself, the early spring, or simply because with me, as with grandfather, another year had gone by, I became a sensualist. First it occurred to me that this holiday, which we celebrated in such worldly fashion with chopped liver and gefüllte fish and chicken soup floating a thick scum of yellow fat, the droplets winking like the glass grapes—even the matzoh had such a lively, freckled brown face—this holiday, I suddenly felt, was something my family could not understand, a celebration not even of this earth, its meaning lying beyond the particular individual, Joe Greenberg, who had a wen on his forehead, or Chiah Gitel, who had hairs growing on a mole on her cheek, or her daughter, Essie, who wore a brace on her teeth, beyond my grandfather, a year nearer death, with his washed beard and new skullcap, and my grandmother who would follow him in death as she pursued him, several pages behind, at the Seder. It was an event only I could understand. And suddenly I saw myself walking on a broad field, not unlike the lawn in the park. Overhead there were the new stars, absent all winter; underfoot was the grass, renewing itself. At a distance, in a lighted area around a table, men were chanting a traditional song about a goat, yellow chicken soup was flowing, children were scampering about. . . . But I walked on in the night, and at my side was a young girl who shared the world with me, whose eyes danced and winked, under whose feet, too, the grass was renewing itself. She smiled when I spoke to her, the tip of her tongue ran over her teeth and lips. She was my aunt Minna, and yet not she. She was all girls in one, all mysteries and delightful things understood and possessed, and mine, all mine. . . .

I rose and spoke out—some thick and silly words, ending in a laugh. The Seder was interrupted.

"He's drunk!" cried my stepmother, not without a certain pride.

"He's drunk!" cried my father, angrily.

The women laughed, the children ran up to me. Willy, roaring, threw his head back, losing his skullcap; my grandfather's smile stretched from one end of the world to the other; my grandmother went on reading the *Haggadah*.

"Come with me," said my stepmother, taking me under the arm and leading me into the kitchen. The children ran after us. I heard my father say, "Shame on you." And I heard him add, "Never mind, now. Let's keep going." My stepmother was giving me water to drink and passing a wet dishcloth over my forehead. "Are you all right? Do you think you can hold it?" she was saying.

"I'm fine, I know what it means," I was saying.

"You know what what means? You're drunk."

"What it means . . . I understand everything."

"Ah, are you *shicker!* Do you want to lie down a little?" She kissed me approvingly on the cheek.

Did she really think I was drunk? "I'm fine, I'm fine," I insisted. "I want to go back, I'll be all right."

The singsong proceeded from the dining room. My stepmother took me under the arm again and steadied me. She was wiping my forehead and smiling, and I thought I heard her say, "Lucky boy," as though she envied me. And why shouldn't she envy me? I had the whole world in my pocket. . . .

"He'll be all right now," she announced when she led me back to the table. She affected a frown. It resembled my father's frown so closely that I wanted to laugh all over again. Willy raised his empty wine glass and waved it in salute. "Shhh," said my father, reading the *Haggadah*.

At the table I was soon sober again. The atmosphere had changed, there was a strain over the Seder which straightened me. When my head cleared I observed that my father and Willy were struggling.

Father glared; Willy smiled. Father sat erect, his skull-cap square on his head; Willy slouched, all relaxed, his cap slung at an angle like a beret. One declaimed the Hebrew text, loudly, punctiliously; the other looked at the pictures, whispered to the women, pinched my knee under the table and cracked nuts with his teeth, disdaining the nutcracker which my father used.

Of course, their opposition was not quite so perfect or so simple. For while my father deported himself belligerently, as if he had been appointed guardian of the Passover, a latter-day Moses, he, too, had his easier moments. He would also whisper and smile, let his attention wander from the text, flip the pages, play with chips of matzoh on the table-cloth. But my father's levities were always followed by stern-ness, by a sharp little cough which announced each change of heart. I never knew whether his digressions into good humor were spontaneous or deliberate—whether his mood would actually change, or whether he simply felt it was time to put on a smile, as a man may take a pill at stated intervals.

He and Willy came into conflict at the very point where the Seder is as gay as comic opera. The point, that is, where the Israelites offer up their great digressions, the better to sing their deliverance. We extol the Lord's virtues one by one and list the blessings bestowed on us, claiming, after

[18]

each, that had this been the only blessing, it would have been enough: *Daiyenu.* There comes chorus after chorus,

Dai-dai-yenu
Dai-dai-yenu
Dai-dai-yenu
Daiyenu, daiyenu . . .

Done with this we sang about a kid "which my father bought for two *zuzim*"—a song in the manner of The House that Jack Built. It grows like a rolling snowball, picking up verses on its way, each devoted to a cat, a dog, a stick, fire, water, an ox, and a ritual slaughterer—until the angel of death comes and with the stroke of the fierce and tribal Jehovah sets things right by ending them. Then we sang the same song over again, with variations,

The master sends
A man to the woods,
A man to the woods,
To pick pears,
To pick pears.
The pears refuse to fall,
The pears refuse to fall. . . .

after which we broke into a chant to honor Elijah, the Prophet,

Elijah the prophet,
Elijah the Tishbite,
Elijah, Elijah,
Elijah of Gilead.

No wonder it took us forty years to cross the desert.

Now while all this gay spirit was raging Willy thrust him-self into the thick of it. He did not know the words—but seizing a knife in one hand and a wine glass in the other he set to work beating out the rhythm.

[19]

"Careful, you'll break the glass," said my father.

But the singing went on, and with it Willy's conducting. And during a pause, Willy struck up a song of his own.

> I believe in the good old Bible,
> I believe in the good old Bible,
> I believe in the good old Bible,
> And it's good enough for me.

He had a Bible-country voice, with a Southern drawl and inflection, a break and a trailing swing in its rhythm. He clapped his hands—and you could see in him the mountain folk sitting in their wilderness in a circle at the tabernacle, following the evangelist with whooping and handclapping. He sang—and went barefoot, his skullcap changed into a straw hat, horse-cropped at the crown. He was professing the faith. . . .

> It was good enough for Paul and Peter,
> It was good enough for Paul and Peter. . . .

My grandfather beamed and melted, snapped his fingers, smacked his lips.

> It's that old time religion. . . .

It was Passover in the hill country, celebrated by the lost tribes.

"Amen!" cried my grandfather.

"Amen!" we all responded.

> It's that old time religion,
> It's that old time religion,
> And it's good enough for me.

Willy got up and stomped around the room, the children after him. The wine glasses trembled; the decanter threw off its rainbows in a fury of winking. "Amen!" cried my grandfather, and even my grandmother, who had by now finished reading the *Haggadah* and looked up bewildered, trying her best to say, "This is not my house anyway, you may do as you please . . ."—even she was smiling, unconsciously nodding her head, approving without knowing that she approved. Only my father sat silent and motionless at the table, diminished, defeated, utterly dispossessed.

In such fashion the Seder ended, with Willy leading us in song. I remember hearing my stepmother say as we drove home that night, "He's such a wonderful man. It's a pity, he should get married again." My head was swimming in wine and in sleep.

Chapter 2

The way things are in the world, Passover often coincides with Easter. The way things are in my family, we buy our new clothes when the holidays are over. Thus, about a week after the last Seder I got my new Passover outfit, a good buy, I was assured, a suit with two pairs of pants and a vest at a saving of perhaps as much as ten dollars. "If you take your time and don't rush to buy when everybody buys you get much better value." So declared my father and stepmother while taking me to a store on Madison Street. They said it in firm and pious belief, as if it were wisdom such as this which blessed their union. But what did I care for wise savings? My suit was a brown herringbone with a pleated and belted back, wide flapping trouser bottoms and four large buttons on either sleeve!

This was the suit I wore when I called on Minna. Believe me, I thought I was handsome—which I have never been, the less so then when my features, first beginnng to sprout into their present proportions, had not yet been pruned and conformed by time. Minna was not delighted to see me.

"What do you want, Bernard?"

My full name always sounded severe to me. Rarely would Minna call me Bernie, seldom show pleasure in my coming, and never pay me a compliment. But since I was now sure that compliments were in order, I imagined that one was concealed in her coldness. This, I thought, was Minna's way of saying, "My, how fine you look!" And, impressed with my own handsomeness, I came into her apartment.

"I'm just paying you a visit." I made myself comfortable on her sofa, pushing aside a blanket and a hot-water bottle, and there I was. I had not neglected to hike up my trousers at the knee.

"You couldn't have picked a better time," said Minna, nasally, and left me, locking herself into the bathroom.

Minna's apartment was the only one I knew which had a fireplace. All the other homes I entered had at best imitation logs with gas vents, in alcoves between built-in bookcases. I had therefore come to identify the absence of a fireplace as a Jewish characteristic, of a kind with dietary restrictions on the mingling of meat and dairy products, or the taboo on pork. Since Jews did not bring fire into their homes, I thought it forbidden. Fire was the image of that raging, destructive spirit, found also in drunkenness, bloody meat not salted or soaked, life without prayer, the freedom of the world without God, against which we locked our doors. True, the women, my stepmother excluded, lighted candles on Friday night. But candles were blessed and prayed over; candles stood upright in the menorah, their flames sanctified, small and clean. Logs, planks, kindling, paper, or coal lay in

[22]

an ashy heap on the hearthstone, their flame crackled and smoked; one did not pray over them.

But I loved fire, and that I thought it forbidden only increased the beauty I saw in it. Presently, I went to the fireplace and poked into the dead ashes, clearing a space, laid on newspapers and bits of unconsumed wood and set a match to them as I had seen Minna do, and when the paper caught I brought more paper and an armful of sticks from a pile in the corner. This was bravery. I had never ventured to touch Minna's fireplace before.

The fire was a good bright one, we reflected each other's pleasure. I stood near it as long as the heat would permit, and when I had to withdraw, its warmth went with me, permeating the apartment. How thoroughly at home I felt! This small room which had little sunlight by day and air at night—my stepmother would have pronounced it unfit to live in—contained the world. The low ceiling, sloping at the corners under the pitched roof, enclosed me in its friendly, personal angle. The pictures on the wall, their wild, broken colors and unrecognizable forms, took on meaning and welcomed me. Here dwelt that spirit which we barred from our lives, and in its freedom it was friendly, not raging, and not destructive, but liberal. This was its natural home. The books on the shelves, not cased in glass, but allowed to gather dust if they liked, the records in albums, or pressed together between sheets of cardboard under the radio, the very coverlet, striped red and green, which lay on the low flat bed that had neither headpiece nor legs—my family would have thought it an abomination—all these were the simple objects of freedom, and yet, like the blue light Minna kept burning in a long-necked lamp on her desk, they conveyed a certain mystery, as if to enter this world were not sufficient when one still had its secrets to lay bare.

I saw a row of bottles near the fireplace. One was not quite empty. I drained it off, choking a little and feeling my throat burn. But I was now utterly happy and, turning off one of the lamps, I went back to the couch, stretched out and watched the fire I had started curl in the grate, crackle and leap and throw its shadows about.

"Why did you start a fire? Who gave you permission?" asked Minna, coming out of the bathroom.

"Do I have to ask permission?" I smiled, and winked.

"Well, I like that! And take your feet off my· couch. If I wanted a fire, I would have had it myself."

"But it makes everything so nice! You should have a fire going all the time. Or at least start one as soon as you see me coming." I spoke slowly, teasingly, in somewhat of a drawl; my voice was completely charming to my ears.

"And the light! Why did you turn off that light?" cried Minna, irritation making her extraordinarily perceptive.

"Oh, come on, you're not really angry." I pulled her over to the couch, grazing her cheek with my lips, and tried to tickle her under the arm.

Minna slapped my face.

I was considerably stunned. The slap was not sharp, but the imprint of its meaning, slower to fade than the outline of her fingers on my cheek, humiliated me. This was punishment for the happiness I had stolen from her world.

"I'll ask you to leave now," said Minna.

I rose, ashamed, fighting back tears. "I'm very sorry." The apology weakened me, and I felt my tears show. I had wanted to hurt her, to damn her old couch, as I would do when my stepmother reprimanded me for keeping my feet on the covers, or call her fireplace dirty and smelly. But there were no subterfuges with Minna—my motives were always the issue.

"What business do you have tearing in here like this?" she asked, not relenting, but detaining me lest something escape her.

"I just wanted to hear some of your records." I realized that this was not the reason for my visit, though I had kept it in mind as the one I would give if questioned.

"That's not what I mean."

"Do I have to have reasons? Can't I just come to see you?"

"I don't care what your reasons are. I want to know why you're so fresh all of a sudden."

I felt myself blush. "I didn't realize I was being fresh."

"Oh, but you were. You were being smart. I don't like little boys who are smart. It's so cheap!"

"I apologized, didn't I? If you want me to leave now, I'll go."

She hesitated, fearing perhaps she had been too severe with me. "Sit down a moment."

I took my place on the couch, sitting upright now, near the edge. I could smell the perfume with which, evidently, Minna had doused herself before leaving the bathroom.

"Don't you know there are certain things you shouldn't do?"

She was defending herself against the possibility that she had provoked my impulse to do "certain things."

"Do you mean because I touched you?"

She ignored my question. "Tell me, Bernard, do you have many friends of your own?"

"Sure, lots of them," I lied. Once Minna asked me to leave, the room itself had dismissed me. Here there was also a locking of doors.

"Do you have girl friends?"

"Of course."

"Well, if you have girls your own age, you won't be coming to see me any more."

Now what was she after? One moment she complains that I have come; the next, that I may not come again. "Not at all, I'll always come to see you!" I protested. Having said which, I was embarrassed, for I now understood her to mean, "I wish you would find a girl your age and leave me alone. And don't go trying cheap tricks on me, your aunt, because you have no one else to play up to!"

She saw how confused I became. I felt myself sweating at every pore. My hands grew heavy, my ears were like saucers, and all that handsomeness I had thrust at her lay dashed and demolished by her insight. But I felt even a deeper shame. With an unaccustomed aggressiveness, confident and familiar, I had made myself at home, virtually taking over her apartment. Had I meant to take over Minna as well? It was in fun, in this same confidence, that I had tickled her, and tried to embrace her, nearly kissing her cheek. But Minna had made a transgression of it and, confronting me with this version of my innocence, destroyed it, compelling my guilt.

"And I see you've been drinking," she went on, friendlier, even rather amused. "From one of those bottles. Nothing is safe with you around. Bernard, aren't you a little too young for all this? You have time enough, sonny. There's no harm in your taking a drink, or smoking, or doing anything you like. But you'll only be making yourself cute, instead of attractive. There's quite a difference, my dear. Most men never learn it."

The fire was smoking itself out. Minna had closed the incident in good humor, but I would have preferred to have her angry. For what of my actual motive, if she was so keen for motives? She found it so easy to put me off because I was young, to mock me with my impulses, which she understood better than I. But I felt at the time—dimly, uncertain of my own defense, and in terms which I can state clearly only now—that she had missed something altogether apart from motive and impulse, a certain innocence which she no longer could recognize. My admiration was too simple and patent a thing for her to know; and perhaps the freedom of her life, its rarest and most precious quality, which I could discover even in the ashes of her fireplace, was also unknown to her.

It was the fault of perfection. Minna had so patiently sought and formed her own life, she could not conceive that it might have value for another. Even love was an intrusion. Another breathing her air would only pollute it. I looked at her, a protest concealed under my disgrace, and found justification. Her expression, tense but clear, held nothing external or imposed; this was her own image, reflecting no other. Her features had none of my family's mark. She rather resembled my mother, whose photograph lay buried in an envelope in my father's drawer; but she was a smaller woman (already I was as tall as she) and would forever look youthful. Her eyes had none of the intensity the picture had given my mother's, and were lighter and colder, with no trace of devotion or family care. Her hair also was lighter and worn differently, more like a girl's; she would remain the younger sister. I already knew her timidity, but I believed her capable of the greatest impudence. Proof of this was her nervous self-concern, as if she knew her restlessness needed watching, lest it do herself, or another, some injury. Sometimes her smile had a fine, cutting edge; she had made it a weapon for defending herself. More frequently, she wore a frown, taking care against its becoming permanent, a mar to beauty, by relaxing occasionally all expression from her face, pressing her hands to her cheeks and drawing her fingers across her forehead. She had no natural defenses—her skin was so delicate, white and clear as to seem permeable—and therefore devised and cultivated a wariness which remained artificial, for all that it had become habit. Shrewd, suspicious, self-contained—how could she know me?

But at least she could forgive me. "Some day I'd like to have a talk with you," said Minna, placing her hand on my shoulder. "There are a few things I'd like to explain. But right now, would you mind getting up so I can lie down again?"

As I was rising, Minna caught me and pulled me back, tickled me and, laughing, put a kiss on my cheek where she had slapped me.

"And while you're up, would you mind lighting a fire under the kettle and filling the hot-water bag? It's gotten cold. And then you can play all the records you want."

As I stood in the kitchen, bag in hand, waiting for the water to boil, I could feel Minna's kiss drying on my cheek. And then I realized that my pleasure in her kiss was so great, I must have desired it all along, and could only have come with that intention. This frightened me. I felt my punishment had been deserved, and that Minna, far from expressing love, had kissed me only to make clear my presumption. And yet I was convinced of an essential innocence; I loved her as one should love an aunt whom one values and whose life is held the dearer for having so clear and admirable a meaning. But how could I admire, and at the same time remain admirable? There was no greater difficulty than to show one's love. For I had thrust myself at her, not in devotion, but in vanity, because a new suit made me feel handsome.

But was it so much the suit? I recalled that I had not troubled to keep myself clean while building the fire and, looking down, I saw ashes on my cuff. No, there was another reason. Trying to invoke again that sense of handsomeness, swagger, and confidence, I felt myself resembling Willy, and I realized that he had been with me, guiding me to her door, and that it was under his influence, in his person, that I had confronted Minna.

From the kitchen I looked back into the apartment, saw Minna lying on the couch, the blue light falling over her, everything bearing her personal quality, dear to me, but withheld, inaccessibly mine. Suddenly I felt a desire to bring Willy into her life—a desire so surprising, and yet so strong, that it too must have been with me from the beginning.

Chapter 3

Willy rented a room downtown at the Y. He was going to look around for a few weeks and if he found a job he would settle in the city. I can't say whether this was his original intention, or the response to my urging. But I was worried, for it was clear to me that Willy did not know what he wanted, and I was afraid he might slip away again.

I met him at his room after school, several times a week. He would take me down to the game room and play ping-pong with me, or we would swim in the large tile pool which smelled of chlorine. We might also play pocket pool or billiards, games which Willy was teaching me and which he would let me win, or go bowling, Willy's favorite sport, where he could not resist trying to outdo himself and where his score was always three times as large as mine.

I would ask him, "Have you found a job?"

"Not yet, my boy. Don't rush me."

"Is it hard to find a job?"

"Hard? Not at all. I could go out right now, there's a fellow who's been after me, and I could say to him, 'All right, Jackson, I'll go to work for you. Only I want forty dollars a week more than that coolie wage you offered me.' And I'd get it, too."

"Then why don't you?"

"Who wants Jackson's old job?"

"What sort of job is it?"

"Well, you know, it's the kind of line that don't appeal to me. It means seeing certain kinds of people, you know, and always being on the run. No, sir—not for me."

"Then why don't you go back on a newspaper?"

"Well, that's an idea, but I ain't decided yet. Here, let me show you a three-cushion shot with reverse English."

And he'd chalk up his cue, lay his cigar down on the edge of the table, the coal away from the wood, and bend over his ball, taking careful aim.

I had only to watch him play billiards, or come upon him in the lobby of his hotel where he always sat in the most comfortable chair he could find, one leg thrown over the arm and his hat pushed back, to know that he would avoid work as long as he could.

Why should this be any concern of mine?

Well, obviously, I had plans for Willy. Not that these plans were clear—we have a desire, and even if it be for a specific end, who knows where it will lead? I wanted to bring him together with Minna. But I could not speak of such a thing with him, any more than with her. Whatever I had in store for him, I needed his approval; which he could give unwittingly, merely by following my lead.

I had plans for Willy. Mind you, I was going to take an

adult in hand and—as these same adults always phrased it with regard to me—I was "going to make something" out of him. I began with his appearance. It was, as you can imagine, slovenly, irregular, motley. Willy wore whatever came to hand: lavender shirts and red ties, checks and stripes and plaids, all thrown together without thought for harmony; collars and cuffs which needed turning, and a serge suit that could use pressing and a little less shine.

To reform him, I had to mind my own appearance. I saw to it, whenever I was with Willy, that I should be wearing my new suit. But I was the victim of my own subtlety, for I had to outdo myself in order to make the least impression on him. And thus I was always brushing and primping before the mirror, picking off hairs and pressing my trousers. (My stepmother was delighted; "He's growing up," she observed. My father said, "That's not at all like him," and suspected something was wrong.) I had every intention, not only to set a good example for Willy, but to shame him and hurt him; to bring it about that people should say, "That man and boy who are always together—why is it that the little boy can keep himself so neat while the man is a slob?" But it had no effect on Willy. He noticed nothing. My hair might have been slicked down so smooth and shiny that the very glare should have been enough to bring light to his eyes. But the most he ever did was this: once when we came to play pool he said, "Better take off your jacket, or you'll get it all full of chalk." Well, yes, he did at least see that I was wearing a new jacket. But this was that partial sight which is worse than blindness. For while he expressed solicitude for my clothes, there he was standing in the pool room in a dirty blue work shirt, the sleeves rolled up, his tattoo exposed, his collar open several buttons down and a striped jersey showing a wide rent across the chest through which his hair poked out. And all this is to say nothing of my efforts to improve his speech, his grammar and diction, to drive away his drawl, his cigars, the habits of a lifetime. I undertook a fundamental reformation, a whole metaphysics of posture, creases and lines. I was exasperated. I saw there was not a thing I could do to prepare the ground. I would simply have to trust to luck when I finally brought Minna and Willy together.

It was a great task I had set for myself. And yet, I now believe that young as I was, I was the person most excellently qualified for this venture. I had the advantage of being under-rated. Willy turned his shrewdness in less unexpected directions, never supposing me capable of the stratagems I employed on him. For one, he was completely unguarded in speaking with me. Realizing that I was of that age when girls would begin to occupy my mind, he undertook to share his experience. He told me of women he had loved, indicating how handsome and popular he had been. Why, when he was just about my age, he had already had about five girls, all of them older than himself. One girl had broken off her engagement on account of him—and, mark his word, he was just my age. Well, no, he must have been nearer sixteen— but that's still plenty young. What a boy he was! Why, he was already over six feet and still growing. Clothes wouldn't last him longer than three weeks, he'd outgrow them so fast. He outgrew his bed, and his desk in the schoolroom; the shoes he wore to church would never fit more than a month. He outgrew everything—except the girls. Ah, the girls, he grew right into them, all right! He was hardly able to walk when he was already tagging after them; his mother would have to go and haul him out of the fields to give him his feeding. Yes sir, he was a wild one! And none of this citified spooning in your dark corners off the staircase in the hall, never knowing when someone would come up, or your crowded little parks in the summertime. He had the woods by day, over yonder by the hill, down past the brook, among the rushes, and by night, the slopes, with hay scattered about, under the wide sky. And then there were the barn dances, the hay rides, the winter sports, the revival meetings with folks coming from miles around, bringing their girls. What a life he'd led!

We would be sitting in the lobby of his hotel in our leather chairs, surrounded by leather chairs, by spittoons, potted palms, tables, and newspaper racks, by the four walls with yellowish marble slabs and a big ledge at the level of your head, painted green the rest of the way up, a clock in one corner, the clerk's cage with the letter boxes off to a side. It would be getting on to suppertime, and I would have to take the streetcar home. Men, pasty and bedraggled, most of them alone, would be scattered about the room reading their papers, picking their faces, staring out the windows where the dusk was just beginning to fall. They would get up, one by one, and leave the lobby. And Willy would be telling me of his youth, drawling and laughing and singing it out, overheard by the men who shuffled by on their way to the cafeteria.

Willy's confidences took such firm hold on me, filled my mind so full, that they replaced my own daydreams. It was I (well over six feet tall) who ran among his hills, loving his girls; and I would never call up the image of a girl without first making sure that she belonged to this world, selecting her so carefully, vividly picturing her straw hair, her eyes, her bare legs, as though I were casting a play.

But just as I was becoming the young Willy, reliving his life, so, it seemed to me, Willy was entering mine. It was nothing short of fatherly feeling which drew him to me;

[33]

and yet—how unlike my own father—the more fatherly he became, the more he was himself a boy.

Now I would claim no false credit for myself; and I have the highest respect for Willy. But which of us, during these sessions, was really the master of the other? Willy, I grant, overwhelmed me, held me captive, completely enthralled. But wasn't he, thus unfolding himself, also yielding to me? Almost without the need for subtlety, and with so much greater success than had met my pains to improve his manners and his dress, I had contrived, simply because I was young and therefore trustworthy, to catch him unawares and set him thinking of women. And since his wife had died but a few years before, this became, I should say, the release of a sorrow, still lingering. Never mentioning her name, nor even in the remotest way referring to her, still he was taking his farewell of the dead by setting forth the memory of his own life. And memory, extended far enough, will bring us to the present. I could have found no better way of drawing him on than by listening quietly. Which I did.

On the other hand, of what use was this to me? I might draw him on as fine as thread, but once I revealed my intentions, gave him even the slightest clue of my plans, the thread would break. I could never manage it fine enough. When Willy discovered where I was leading him, or when he saw where I had made him lead himself, he would throw me over, traps, plans, and all. Then, not only my subtleties, my very innocence would condemn me in his eyes.

Again it was Willy who came to my assistance, falling victim to his own experience. We were in his room, having just come up from the swimming pool. Our hair was wet, freshly combed, mine, of course, much more neatly than his. I had obtained permission to stay and have supper with Willy, who was going to take me to "a real restaurant—none of these here nickel-plated railings and tile floors like we got downstairs in the cafeteria." My stepmother had given me two dollars—"Here, and make sure you pay your own way. Willy isn't working. And we won't tell Pa about this."

We sat on Willy's bed in the room which was hardly large enough for the two of us. It contained a combination desk and dresser, a chair, a wardrobe and a washstand. The walls were a dingy yellow. By the side of the door was an oblong card bearing instructions for the guests, in large type: what to do in case of fire, when to play and when not to play the radio (there was no radio in the room), where to deposit jewelry and other valuables, etc. A black Bible stood upright against the mirror on the dresser top, in the company of the hairbrush, the toothbrush, and the shaving brush; on its spine was stamped, in gold letters, Holy Bible; on its side, YMCA. The single window had a green blind, which was raised. I looked out into a deep window-lined shaft, or court, which was filling with a bluish mist.

I had got water in my ear and was shaking my head, making the iron bed rattle under me. I struck myself a blow with the heel of my palm above the ear, hearing a dull sound; I gasped, wagged my jaw. At last the water came out in a warm gush. I continued to look out the window, watching lights go on, seeing men move about in their rooms.

Willy was sitting at the other end of the bed, leaning against the post, and looking in the opposite direction, at the door, the Bible, the mirror, the instruction card. We were in a pleasant fatigue, drowsy and melancholy.

At last Willy said, "Ever read the Bible?"

"Some," I replied.

"Go on, I bet you never did. Who was Barabbas?"

"I don't know."

[35]

"There. He was the thief whom the Pharisees asked Pilate to release, instead of Jesus. You'll find it in Matthew. No, really, don't you ever look into it? Your part, I mean. There's Ecclesiastes, the Song of Songs, the book of Esther. You should read it. There's the story of David and Bath-sheba. Do you know what that is?"

He got up from the bed and reached for the Bible; fell back, rattling the springs, and leaned against the window sash, fingering the pages in the bluish light. "That's a wonderful story." He smiled. "I remember it every time I go to the swimming pool. Seems that David was a powerful king, had everything he set his heart on. Palaces, a big army, and gold and riches. He used to go walking on the roof of his palace. One evening, when he was up there, he happened to look down into his garden and he saw a woman bathing in the pool down below. 'And from the roof he saw a woman washing herself,' read Willy, " 'and the woman was very beautiful to look upon. And David sent and enquired after the woman. And one said, Is not this Bath-sheba, the daughter of Eliam, the wife of Uriah the Hittite? And David sent messengers and took her; and she came in unto him and he lay with her; for she was purified from her uncleanness. . . .' "

He snapped the Bible shut, tossed it down on the bed toward me. It had grown darker; loneliness filled out the time. "We're going to have some meal tonight," said Willy, and stretched and yawned, and fell back again. "I'll take you to one swell restaurant, a beaut. You needn't be ashamed to bring your girl there. . . . Tell me, you interested in any girl?"

"Oh, maybe one or two."

"Tell me about them."

And then, before I had thought of what to say, I blurted out, "I really like a certain woman."

[36]

"Woman?"

"Well, that is, she's a little older than me, I mean. . . ." I blushed, avoiding his eyes.

"Who is she? Tell me about her!"

"Well, that is, she's my . . . I mean, she, she lives on the North side . . . alone."

"What do you mean? Do you know her well?"

"Well, I . . . yes, sort of. I've been to her house."

"What's that?"

In my mind was the image of a woman, bathing in a pool. "Well, I mean I just like to go and talk to her. . . . She likes me."

"Look here, is she really a *woman?* Is she nice, that is, you know, refined, good-looking?"

"Yes, she is."

"Oh, what a lad, what a lad he is! Why didn't you tell me? Knows a woman and keeps her from me! Where is she? Lead me to her!"

It was as simple as all that.

Chapter 4

But Willy would have to wait, for I still had my work cut out for me. Minna must be prepared and her consent obtained.

My last visit had had curious consequences. Though I felt closer to her than ever before, I had put her even farther beyond my reach. Somehow, I had grown older; perhaps because my feeling for her had revealed itself. For, if I had once had access to her house in virtue of a simple affection, now my affection was spoiled—light had got at it and I therefore stood in shadow. I had expressed my affection in a manner for which she judged me too young, out of an intention for which I was too old. Children's emotions and actions are one; adults have mastered the art of conforming them. I stood between, having lost a gift and not yet learned an art. To see her again, I would need a pretext.

Had Minna been a doctor I could have gone to her with a sickness. Had she been a schoolteacher I could have brought her my French. A painter would have called for paintings; a writer, for stories. Were she even an ordinary aunt, I need only have been a nephew. But Minna was Minna. True, she was a dress designer. But could I come to her and say, "I want you to design a dress for my stepmother"? My stepmother herself would not have been able to do this. Minna could not be reached.

It now seemed to me that this had always been the case, although I could still remember the time when Minna, on close terms with the family, had been friendly and available to us all. In those days she was a dressmaker. I always saw in her room a clothes dummy mounted on a stand. It had the shape of a woman, but was without head or arms, and had a hooped wire skirt in place of legs. I was afraid of it. Minna, to reassure me, one day put down her work, took the pins out of her mouth, and told me the story of the dummy, whom she called Sonia.

"When I was a little girl," went her story as I remember it, "I lived far away on the other side of the ocean in a big big country called Russia. My mother was very busy all day long in the kitchen and my father would go away for long long trips. I had no playmates. My brothers would not play with me because I was a girl, and my little sisters were not yet born. I was very sad and lonely and I cried all day."

I did not notice the discrepancy here with the fact that she was my mother's younger sister; instead, I wrinkled up my chin as if I, too, would cry. Minna patted my cheek and smiled at me and went on.

"I wanted so badly to have a playmate and I didn't know what to do. One day I went out into the woods and I said, 'I'm going to walk and walk until I find a little girl to play with, and I don't care if I never come back.' But then I remembered that a wise old woman lived in the woods, so I went to her and told her how lonely I was and the old woman told me not to cry. She said, 'Minna, why don't you make yourself a little girl to play with?' And she gave me a big box, all wrapped up and tied with a string, and she said, 'Take what is in this box and make yourself a little girl out of it.' I ran home as fast as I could and I untied the box and I made myself a little girl and I called her Sonia. Sonia was very pretty and we played games. Only I didn't want my mother to know about Sonia, and I didn't want my father and my brothers to know. So I used to hide her in the garden every night before I went in to supper. And before I went to bed I used to sneak out and feed her with food that I had saved from my own plate. Sonia was a good little girl, and I was very happy with her.

"But one day the old woman came to me and said, 'Minna, would you like to have a little sister?' 'Like Sonia?' I asked her. 'Just like Sonia,' said the old woman, 'only she would be your own little sister.' 'Yes, I would like to, very much.' 'Then give me Sonia's head,' said the old woman. 'Your little sister has to have a head.' I didn't want to give her Sonia's head. I was afraid it would hurt Sonia, and I cried. But I wanted to have my own little sister, so I took off Sonia's head and gave it to the old woman.

"Then the old woman came to me again and said, 'Give

[39]

me Sonia's arms. Your little sister has to have arms.' Again I cried. But maybe Sonia wouldn't mind so much because I had already given away her head. So I took off Sonia's arms and gave them to the old woman.

"Once again the old woman came to me and said, 'Minna, your little sister has to have legs so she can run and jump and play games with you. Give me Sonia's legs.' 'But what will Sonia do without legs?' I asked her. 'Here, I'll give you some wire,' said the old woman, 'and you can make a skirt for Sonia, so she won't need legs.' I took the wire and made a skirt for her. And when my little sister was born she had Sonia's head and face and arms and legs. And that is why Sonia has no head, no arms and no legs. But we have remained very good friends."

In those days Minna was always sewing, by hand, or bent over a machine which she ran with a treadle. Her room was full of cloth, silk and satin and pieces of lace. She would let me have the snippets that fell from her scissors, black and red and green little squares and triangles. I would stuff my pockets full, but could never find any use for them. She wouldn't mind having children around while she worked, and sometimes I would call in my friends. She would give us each a penny. Minna worked hard, and her hair was disheveled, and sometimes she would be sweating. And she always kept pins in her mouth.

Thus I remembered her, most clearly in the year my mother died. I was about five years old.

But I was never too confident of the reality of these recollections. For they made the present Minna utterly mysterious, and the more I relied upon them, the more inexplicable became the woman whom I knew. Memory resembled the old photographs lying about the house, pasted in albums, buried in drawers, pictures which begged to be believed, showing my father as a young man, my mother as a girl, myself as a baby. These images were too oblique a version of the familiar, too greatly altered, completely negated in life. I would sometimes stare at the snapshot of my father, my eyes fixed to the softer and younger face, each line and hair of it, hoping I might thereby gain some understanding, a clue, perhaps still available in the past, to undo that in the present which was entirely a secret. But even the younger face denied me; I would stare until my eyes teared over and the image began to dissolve. So with my own snapshot, a baby, ball in hand, seated on a rug. This being I might never again enter. And if I were cut off from myself, what hope could I have, despite all my striving, to re-enter what would at best be only a partial knowledge of Minna?

I had many times tried to account for the changes that had come over her (epitomized by the transformation, dressmaker—dress designer), her withdrawal from the family, her dislike of children, her striking out into a cold, aloof, inaccessible world, essentially Gentile, where one became, as my stepmother put it, *"wie die goyim,"* or, even worse (I translate literally), "like dogs and pigs, low, false, besmirched, without heart and soul, without love, without self-respect, without a care for anything human, and as hard and selfish as a stone." But how could I account for a change which I myself gladly would have undergone? And if my stepmother's imprecations, supported by the strictures and fears I had known throughout my life, put restraint on me so that in my love for Minna there was always some element of guilt, the very nature of my love was such that I would have insisted that she stay remote from me.

There was therefore no telling how I should approach her.

A telephone call from Willy.

"How are you, old man? Ain't heard from you, where you been? Why don't you come to see me?"

I am well, I've been busy all week, I've been meaning to look him up. I speak in a low voice, smothering the mouthpiece. I do not want my father, who is sitting in the living room with the evening paper, to know that I'm talking with Willy.

"What you been busy with, eh?"

With school. Homework.

"Oh, I see. How are the folks?"

They are fine. How is he? Has he found a job? That's right, he should just keep looking and he'll find one. Oh, by the way, that nice sport coat we saw in the window, some time ago, which he said he was going to buy—did he buy it?

"Ha ha, you're a rascal. I'm on to you, all right. No, I ain't had a chance to buy it."

Haven't had a chance.

"All right, haven't. So you want me to be a gentleman. . . . Well, what about it?"

What about what?

"Now *aren't* you clever! You know, what's her name. You holding out on me?"

No, I just hadn't had a chance to speak to her.

"Well, hurry up, I'm a lonely man! No kidding, I've missed you. Come around."

I will, soon. Good-bye.

I heard my father rustling his paper as he folded it carefully before putting it aside. He came to the phone as I was hanging up.

"Were you talking to him again?"

"To whom?"

" 'To whom?' " he says. "To Willy."

It would be useless to deny it. I remain silent and slowly begin disengaging myself, retreating a step at a time. My father goes on, his voice rising as I draw away from him.

"You couldn't find a better friend? You have to hang around with a tramp, a bum? Fine tricks you'll learn! I'm warning you, be careful, watch out! Look at you, look how excited you get when he calls up. Your eyes light up, your face gets red. The whole world depends on Willy! Ha? What does he want? Maybe he wants to take you out to the girls? You stay in the house tonight, do you hear me? You stay in! A fine way you'll end up! Watch out!"

I was by now at the door of my room. My father turned and went back to the living room, sat down violently in his chair, and took up his paper without opening it. I went into my room.

My father's injunctions—watch out, watch your step, I'm warning you—were meaningless, but pertinent. Fathers believe their sons to live under a constant danger. They warn us against their own temptations, their own anger and violence. Still, he was right, absolutely right despite his error in thinking that it was Willy who was bringing me to girls. He had observed my excitement, my face flushing and, resenting it, understood what it meant. And he knew when the phone rang that it was Willy calling me. By what science, by what knowledge was my father preponderantly in the right about his son? What gave him his insight? Was it the fact that he had to be angry—without anger he could not be a father—and anger must have its grounds, its certainties?

I grant that he understood me. The only person he could not understand was himself, and this made his understanding partial and blind.

I called at Minna's house the following night and found her out. I returned the next evening and saw a light in her window. There was no answer to my ring. I rang again; no answer. I was afraid of her as I stood in the vestibule, and

[43]

I was afraid of my own resolution to see her. I rang again, and when there was no answer I tried the door in the hall. It was open and I went up the stairs.

The transom over her door showed light. I remained still, undecided whether to knock. I listened, unsure whether I heard anything. Perhaps I had heard a sound, a muffled creaking, like a movement in a chair of someone trying not to be heard. The sound was not repeated.

I touched the door once with my knuckles, softly. Suddenly panic took me and I turned and ran down the stairs. I was convinced that she was home, that someone was with her, and that she knew it was I who had been trying to get in. I lurched down the stairs, scuffing and hitting the banister as loudly as possible to disguise my step and tried, as well as I could, to imitate a drunkard.

Chapter 5

The next night Minna received me.

From the amusement and annoyance which were mingled in her greeting, I gathered that she knew I had come the night before. But now the pretext I had been seeking suggested itself. The immediate result of seeing Minna's fresh, clear face was this: I thought of the hot-water bottle of my previous visit. I could therefore inquire into her health with more than mere politeness, with purpose, with a useful sincerity.

"Thank you, I'm pretty good for an old lady." She smiled, yielding to an occasion for self-appreciation which momentarily put out of her mind the hostility I knew she felt toward me. But she had not put down the book she was reading; she closed it on her index finger. I glanced at the title and made out nothing. Minna, catching me, had turned the book away.

"Are you feeling better now? You were sick last time." ("Last time" was an involuntary admission that I knew myself to be a pest. How I wished I had the courage to forego pretexts!) "Was it a stomach ache?" (An absurd remark.) "I mean, because of the hot-water bottle . . ." (Even worse.)

Minna's response startled me. I had not thought it in my power to disconcert her. For a moment her expression of indulgence and impatience changed utterly, and I could not believe that I had seen her in fear, worried and suspicious, hastening to the memory of that evening as if to make sure she had not betrayed herself.

"I wish," said Minna, "you would call up before you come."

"But I don't know your phone number. It's not listed . . . and you'd never give it to me."

She put her book down, losing the place. Out of her desk drawer she took a calling card and pressed it into my hand, tapping it against my palm with her fingernail. "Tell them this is a more businesslike way of doing things!"

"*Them?*"

"For your own self-respect," said Minna, flushing and angry but not raising her voice, "you oughtn't to do this. You're young and I don't suppose you know what you're doing, but if you did, you'd regret it!"

I was terrified. Not by her anger, the words which I failed to understand, but by the realization that she might now reveal herself.

"Do they send you here? Your father, does he tell you to come here?"

[45]

"Minna, no, he never knows. He wouldn't let me come!"

"You're lying! He made you promise not to tell me."

"Minna!"

"He sends you to spy on me. You were at the door last night."

"I was not! I was never even near your house." I lied for the sake of the truth I had to impress on her. "Even if he did send me, I would never go. I swear, Minna, I should hope to die, I wouldn't! I hate my father! Honest to God, I hate him like poison!"

"You mustn't say that about your father," said Minna, repelled by excess, however my words may have pleased her.

Sincerity and design had coincided in my outburst. Minna took my hand and led me to the couch, making me sit down beside her. She smoothed my hair, abstractedly, hardly aware of what she was doing, fixed my tie, brushed a few specks from the lapel of my new suit on which she had not commented before. These gestures now served her as a commentary. Her caresses were awkward, strange to her. . . .

"Are things so bad for you at home?"

"No, no, they're not!" I was repelled by her sympathy. I knew I should never have revealed hatred for my father, the more so as revealing, in part, created it.

"How does she treat you?"

"She treats me fine. Really, she does."

"She is all right. It was never her fault. He took you away from me."

"Took me away?"

"You won't remember when your mother died. You were too young."

"I remember a little."

"No, you wouldn't understand. You're still too young. Don't contradict me!" She paused, apparently embarrassed by the new, or renewed, relationship that was springing up between us. When she resumed, it was with an effort to detach herself. "He chased me away. I was to have taken your mother's place, but he wouldn't have it. . . . But some day you'll know the whole story."

"What is it? Tell me now."

"No, I can't tell you yet. I can't ever tell you."

"Then how will I know?"

"Maybe you won't know." The possibility had first occurred to her. She accepted it. "Then you won't know. It's not my worry."

"But what am I supposed to find out? Tell me. Maybe I'll find out for myself."

Minna laughed. "You're at such a wonderful age!"

"What's wonderful about it?" I asked in resentment, feeling cheated, exploited, brushed aside.

"I mean it. It is wonderful. I thought last time that you'd been spoiled. But you haven't. You're still a child."

"I'm not a child!"

She sighed as if to assure me that it was merely the ineptitude of her remark—not its intention—at which I need take offense. "All I mean, my big grownup, is that you don't know anything about your aunt. And it's better that you don't."

It was the first time I had heard her refer to herself as my aunt. It made me feel slightly uncomfortable; precisely why, I could not understand. I too was struggling against our relationship.

"But tell me," said Minna, "your father does know that you come to see me?"

"I think he suspects." It was to preserve my own dignity that I refrained from telling her that he knew everything about me.

[47]

"And he doesn't object?"

"He lets me do what I want."

"And that's the same as not letting you do anything at all?"
I did not understand this remark, but replied, "I guess so."

"Does he ask about me?"

"No. He's never mentioned your name."

"He's got good reason not to. Let me tell you he has! Does
he ever talk to you about the time when we were all living
together?"

"Never says a word." I could not be sure whether her
questions reflected suspicion or disappointment. Minna, evidently, had as much to learn from me, as I from her. "I wish
I could tell you more," I added. "But there isn't anything
more."

"Then let's drop it," she said suddenly, resenting the fact
that I had noticed her curiosity. She had seemed on the
verge of telling me "the story"—that which I would have to
know in order to remain attached to her and not, unconsciously, do my father's bidding. But it was no longer necessary. She slipped out of all involvement, was free again, no
longer "my aunt." I was surprised to find that I regretted this.
Then I had really not been struggling against our relationship, but had actually desired it.

She rose from the couch. "May I fix you something? Would
you like some tea?"

"No, thank you." But I was delighted by the offer. Our
new relationship still existed, after all. It struck me that
there was an extraordinary politeness and consideration, both
in her offer and my refusal. I thought, people who have just
got married talk to each other this way.

"I know what you'd like to drink," said Minna, smiling,
"but you're not getting any."

And yet she was still capable of dismissing me, locking

me out. She took up her book, again, although this time perhaps unconsciously, concealing the title. I would have to leave now. Suddenly I remembered why I had come.

But Minna said, "Was there anything you *wanted?*" emphasizing the word with a not unfriendly, but suspicious accent as if she were unable to believe that my visits were without motive.

I would be bold. "I wanted you to meet a friend of mine," I said, getting up.

"A friend?" The idea seemed repugnant. "You mean from school?"

"No . . . he's older than me."

"What's his name?"

"William Harpsmith."

"That's a pretty name. But why do you want me to meet him?"

"Because, well . . ." I tried to remember what I had said to Willy under similar circumstances. But it was useless. Minna was not a person I could control, nor one who, unconsciously, would yield to me. We were back at proper proportions. I finally brought out that I liked my friend very much and that I believed she, too, would like him. (I knew it would be disastrous to let on that he was a member of the family.) "He's interested in meeting you," I added, realizing at once that this was a mistake.

"Why?"

"I've told him about you," I replied, repeating my error.

Her suspiciousness flared up again. "What have you told him?"

I knew one thing and another about Minna; what to expect, what to avoid. But if I could only have known her simply, in a word, in a single gesture, I would have known exactly what to say. This seemed very comical to me. I

remembered Willy cracking nuts with his teeth at the Passover table.

"Why are you laughing?"

I thought for a moment she might slap me again. I would
always have to pay the penalty for imposing myself. Whether
she really was or was not "my aunt" was immaterial. I might
only strive to know her, never actually dare to disregard the
barrier that confronted me. But my striving was so integral
a part of my feeling for Minna, so very much the condition
of my love, that I took pleasure in it, and could not believe
I was defeated.

"What did you tell him?" repeated Minna.

"Just that . . . that you have nice records, and books, and
a fireplace . . . and that we have a lot of fun." (I would never
have dreamed of associating Minna with the idea of fun.)

She seemed relieved, and even smiled, herself recognizing
the incongruity. "Does he like records and books, your
friend?"

I could see by her question that she was still taking Willy
to be a youngster, at most only a year or two older than
myself. But as she was on the point of yielding, I did not
correct her.

"He does. He's very intelligent. Can we come over tomorrow night?"

"I have a date tomorrow night."

"The day after tomorrow?"

Minna went back to her desk, picked up a small calendar
and began turning the pages under the blue light. "I'm
going to a concert. . . ." She read a list of appointments,
indistinctly, half-aloud. "I'm sorry, I'm going to be busy
until a week from this coming Wednesday."

"But that's so far off!"

"Well, then the Monday of that week." And she added,

still leafing through her calendar, and as if to justify its existence, "I simply have to have things in order. Otherwise people would be dropping in at all odd hours and I'd never have a minute to myself."

"We won't stay very long."

"But you don't understand—your family is different. I just have to be by myself. I'm more of an individual in this respect."

"You are different," I ventured to say. ". . . Do you remember telling me the story about Sonia?"

She frowned. "Enough, now. Good night, Bernard." Taking my arm, she led me to the door.

One never knows where one stands with Minna. For a moment I could even wonder if I was expected to kiss her, in virtue of our new relationship. But it had that ambiguity which called only for politeness and patience, and as I left her I thought, it will always be so.

Chapter 6

The night before the meeting of Minna and Willy, my father came into my room. I knew why.

He had been restless all week; had stared at me at odd moments, wanting to talk with me, and then, at other times, had seemed to avoid me. On Saturday—the previous day, that is—he came home from work in the early afternoon. "I took a half day off. Would you like to go to a ball game?" he asked. I did not want to go. He was hurt. This had been our one common understanding in the past. He shrugged his shoulders and a sigh of resignation caught in his throat.

[51]

Then he went into the kitchen to my stepmother, where he was not needed and found himself in the way. He returned to the living room and stretched out on the sofa. There was at least some solace in a nap on a Saturday afternoon taken off from work. But he could not sleep. Fifteen minutes later he was back in my room. "Let's go for a walk in the park." He made the suggestion appear as terse and confident as the first, trying to conceal the disappointment which, could he speak freely, would have led him to say, "Look at the way things are with us. Why must I always come to you?" My father was obliged to assume the various guises of authority and good faith, none of which, however, could overcome our mutual embarrassment. This embarrassment was the source of my obedience. I could not long endure his disappointment or my own sense of guilt, and, eventually, would accept the terms he offered me, hoping it would improve our relationship.

We went to the park. Women were strolling beside the lagoon, pushing their buggies; children played on the lawn, tearing up handfuls of grass and showering one another; the tennis courts were taken by players in white; an orange kite sailed high in the distance, its rag tail curving, the string which related it to the scene below barely visible in the sunlight. We walked over the hill and around by the bridge to the flower garden. Flowers were already up—tulips and irises were the only species I could recognize—and in other sections of the garden men were turning the earth in black crumbling lumps. I asked my father if he could identify any of the flowers. He could not. This was the first time we had spoken.

It was pleasant walking in the sun, even though our embarrassment had not subsided. I still have the habit of drinking at every bubbler that I pass; on that day my father must have thought I was dying of thirst. He never drank once, but I would stop and even if there was a crowd of children splashing around the fountain I would wait my turn, bending over for a sip or two, each time seeing in the base of the fountain the same pattern of tiny chipped stones worn smooth and covered with algae just above the level where the running water reached. Even so simple a habit marked me off from my father. When I was a child he would raise me to the wide rim and hold me over the bubbler while I drank. Everything I did marked me as his son. My whole life was an acknowledgment and a denial.

We went on, my mouth cool and sweet from the water I had been drinking. My father, apparently, had given up the attempt to have a talk with me. He spoke only to know if I wanted anything, making an effort to please me. Thus, when we came to a kiosk in the center of the park where candy and ice cream were sold he stopped and jingled the coins in his pocket. "What'll it be?" he asked. I did not want anything. He looked at the Cracker Jack boxes piled on the shelf inside, at the popcorn machine turning on the counter. "You used to like Cracker Jacks," he remarked. Later, when we came to the boat house, he merely said, "Well?" I consented.

The boats had just been put out for the season and were newly painted white, with the inner surfaces and the seats green. My father took the oars and set to work, keeping an even rhythm, rowing expertly, without splash. We spent over an hour on the water, alternating at the oars. We had taken off our coats, loosened our collars, rolled up our sleeves, and tracked ripples and a slow churning wake back and forth over the lagoon, near the water lilies, under the bridge, around the island, at our ease and heart's content, our embarrassment forgotten. But when we were back on land again (the ground swaying underfoot), I realized that except for saying, "May I have the oars now?" we had not spoken to each other.

He sat in my room, on my bed. In the outer light, which reached him from my reading lamp, he looked aged, without color. Shadow had returned some of the black to his gray hair, but his face was leaner, hollowed and more heavily lined. (On Sundays he would go without shaving. When I was a child, the stubble of his beard would prick me as I kissed him—one of a number of distinct Sunday qualities, along with comic strips and lying late in bed.)

He said, "Could you put that book down a moment?"

"It's homework."

"I won't bother you long. I just want to have a talk with you."

"What's the matter?"

"Nothing's the matter. Must something be the matter if I want to talk to you? I just want to know how you've been getting along."

I swung around in my chair, facing him, but left the book open. "I've been getting along all right. I got an A in my last French exam."

"I don't mean school. I know you're all right in school. . . . All the same, you didn't do so well in geometry."

"That's nothing. It wasn't the final."

"All right, I know you'll do better. But I mean in general. A good heart to heart talk . . ."

Silence, discomfort. I avoided him, looked at the other end of the room, and through the corner of my eye I saw him only as a gray figure, featureless.

"I want to know, for instance . . . Well, you see, you're growing up, you're going on fifteen. . . . I don't have to worry about your studies, but I think a boy your age should

[54]

take a certain interest in life, go out more. You don't go out enough."

He had not come directly to the point, but these premises would also serve. I saw where they would lead: I don't have enough friends of my own age, I spend too much time with Willy, therefore I should stop seeing Willy. I cut him short, not only to answer his objections, but to justify my leaving on the following night. "I'm going out tomorrow with the boys."

But my father was dissatisfied. He recognized my deliberate refusal to acknowledge the spirit of his inquiry. I was taking him literally—and thereby exploiting his inability to say directly what he wanted to say.

"Look, now, it isn't that I want you to run around. I know you're not like other boys your age, and I don't mind telling you this—I'm proud of you. I suppose it's natural that you should like older people. . . . See, your father isn't so ignorant after all. I understand you, it isn't so hard. . . . But all the same—

"All the same, there's a limit to everything. How much do you really have to be with that Willy? . . . And that's not all. Don't you think I know you go to see *her?*"

So he knew. In itself this was not surprising. But how well did he understand? How much, actually, did he know? I had never stopped feeling superior to him. Even though his understanding penetrated so much farther than mine, and with such definitely greater weight and authority, I always felt that his insight was blind. But at times it was a weight greater than I could bear.

"If you want to see her, all right, fine, go ahead. I won't say a word against her. She's your aunt, see her all you want, go ahead, go ahead! But into this house she can't come!

[55]

. . . But all right, all right. Only, the thing is, is it right you should see older people so much—especially her?"

"But you just said I could see her all I want!"

"Ahhhh . . ." It was useless talking to me. Talk to me, and talk to the wall. But today he was incapable of anger; he was aware of the distance which had spread between us, and was feeling it too keenly. It was yesterday in the park over again —the father kept off by the son he was striving to know and, consequently, harboring his patience, imposing an additional restraint on himself, cautious, counting on good faith and trying not to press his authority. And thereby weakening himself. For I could ignore his gentleness, but his weight would have borne me down.

He remained on the bed, motionless, his hands gripping his thighs, his head somewhat lowered. I stole a direct glance at him. I thought he would leave.

"Grown-up people," he said suddenly, "have to lead their own lives. It isn't right that you should be butting in all the time."

"But I don't butt in. They want me to come." With the word "they" I feared that I had given myself away.

"Does Willy know her?" asked my father, eagerly seizing on the word.

"No."

"Look at me. Tell me the truth. Does he know her? Do you go to her house with him?"

"No."

"Why do you lie to me?"

"I'm not lying."

"Don't I know by looking at you? Don't you think I can tell?"

"But I'm telling you the truth!"

"All right, so you're telling me the truth. All the same,

I don't want you to see them. Let them lead their own lives."

"But you and ma are grown-up. Am I in the way here?" Though I could not exactly say why, I knew my question was dishonest. I saw that he had taken this remark poorly, without actually perceiving its dishonesty. The reference to my stepmother must have hurt him, although as far as his immediate feelings were concerned, I am sure he was pleased that I called her "ma" just as I called him "pa," and never confronted him with the fact of his second marriage. I did not remember my mother and could not, therefore, bear him any rancor on this score. Yet the very ease with which, as a child of seven, I had accommodated myself to my stepmother, as well as the obvious fact that I was more generous to her than I was to him, must have provoked that envy of the heart from which my father constantly suffered. Besides, I had touched upon that very aspect of his marriage which he always found it necessary to veil. And had done so flauntingly, playing the innocent.

"Now what are you saying? Who's put that idea into your head? In the way here, in my house? I suppose there's something wrong here, something doesn't suit you, you can't have everything you want! Sure, sure, the grass is always greener in a stranger's garden. It's a wonder to me you don't run away altogether. Go ahead, go to your Willy, go to them, go!" He looked at me in wounded faith—again without anger—as if he had caught me in a conspiracy to forge a new issue of parents.

He rose, on the verge of leaving. But his object, not yet achieved—he simply wanted to have a talk with me—detained him, and the fatherly mood of it still enclosed me with an unreleased emotion. "Do you know," he said, "it's impossible to talk to you. I've tried, many times, when you didn't even know it. I don't know why it is . . . a boy as

[57]

young as you after all . . . But I suppose there's nothing I can say to you. You know it all already. Is there something you don't know?"

I wanted to break out of my arrogance, above all to be honest with him. But so long as he stood before me, I felt my every action was a deceit. I replied, "I suppose so."

"You've had your education already. In the street. I guess you know all about . . . about life, too. Very fine." And he went out, slamming the door.

Over all the conversation, accounting for my sense of dishonesty and shame, had hovered the subject which he could never mention openly to me. Curiosity to know and share my experience motivated his fatherliness, making him eager to confess me, to have me at his wisdom and—as if it were ultimate—his virile authority. I believe this underlay his distrust of Willy who, he feared, had robbed him of his last influence. Hence his pryings and suggestions, the veiled accusations, the open hints. Therefore, also, his fear of Minna. I did not know at the time what ground he had for fearing her, and with what good reason he regarded her as an additional threat. But Minna, however dimly I realized this, had already become for me the image of experience, of knowledge to my ignorance, the person in whom mysteries were both contained and cleared. I am sure he perceived that it was through Willy, rather than himself, and through Minna, rather than the poor figure of a stepmother which was all he could provide, that my maturity would issue. As he saw me falling away from him his curiosity must have grown ever greater, requiring always more, endowing me with secrets and then demanding to know them, wanting dreams, wishes, fantasies, the very girls who came to me in sleep. My own sexual awakening had stirred my father's blood.

And yet, as I remember, I was still fairly innocent; and

[58]

if not of knowledge, then of desire. I had not yet come by my own longing, and it is longing which makes mysteries impossible. I still found mystery in connecting what I knew with what little I perceived. I was more eager for insight than experience. I lived in a world in which, it seemed to me, people understood one another perfectly. Men spoke with complete assurance of women, and women of men. Their sex was divided and shared, subsumed under and related to their entire lives. I felt awe in this; and I was drawn in awe to Willy and Minna, exemplars, connected beings.

But I told myself, "I know what it is." And I thought, "I know the truth." Yet, if I knew the truth, why should it mean less to me than to anyone else? The mystery was not to know the truth, but to be moved by it.

Chapter 7

Willy had at least tried to meet specifications. He was perfectly clean and he was wearing new shoes. His cleanliness startled me when I met him in the lobby (where, for once, he was standing beside a leather chair, instead of slouching in it). I had always assumed that his skin was a shade darker. His new shoes were so obviously new, I expected them to squeak when he walked. They were pure orange.

"How do you like the outfit, son?"

But I saw no outfit. His suit was the same serge he had always worn, albeit with the shine and the wrinkles pressed out of it. He wore a white shirt, perhaps in deference to my distaste for lavender, and it was new, but again—as with his shoes—its newness was its defect. The unshrunken collar was too wide for him, and bore a crease down either side where it had been folded. Drooping from the collar was a large red bow tie, its ends uneven and tucked under like a pair of wings.

I sighed.

"Wait, here's the pay-off." Out of a paper bag on the chair beside him he drew a straw hat, twirled it around his finger and with a flourish set it down on his head. The flat crown and the flat stiff circular brim gleamed with varnish and were divided from each other by a speckled band.

"Think the old gal will like me?" He took me by the arm and marched me out of the lobby, stopping only at the cigar stand where—my heart sank to see it—he bought a two pound box of chocolate-covered cherries. "We're going to have a blow-out."

I did not know what to make of this, unsure whether he was mocking me or himself or—what was worse—whether he was serious. I blamed myself for not having better prepared him to meet Minna. And as for Minna, there I was even a bigger fool. For if Willy did not know what to expect, she knew even less. Besides, she would have to reckon with Willy's own perplexity which, as it made him uncertain of himself, removed him even further from her expectations. I sat in the streetcar in silence, dreading the evening toward which I had been devoting all my hopes.

Minna hardly looked at me when we came in. Her eyes were on Willy. She took in his hat, his bow tie and his shoes, and the immediate judgment she had formed of him was summarized in the exasperated glance she directed at me. Suddenly she burst out laughing.

Willy, who was no doubt prepared to play the clown, was nevertheless startled to find that he could draw laughter even before he had called for it. He removed his hat, awkwardly, holding it so that it concealed the box of chocolates, and, in his turn, cast a glance at me.

"Is this your friend William Harpsmith?" asked Minna, her tone indicating to Willy that she had been awaiting a boy my age. She had turned a light pink from laughing.

"Yes ma'm," replied Willy, coming forward with a slight bow and presenting her with the box of chocolates.

"For me? How sweet!" she exclaimed. She undid the wrapper, showing great surprise and delight. "I simply adore chocolate-covered cherries!" Affecting a child's enthusiasm, somehow even making her eyes shine, she offered the box to Willy and me, and took a candy herself, cramming it whole into her mouth.

How their insincerities wounded me! Perhaps as a result of my own insincerity toward them—while not repenting, I felt it all the more strongly—I sensed only the embarrassment, even hostility, which, in an undertone, formed a commentary on their actions. Moreover, the candy was very bad. The syrup had crystallized, the cherry tasted waxen and stale. We ate rather grimly. I blushed for Willy who, I could see, was suffering.

"Will you have another piece?" asked Minna, offering him the box with what seemed to me excessive cruelty, as soon as he had finished his piece.

"No, thank you. They're for you. I've just had a big meal."

"But I can't possibly eat them all by myself! Here, Bernard, do have another. Oh, I'll get fat and you won't come to see me any more!"

It was becoming a game, at which, however, we had not the courage to play long. For we were under too great a strain; and presently we all gave way, as at the snapping of a string, and fell back into lifelessness, silent and stiff, and as frank as wood.

[61]

To break the silence, Minna turned to Willy and asked, "How come you know Bernard?"

I had no time to warn him. He replied, "I'm his cousin."

"Cousin?" Minna was frowning.

"Sort of. That is, I was married to his second cousin."

"Well, how interesting!" declared Minna, 'in sarcasm which was lost on him. "I'm his aunt."

"Really!" cried Willy, springing up from his chair and rushing forward, as if to embrace her. Which he did not do. The emotion that had preceded him rebounded as from a cold surface. Willy hovered over her, distinctly puzzled. Again I was struck by his color, the cleanliness which showed none of the ruddy underglow of washing. Rather, he looked as if he had peeled away several outer layers and emerged like an onion, green and smarting, in his underskin.

"Well, that's very funny," said Willy, retreating to his chair, "that we should both be related to Bernie."

"He never told me you were his cousin," said Minna, looking at me reproachfully. "I expected you were a child."

"He never said anything to me, either. He just said you were some woman that he knew."

"Bernard, is that the way you talk about me?"

On such occasions, I am told, one wishes there were a hole in the ground into which he could sink. This is untrue, at least of my own experience. It was not myself I would have debased in submission before an overwhelming and unbearable reality. I would rather have stuffed reality itself into your hole in the ground. I was oppressed not so much by reality as by frustration—unless the two are one. Never having had great respect for the real, that evening, instead of fleeing, I would have driven it from me, torn its film from my eyes, dispelled its mists, myself remaining inviolable, incapable of error, illusion, or embarrassment, remote in a true world where plans prosper.

But although I considered myself the logical cause and center of events, both Minna and Willy, from this point on, ignored me. They had begun to take an interest in each other —which would have put the spur to my hopes, had the interest not been qualified by uneasiness, apprehension, resentment, and devices of hostility or contempt as only adults can employ them, for these are the fruits of their experience.

Willy asked, "How come I've never seen you before?"

"This is a fairly large world—and a fair-sized city." Her smile, too fine for other uses, was a weapon.

"But then, you've never heard about me either?"

"Of course not."

"Not so fast. Why haven't you ever heard about me?"

"I don't hang around pool rooms."

"Oh, are you smart! But the family, they never mentioned you. I didn't even know you existed. Why weren't you at the Seder?"

"Isn't that more or less my own affair?"

"But don't you ever go to see them?"

"If it would interest you to know, I'm not on speaking terms with the family."

"Not on speaking terms! What a shame! But why? They're wonderful people!"

Minna ran her hands through her hair, drawing the strands out full length and letting them fall—a woman's reference to her charm under circumstances which indicate her boredom. "Don't you suppose I might have my reasons?" she replied wearily.

"But what are your reasons?" Willy was at the edge of his patience, feeling she had mocked his good faith. "Why did you break away from them?"

"And why are you entitled to know?"

"Lord, what a suspicious, spiteful creature. All right, don't tell me. *Is nit gefüllte fish*—isn't that the way you say it? But all the same, I think you're wrong about them. The Millers are a swell crowd."

"Even his father?"

"Well, he's all right in his way. He's peevish, but he's had lots of hard luck. I can sympathize with a man who's lost his wife."

"But that's still not my idea of wonderful people."

"Now what a way to talk about your brother."

"He's not my brother."

"You mean . . . you're his mother's sister? Oh, I'm sorry, I didn't realize . . ."

This momentarily halted Willy. But the apology did not put an end to his resentment. His color had returned, even higher than usual, a full-blooded and angry shade. Had he actually been so nervous at the outset of the visit as to turn pale? This did not agree with my admiration for him as a brave man, unhesitating and self-possessed. And while I preferred to see him once more in command of his courage, I felt that he had overcome his uneasiness only by the strength of his dislike for Minna. If he had liked her he would have remained smarting and green, shy, his tongue lost, a fool. One way, and not the worst, of showing one's love for a woman is through foolishness; but Willy rather was hoping he might make a fool of her. Yet how could one possibly dislike my aunt Minna? And, what's more, how could Willy, whose feelings I would have accepted as my own, be the one to break my trust in her? I could only believe I had misinterpreted his attitude.

But Willy's dislike seemed only to grow. "What's your idea

of wonderful people?" he asked arrogantly, resuming the conversation.

"Oh, my friends, for instance."

"Who are your friends?"

"Oh, they're very nice," replied Minna in the tone of voice that she had often used with me, implying she did not share her friends with outsiders. Minna was colder, more restrained, and had a greater capacity for dissimulation than Willy; she employed her hostility like a talent, improvising gestures of annoyance, disapproval, and superiority. But again, how could they prove disagreeable to each other— and how could my loyalty contain them both?

She had now set about revealing the contours of her private world, glimpses of which had always delighted me. She described a few of her friends, mentioning them by name as if to show that though named they would still remain anonymous and remote in her possession.

I had always felt privileged merely to consider that I stood, no matter at how great a distance from the center, somewhere on the periphery of Minna's circle. But now, for the first time, and because Willy was with me, I felt excluded. I need, however, only to have yielded on the single point of my loyalty to him and once more I would have been her confidant, sharing secrets all the more intriguing for being but vaguely known. I need only to have said what her manner— if it was at all directed toward me—seemed to require of me: "Yes, he is ridiculous, he is dull, uncivilized," and I would have become at once the most civilized and desirable of all Minna's friends. Therefore, I could now feel no resentment at being excluded from her intimacy, for I understood that the present rejection was also an invitation, and the more my loyalty called me to the support of Willy, the more I was tempted by her.

"The people I prefer are, naturally, the ones with whom I have something in common," said Minna, shrugging her shoulders in summary after she had presented a list of her friends, whom she had identified by their talents. One name stuck in my mind, "Doogie Lucas, a painter." I could not tell whether Doogie was a man or a woman; the name combined exotic with homely qualities, as if to bear such a name were already an accomplishment while, at the same time, it remained a foolish thing.

Willy was silent while an indulgent but rather contemptuous smile spread over his lips. I don't know whether he meant to provoke her, or whether it was simply a kind of artlessness which persisted in spite of his anger that led him to say, "Well, I don't call that much of a happy life."

"But I don't particularly care for your opinions," replied Minna.

"Now don't get mad." He had evidently decided it was best to treat her like a child. "It's just that my own idea of a good life is something with a lot more to it. I don't believe you really get much satisfaction out of yours."

"And why not? I've been perfectly content to lead this life for years."

"Oh, but what's there in it? A blue light and a fireplace and a lot of trash on the walls."

"You have more than a little streak of boorishness," observed Minna.

I found myself agreeing inwardly, astonished by Willy's desecration of this temple, this cell of the spirit, and surprised at my own willingness to admit that I now could, conceivably, break with him.

"Look, lady, don't get mad. Why don't you get married and raise yourself a family?"

"Oh, how dull." Minna, restraining herself, still pretended she was bored, detached.

"Not at all. You only think so. Fact is, women like you always kid themselves. You think you're being free and having experience and taking life as it comes. But it's the ones like you who are really afraid of experience. You never settle down long enough to let it catch up with you. There's only one kind of experience, anyway—for a woman especially —"

"What makes you so sure of yourself, so smug, so damned certain," cried Minna, exploding at last, "and where do you get that 'women like you' stuff? One might think that you knew something, especially about a certain Minna Goodman. You're an idiot! An egotistical, simple-minded idiot! If you'd like to know something, that's what people like yourself are always doing. You always see things in black and white. If you meet a woman who's just a day over thirty and she's not married yet, that's the first thing that pops into your head—she ought to get married, she needs a family, she's lonely, she's miserable, bla, bla, bla. It's all so sweet and simple, such impertinent childishness, A, B, C—"

"Well, I don't care," said Willy, interrupting her, and proceeding in a drawl, the better to set off her provocation, "I don't care how simple it sounds. And that's another thing —say something simple to a woman like you, and she turns up her nose. It ain't complicated enough for her. But the point is, is it true or not? I say it is." He nodded, approving of his own sagacity. "I can't see where any life is worth a damn unless it has some real emotional feeling in it."

"Ouch!" said Minna. "It's actually painful to listen to that bilge. I've heard it a thousand times already, and it just keeps coming on and on and on—you don't even begin to know what you're talking about. How do you know that

I haven't a complete life? You don't know anything about me, you don't know how I live, what I do, what I've been through. You should have had to go through what I've been through and then maybe you'd have a right to talk. You're narrow-minded. You just see one thing, you think of one thing, and you say one thing—a woman's place is in the home. The point is, you really don't know the first thing about women. You haven't ever really known any. That's why you're so eager to see women in their place—you're afraid of them. I'd say, just as I'd say it to Bernard if he started up like this—only I think he's got more sense—I'd say you should find out a little more before you go around giving women advice. Sure, creep out of your little shell, find out what it's all—"

"Oh," said Willy, "I've done a bit of knocking about, and I think I've known more people than you'll ever know. And I mean women. I was a sailor once, you know."

In perfect good humor, pleased with himself, he rolled up his sleeve, exposing the tattoo. A blue anchor lay imprinted on his forearm, over the veins, light hair growing around it. Willy held his arm out in the light, smiling at the mark. "I could show you a few more."

"No, thank you," said Minna. "It's very esthetic, but one's enough. Enough to show what a fool you are. I don't care what you've been or how many women you've known. That's just childish bragging, anyway. You're a complete child. And a bit of a Philistine, too, if you'd like to know. Art doesn't mean anything to you. You sneer at it. And you're prejudiced against women—my kind, of course, and I'll bet you can't stand city life either, but would just prefer a nice little chicken farm somewhere—and I don't know how many prejudices you may have, simply as a Southerner—"

"Now hold on a minute!" broke in Willy. "That's all a

lot of bunk. You remind me of some communist women—"

"Speaking of prejudices," said Minna, scoring her point.

"—I know whose minds are the damnest one-track little trolley cars you ever saw."

"Now what's wrong with the communists?"

"Plenty. The women especially, the real devoted ones, they're all wrong. They think that just because they've found a cause they can devote their lives to, that takes care of their lives. The hell it does. Such lives, such awful mixed-up stinking messes. Take it from me, stay away from causes. I hate causes. Any person who finds a cause he can devote his life to is a goner."

"Oh, so now we're against causes."

"Lay off, lay off, sister. All I mean is, a person either believes a certain thing because it's really in him—and then it's not a cause, it's his nature—or else he's only faking. And trying to cover up a lot of dirt, most likely. When I was in France this last year, for instance . . ."

He paused, as if at the point of launching a narrative, and with an air of considering where he might best begin. I had not known Willy had been in France, which, of course, Minna had also not known, and we now fixed our attention on him, waiting—myself with an eagerness to learn something new about Willy, and Minna, so it seemed to me, with a trace of envy.

But Willy made use of the pause to stretch and yawn, to crack several joints with his stretching, and sprawl out at greater ease in his chair. As by an afterthought, he drew a cigar out of his breast pocket, removed the band and tossed it into my lap, and lit up, blowing smoke into the room.

"This was in Paris, about a year and a half ago," he began. "I knew a printer, a certain Charles, the most decent sort of chap you'd ever want to know. Now this Charles killed

[69]

himself on account of one of your devoted women, a communist organizer. It seems that he fell in love with her—"

"What were you doing in Paris?" Minna interrupted him.

"I was a newspaper correspondent."

"For what paper?" She was treating him with greater respect.

"*The Daily Jewish Tribune.*"

We both burst out laughing.

"What's so funny?"

"What do you know about Yiddish?" asked Minna.

"Nothing," said Willy. "And I didn't know anything about French either. But what of it? I wanted to go across. I hadn't seen France since the war, and somehow I'd always missed it when I was sailing. Got as far as China and India, but never France. And the paper I was working on wouldn't send me. So I went on my own. I had a friend of mine who works on the Jewish outfit fix me up. Just a matter of signing a few papers, and so on. It didn't mean anything, but I was able to get around a lot more. I did cable a story over—in English. About a synagogue in which the basement got flooded. They never used it, though."

Minna went right on laughing. It seemed to me she had overcome her dislike for him, forgotten her suspicions, and for the first time that night I felt some hope. She had suddenly grown kinder, as if she had suddenly realized, with the unmarried woman's inevitable forgiveness and indulgence, that Willy, whom she had considered a child, was, after all, a man. Her irritability, most noticeable when she was arguing with him, had all but disappeared. Her hands, at one point, had been trembling, and her eyes blinking violently. Now, having pressed her hands to her cheeks and drawn her fingers smoothly over her forehead, she was more fully composed; she sat back on the couch, her legs tucked under, and it even

[70]

appeared to me that there was an unusual softness and roundness to her face. This, however, she may have owed to the light. As I recall, there was a wall lamp arranged at an angle over the couch, so that she need only have sat in a given position, with her head and shoulders properly inclined, to have the light strike her hair, her face, and her arms where it suited her best. Not until this moment had she availed herself of the lamp. She looked at Willy with a curiosity far less critical than when she had observed his ridiculous costume. Her laughter, it seemed to me, was even a little unnecessarily prolonged, as if for his benefit; or, perhaps also for her own, for, while she laughed, I noticed that her eyes remained rather distinctly focused upon him, as if she were using laughter as a means of concealing her interest.

But Willy was undecided whether or not to respond to her friendliness. He was now a good deal more at ease, well reinstated in his own esteem and apparently unwilling to relinquish the advantage that he felt he held over her. The placidity with which he accepted her gaze showed him content to remain as he was now, satisfied with her attention. But at the same time I believe he was tempted to return her emotion, perhaps to come up to her, sit down beside her, even put his hand on her head, as he might do to me. In the complexity of his feeling he must also have been unwilling to relinquish the pleasure it had given him to quarrel with Minna, and I could not be sure whether he would return her softness, or again show spite, vindictiveness, mockery, perhaps even resuming his story about Charles in order to destroy the sympathy Minna had finally surrendered to him.

He put it as follows: "You see, miss, I don't mind your laughing, because it is funny in a way. But I have the feeling that I'm a better Jew than you are." He sat back, regarding her somewhat wistfully, and chewing on his cigar, then drew

[71]

it forth and held it between thumb and index finger, extended like a pointer. Through his mind there seemed to pass a final comment on her existence, as if he had settled it to his own conviction that she was cut off from the source of life and warmth and human solidity as represented by the Miller family.

But Willy sprang up. "Come on, let's not be so serious!" He winked at me, to assure me that I was not forgotten, and approaching Minna with an exaggerated bow, in which there was a little of the triumphant, a little of the ironic, and much of the self-flattering, he remarked, "Will my esteemed relative please forgive me for talking too much? Let's do something. Get up, we'll dance!"

Minna gave him her hand and let him draw her up. She found a program on the radio, hesitated a moment, then turned to him and stepped into his arms. She was very small and frail beside him, a full head and shoulders shorter than he. The palm of his hand, spread stiffly but carefully at her waist, enclosed her.

They circled around the room, smiling, talking to each other. I could not hear them but, I thought, they must be saying nice things to each other, they seem happy. His face was wide with a grin, and he held one eye half-shut in the expression of competent wisdom that I had seen in the game room when he was laying out a shot in billiards. It occurred to me that this, which was now before me, must be the very event I had so desperately wanted to bring about, and I tried to recall my feelings on the night soon after the Seder when I came to Minna with the still not fully conscious intention of bringing her together with Willy. I could not re-enter that earlier evening, the emotion of that time was gone, and I therefore had nothing with which to compare my present state. But I remembered the awkwardness which the grace

[72]

and freedom of her life had brought out in me, the penalty I had paid for my happiness and for venturing to express it. Was this, then, any nearer the true expression? Except that it was strange to me, and that I did not know how to accept and evaluate what had taken place tonight, I was satisfied, and I believed—since I could not be sure—that I was happy. I watched my aunt dancing in Willy's arms. It was very strange, even difficult to believe. To understand exactly what it meant—though, obviously, this was so full of meaning —or to know why, in looking at them, I experienced so deep, yet satisfying an embarrassment, was impossible. I watched Minna kicking her feet about, sliding and whirling, her heels flying, and Willy moving with her, less skilfully, with none of her grace and ease and yet perfectly in rhythm, and I felt, though I did not know how to dance, that I should very much like to be in his place.

We left soon afterward when Minna, in one of her complete changes of mood, just as she was about to mix drinks, looked at her wrist watch and declared, in great anxiety, that she hadn't realized how late it was and that she must go to sleep at once, for she had to rise early in the morning. I would have protested the loss of a drink, but as Willy showed no regret and at once made ready to leave, I put myself under his guidance, shook hands with Minna, and went willingly enough down the stairs.

"It really isn't as late as all that," said Willy, when we reached the street. "It's just after eleven. Care to go for a walk, kid? I'll fetch you home."

We went down to the lake, a few blocks away, and climbed up on the rocks. The waves played below, visible for a few yards as they came in with a small break, occasionally showing caps. It was a clear night; channel lights burned, in the

[73]

distance the piers were lit, and overhead a beacon crossed at regular intervals, cutting a blue swath.

I had been waiting for Willy to speak, but as he kept silent I finally said, "Well?"

Willy was staring at the water. I could feel he was sad. At last, rousing himself and sighing, to dissipate rather than express his mood, he replied, "I don't know, son."

"You don't know!" I thought he had finally taken a liking to her. "Why not?" I demanded.

Willy put his arm around my shoulder. I could feel the water drawing him, maintaining his sadness. It occurred to me that he must be thinking of his wife.

"It isn't that I dislike her. . . . But she's a very sad woman. Very unhappy."

Minna had never seemed particularly unhappy to me. I mentioned this, trying my best to hide my disappointment.

Willy, knowing how I felt, and not wanting further to depress me, smiled his better insight and did not argue.

A wind was blowing off the lake, mildly penetrating our clothes. From time to time spray fell, wetting the rocks, settling on our cheeks and hands.

"But didn't it strike you funny," said Willy, presently, unable to contain his insight, "the way she shooed us off all of a sudden?"

"Well, I suppose she had to go to sleep."

"No, it wasn't that. It's still early. She never goes to sleep before one."

"How do you know?"

"Oh, there are certain things a person knows."

"Then maybe she wasn't feeling well."

Willy smiled. He drew me tighter at the shoulder. His sadness seemed to grow, and yet lay more lightly on him. He could throw it off by talking to me.

[74]

"Tell me," I insisted.

"No, kid."

"Why was it funny? Why did she send us away?"

He would not answer me. The waves continued, meager and intermittent at our feet.

"Maybe you should know," said Willy, tempting himself. "She is your aunt." He considered this for a moment. "She's a very unfortunate woman," he went on slowly, hesitating over the words. "The trouble with her is . . . But you're too young. . . . It was very nice of you, though, to bring me over to meet her. I appreciate that."

"I wish you would tell me," I persisted.

"All right . . ." he said at last, and spoke slowly and carefully, as if to gauge his words by my understanding. "You know how it is with men and women, don't you? You're pretty grown-up by now. Well, you know, most men and women get married and live together. That's the only way they're happy. Your aunt never got married. There's probably some reason for it. But she's lived a woman's life anyway. . . . That is, I mean she's lived with men. She's probably living with a man right now."

"But she lives alone!" I exclaimed. At once, however, I understood him, and I thought I had no right to learn this about Minna.

"I'd say she's lived with lots of men," continued Willy, his sadness and restraint yielding before the pleasure of elaborating an insight. "You see, you got to look beneath the surface, otherwise women are very hard to understand. I bet you thought she had me buffaloed for a while. Not me, my boy, I know women pretty well. She's not what you think she is. . . . Of course, don't get me wrong, I don't hold anything against her. I've lived with a lot of women, and so will you when you're older. It's got nothing to do

[75]

with right and wrong. She can have lots of men if she wants to; why not? But it just hasn't made her very happy. I have the feeling that she just can't find happiness in her life."

I saw Minna isolated, lonely, cut off from human life and I felt sympathy for her—but also, and for the first time, abhorrence.

"The way I see her," went on Willy, taking an ever greater pride and pleasure in the exercise of his understanding, "she just can't find any satisfaction, and it just keeps driving her on and on. It's driven her from the family, from her friends, from man to man. . . . I know the type. . . ."

I felt myself on the verge of a shame and an enticement that I had never suspected to exist.

Chapter 8

Summer had come, and with it, vacation. And I, as was always each summer's case with me, was sitting about the house. Strictly, this meant my room. It was a large room, much larger than Willy's hotel cupboard. I had at my disposal bed and desk, and a bookcase nearly filled with books that I had bought with accumulations of my weekly allowance. There were a few prints on the wall, none of which I have kept or remembered. Other furniture was present, such as a reading lamp, soft chair, and footstool; but although I recall that my room was always cluttered, nothing else comes to mind when I think of that year—except a rowing machine which stood up-ended and abandoned in my closet. My room was an island in the house, the more so as I had come to regard as vulgar the surrounding area—where flourished statuettes, rubber plants, and stuffed furniture covered with lacy antimacassars.

I was not required to work during vacation. True, it had been pointed out to me that work was far from harmful. But as my father's business was still doing well (he sold hardware to dealers who, in turn, sold it to customers, an arrangement I never understood; a few years later he went bankrupt), I was free to do as I liked with my time. But during the first few weeks of that summer, I found leisure a burden. Though I sat, I could not sit still; and if I walked in the park, or played a few games of tennis, it was only because I did not know what else to do with myself.

It was late on a Friday afternoon, and my stepmother, having finished with the house, had just come out of the tub. She never spoke of bathing; she "tubbed" herself, or gave herself "a good tubbing." In general, she was a woman with an enthusiasm for health, full of vegetable greens, and attracted by nature to all healthful things which she identified by their shine and glow: tomatoes, red apples, oranges. (She had been the last of our household to abandon the rowing machine.) But her observation of personal cleanliness was more than a measure of health. It was, to begin with, an extension of her housework—done cleaning the floors and the furniture, the rugs, the dishes, and the woodwork, she would begin on herself, and in this extended ritual the same motive would continue to operate. For it was no mere going-over she gave to the house; it was a religious ceremony. Every Friday, the eve of the Sabbath spring, was a release from a winter of weekdays. And as she made the house ready, so she prepared herself for the coming of Queen Saturday, the *Shabbes*. I don't know what women in the old country would do of a Friday toward nightfall; whether

[77]

they went to *mikvah,* the ritual bath, for purposes of puri-
fication. We, however, had none of the usual concomitants
of an orthodox Sabbath. My stepmother baked no *chalah,*
traditional woven loaves, billowy or braided like wigs and
covered with a glossy patina of egg; nor, covering her head
and cupping her hands, did she light candles after sundown.
All this was left to my grandmother. Stepmother's tabernacle
was the toilet, and the tub was *mikvah* enough; she braided
her hair in place of dough, and as for the gleaming of
candles, she found an equivalent in cold cream which, when
applied to her nose in particular, was as good a substitute
as you could want.

My stepmother had flung open the bathroom door and I
saw her standing before the mirror plaiting her hair as I
was on the way to the kitchen for a drink.

She called to me. "Bernie, be a good boy and bring me
my hairpins. You'll find them in a little red box on my
dresser."

I went for the pins, and when I came back she already
had her hair woven in two strands, which she had looped
together on the top of her head, and was holding them in
place with her hand. She opened the box with her free hand
and stuck in the pins without messing a hair, meanwhile
saying to me, "Maybe you would take a tub, Bernie. Go
ahead, you'll feel *so good.*"

I did not want a tub.

"Go ahead, you'll cheer up. Shall I run the water for
you?"

No.

She gave her hair a final touch—it was dark and wet,
with here and there a thread of lighter color showing but
no trace of gray—and reached for the cold cream, scooping
a blob out of the jar. She worked the cream into her face

[78]

with both palms, rubbing vigorously, and with her fingers patted the wrinkled but not yet paunchy skin under her eyes.

"I think something is bothering you," she remarked while creaming her neck. It was an observation neither curious nor solemn, and had almost the same heartiness as her recommendation of the tub.

I did not deny it. In view of which she again offered to run the water for me. She had now finished with the cold cream and wiped her hands. My stepmother was wearing a clean pink apron with a starched collar and pearly buttons. Her face gleamed, her nose shone, her hair was as tight and neat as a cap. She was ready for the Sabbath.

Her next remark, as we left the bathroom, did not surprise me. "Bernie, why don't you ever read a book?"

I knew what she meant, and it was pointless for me to say, "But I read all the time."

"A Jewish book," she explained. "At least you should read, you just sit around the house. It's a shame the way you've wasted all your Jewish education. Ah, there are so many nice things—Sholem Aleichem, Peretz, Mendele. If that's too hard, your father could read them to you. You should take more of an interest in Jewish life."

She went to the stove, looked into the pot of boiling chicken, and regulated the flame. On the window sill a plate of fish had been cooling; she now put it into the refrigerator.

The kitchen was brilliantly clean—the linoleum scrubbed, the enamel table top wiped spotless, the checkered towels hung out on a rack on the pantry door. Sun was slanting in through the porch; the odor of chicken soup filled the room.

"You shouldn't be blue like that," said she. "A young boy like you should find plenty to do in the summer. No wonder you're downhearted, the way you sit around the house all day. Ah, when I was your age we used to have such good times. We'd dance the Hora and sing Hebrew songs and take courses in farming. We were young Zionists. Such a spirit!"

I ran a glass of water at the sink.

"Let the water run," said my stepmother, coming up with a head of lettuce which she doused under the faucet. She tore off the wilted outer leaves, shook the lettuce, and began to cut it into a bowl. She seemed to enjoy the feel of the crinkly leaves, the water standing up in distinct drops, and the green, yellow and white of the vegetable as she cut into the heart of it. At the same time, she was completely unconscious of her movements.

"At least you could spend a day or two at your grandfather's. Don't shut yourself off altogether from Jewish life."

She sliced several tomatoes into the bowl and stirred them up with the lettuce. A few of the round slippery seeds clung to the knife, and she washed it off, dried it and dried her hands. Then looked at the clock.

"Your father's coming soon. Bernie, be a good boy and put out some tissues for me. You'll find them in the upper left-hand drawer of the dresser."

She would now wipe the cold cream off her face.

To grandfather's I went. I packed a small suitcase full of a week's supply of shirts, socks, and underwear, took along a book to read, an orange, at my stepmother's insistence, to eat on the way, a tie for my grandfather and a lace-trimmed handkerchief for my grandmother.

The trip was by elevated train, over an hour long. I settled myself on the seat, looked out over the roofs and yards and soon lost sight of them. I had developed a tendency to stare off into space until objects fused and became meaningless;

but in actuality this was only a way of staring at myself. My eye fixed, unseeing, at some far point on the horizon, I would take account of myself as at a long distance; and the space which intervened between the place where I sat and the place in the world where I imagined myself to be, corresponded to the vacancy that had spread itself within me. My life was interrupted.

I could easily have patched it together again had I suffered, say, some minor but definite disappointment, such as losing the chance to visit another city, failing in an examination, or having a girl I was interested in go to a dance with someone else. But I had no girl, and never went to dances; nor did I fail my exams; and the opportunity to go traveling never presented itself. I might even have enjoyed frustration on any one of these counts. Then, at least, I would have known a form to my existence as something which could be increased or diminished by gain or loss. But I could not tell what I had lost; and even in moments when I thought I knew, I could not be sure that I understood.

I don't know what made me suffer more, whether it was loss of hope or loss of faith in Minna. I could not even be sure that what Willy had told me was true. I had, of course, no way of knowing. But I was more concerned with the sentence itself than with the person on whom it was passed, and this alone was sufficient to induce a loss of faith. I was repelled by the image of Minna that Willy had put before me. And while I tried to regain the pity I had felt for her as a lonely and unhappy woman, I found I could no longer extend my sympathy to the life she was presumably leading.

But I was involved in a curious duplicity. As I say, I knew the truth. I knew there were "all sorts" of women in the world, as my father might put it. Thus, I knew there were prostitutes, and I even understood their function. Not that

I had ever seen a prostitute—but there was a girl in high school, a certain Ruth Mary Kaufer who, I had heard, could be had for the asking, and I therefore imagined that prostitutes were all like Ruth Mary; dark-skinned, with large legs and breasts, and rather poor in American History. Such women were concrete figures and I accepted them. But it became increasingly difficult for me to see Minna in the light which they reflected. Prostitutes might even share a weakness in history with Ruth Mary, but there was nothing which I could allow Minna to share with them.

So long as I drew a line between Minna and women at large, I could look with composure at either side of the line. But the moment I brought Minna over the line, I would feel guilty, as if I had degraded her. Therefore I felt—if what I had been told were true—that she had degraded me.

This loss of faith brought on the loss of hope. It now seemed impossible that my desire to unite Willy and Minna should ever be realized. Willy had rejected her. Even if he were proved wrong, the fact that he could think such thoughts of her plainly showed his rejection.

But what if he were proved right? I knew that men pursued such women; the older boys went after Ruth Mary. All this, of course, could make Minna so much the more attractive to Willy. But then my original desire to bring them together, and all my plans and pains, would appear so foolish, so childish and naïve, that I should rather have kept them apart. I preferred disappointment to a downright humiliation.

Grandfather's greeting differed from grandmother's. For both of them the most significant thing about me was the suitcase I had brought along. But the old lady, who immediately understood its larger meaning, took it as a further

[82]

opportunity to express her resignation. "If you've come to stay, you may stay. Do I have a say in the matter?" was what her expression conveyed to me. Grandfather, however, immediately wanted to know what was in the bag. "Here, let me help you into the house!" he exclaimed, grabbing it out of my hand when I was at the door, and carrying it all of two feet over the threshold.

"Ah! It's so good to see you!" he went on, pinching my cheek and twisting my ear. He gave off a strong tobacco smell. "A pleasure! Here, make yourself at home right away! Wait! First change into something comfortable. You look hot and all worn out."

"So maybe you'd give him a chance to breathe?" said grandmother mournfully with her special talent for perceiving the old man's motives, which, however, as her expression indicated, was of no use to her. She went quietly back into the kitchen.

I opened the suitcase without delay and took out my grandfather's present.

"This is for me?" he asked, holding up the tie, fingering it and bringing the weave against the light. "Very nice, but it's not practical. What do I want with a tie? I have a beard." And he tucked the tie under his whiskers.

"You can still see it," I assured him.

"What are you talking about? Through my beard? Who can see it?"

He thought a little too well of his beard. It was dense enough around his mouth and chin, but the edge was scraggly; he trimmed it infrequently, only before important holidays. All the same it was a good beard, its thickest parts reminding me of the coat of a wire-haired terrier, a resemblance borne out by brownish tea and tobacco stains. Grandfather also reminded me of Socrates, a bust of whom stood in

[83]

a niche in the assembly hall at school. Except that his beard was better than Socrates' poor chop, grandfather had more or less the same features—the same knob of a head and bulb of a nose, the same fleshy and myopic turbulence about him.

My grandmother came into the room with a glass of seltzer into which she had lowered a spoonful of strawberry jam. I gave her the present and watched her, first over the rim, and then through the glass, as I drank. She had developed a ritual of acceptance, the result of years of dependency. First she would make herself unworthy, pursing up her lips, frowning, and disclaiming all title to gifts; then appear grateful, smiling, and finally, humiliated, saying "Thank you" in a hurt voice. Sometimes she would kiss her benefactor on the forehead, cheek, or lips, and occasionally—though she tried to make this appear casual and frivolous—she would kiss his hand.

Now she made the usual protests and stooped over my chair to kiss me on the head. "Haven't I been shamed enough?" said her kiss. And at once she put the handkerchief to use, blowing her nose as if to show that if we would force gifts upon her she would defend herself by taking them at their most common utility, preserving her pride by lessening their value, and thereby reducing her indebtedness. But as I saw her blowing her nose it occurred to me that her refusal to value the handkerchief may have been no pretense at all; for, very likely, the handkerchief was a cheap one, so that beneath all her complex humilities there may have lain the simple disappointment in receiving a worthless thing.

Now all this displeased grandfather, for it reflected on him. The old lady's sense of disgrace—though he did not share it—was, after all, as established by an old and bitter implication, a comment upon his failures. So he grew angry, glared and bristled and scuffed about the room in his straw carpet slippers. (In summer he changed his slippers to straw as other men change their hats. Grandmother still wore her boots.)

My grandfather disliked all display of emotion. Not that he would hold himself in on anyone's account—but then he was different. You could rely on him. If he was angry, you could be sure there was something to be angry about; and so if he was morose, sad, sulking, or happy, it was all with good reason. But what business had grandmother to stand there embarrassed, making faces of gratitude and shame?

We witnessed one of his famous rages, spontaneous, effervescent and, at least as far as he was concerned, a great delight. "Aaah!" he shouted, and "Gaah! Ha? What? Never mind! Let that be enough!"

The old lady ran into the kitchen giggling, I should say, in fear, were it not that her apparent emotions were too much of a piece with his. For in the same sense that he concocted a rage, so she contracted a fright. Neither, actually, could feel anything so strong. They quarreled because they were alone in the world.

"Now, well now," said the old man, whose anger died as quickly as it sprang, "I don't expect you to stay in the house with that crazy woman. You can't trust her a minute. There's no telling what she might do. She might sneak up on you with a knife while I'm not looking, and then where would you be? So, should we give her a chance to cool off for a while? Let's go out."

As we were about to leave, the old woman sneaked up on me brandishing nothing worse than a slice of bread, heavily smeared with chicken fat. "Eat, I beg you. It's a long time to supper yet."

Out of politeness, I offered a bite to my grandfather

[85]

when we were already out of doors. I did not expect him to accept, which he nevertheless did. I felt rather disgusted as I saw him tear out a deep, doughy chunk, avoiding the crust, chewing with his mouth open and rolling the bread over his gums. He smeared his fingers and his beard, and wiped his hands on his jacket before drawing out a crusty handkerchief with which he dabbed at his lips. Not that I was fastidious, but it offended and embarrassed me. I hated to see him placed, by his weaknesses, in a position of such obvious inferiority to myself. And now that we were out in the street, he should at least have preserved some trace of dignity. I was his grandson, he owed it to me.

But I felt no real shame in his presence. He lived in the heart of the Jewish neighborhood, where it was no uncommon sight to see old Jews in the street, bearded and slippered and wearing derbies. Once when he had come to our house— we lived farther North and West, among Gentiles—I had been ashamed to meet him at the elevated station and walk down the street with him, and had kept a few paces ahead, not letting him take my arm. He now held my arm, dragging after me and complaining of grandmother who, so he was telling me, was a silly woman with the brains of a twelve-year-old.

I was tired of it, tired of this poor, overdone figure of an old man, his endless complaints and ironies, his arrogance, wit, familiarity, his pinchings and pettings, angers and cranks, his constant, unalleviated *schlepperei*. His age was decay, a matter of loose teeth and gaping gums, blackheads, tobacco smell, seediness. And for all this he was vain, forever soliciting compliments and demanding gifts, picturing himself the very devil, the only man of his kind. Ah, how he thought well of himself!

And what was worse, how far from Socrates he was in

[86]

knowing himself. He believed to the letter his smallest pretenses, tormenting grandmother, I was sure, even when there was no one about to appreciate his wit, and thinking all the better of himself for the generous encouragement of his own applause. For he was a miserable man who happened to be profoundly satisfied with his lot. And therefore what else could he do?

I regretted my visit, not yet an hour old. Was this, then, that Jewish spirit from which I had shut myself off?

My grandfather did not care for parks. He crossed the boulevard which would have taken us to Douglas Park, and turned, instead, onto Kedzie Avenue. This was his favorite walk, down the dense street, past chicken coops, their wire and wooden sides stuck with feathers and droppings, past dry-goods stores, rummage stands, herring barrels. Here his contentment spread, like a golden dust, into all corners and doorways, over each dilapidated merchant and stall; this was his permanent fair, the bazaar of his senses. He elbowed his way along, calling out a greeting now and then, occasionally stopping to introduce me to a storekeeper. He presented me as if I were a bargain, some rare stroke of business, a young boy in good condition. And again he would push off, commenting under his breath, entrusting me with the secrets of the street, "Lazarus, a miser, a black heart; Fishman, a millionaire, I should have a penny for every dollar he makes in his stinking grocery; Waldman won't see another month of business, he's going bankrupt, mark my word."

We stopped before a store window which bore, in large gold lettering, the sign, P. MACHLISS, BUTTER AND EGGS. "Do you remember this place?" asked my grandfather.

Here once his own store had stood. Some four years ago he had closed down, bankrupt. I remembered the window, covered with dust and fly specks, where newspapers always lay scattered. My grandfather had filled about a dozen milk bottles up to their necks with flour and to the top with corn meal. This was to represent pure white milk floating a layer of thick cream. He had arranged the bottles in a pyramid in the center of the window, and for a month or so people would stop and remark how clever this was. But dust seeped into the bottles, streaking the flour gray and discoloring the corn meal. He never removed the bottles. They were his display, his novelty—and as for changing the flour, that would have been a waste. They remained, growing dirtier, marking his fortunes.

Besides the milk bottles there was another pyramid of orange coffee cans, and a layer of Yiddish newspapers spread in the window. The newspapers turned yellow. A long strip of fly catcher curled down from the ceiling. It had caught many flies.

The store itself was as discouraging as the window. Some of the shelves stood empty; the rest were sparsely populated by cans of peas and salmon—what else I cannot remember. Flat tins of sardines he had in profusion—little oval cans, key attached, wrapped in wax paper with red labels pasted on, bearing the portrait of a Norwegian king. A tub of butter stood in the window of the ice box, tilted toward the customers. Eggs lay in a trough behind the counter and in unopened crates on the floor. The ice box leaked, and the scattered sawdust always turned damp and gave off a sour odor.

My grandfather studied Machliss' window. It was neat, attractive, clean—no fly catcher, no fly specks, no dirt, no Yiddish newspapers. Cans and containers were piled up, not only in pyramids, but in rows, curving lines, zig-zags, steps, tiers, and balconies. Colored posters announced picnics and dances. There was an electric clock in the window, the long red second hand sweeping the dial.

"Ah, that man, is he a faker!" said grandfather. "Come on, would you care to go in a minute?"

P. Machliss was waiting on a customer. He wore a clean white apron, he was clean shaven, there was no derby on his head. He joked with the woman, inquired after her husband, her daughter. "I haven't seen her for awhile. Is she still going with the engineer? And what else, Mrs. Silver?"

Grandfather led me up to the counter, put his arm on my shoulder and winked at Machliss, who paid no attention to us. He laid out the purchases, added them up with an ever-sharp pencil, loaded them into a bag.

"Ah, Pinchus," said my grandfather as the woman was leaving, "are you a *goneff!* Highway robbery!"

"What's the matter?" said Pinchus, drily.

"What did you charge her for the lox?" demanded my grandfather.

"Why, do you want lox?"

"Pinchus, I should buy by you yet! I just want to know."

"I don't charge a penny more than you'll find all over," said Pinchus, righteously.

"Nu, Pinchus, why don't you ask me how is *my* family, ha? You see this boy, that's my grandson."

"Fine boy," said Pinchus skeptically. He smiled briefly, showing a gold-capped tooth, and looked out the window in the hope of a customer.

Grandfather took a dried apricot from a box on the counter and began to suck it. "Look here, Pinchus, I don't remember any more, is that a new ice box, or did you paint the old one?"

"A new," said Pinchus. "All the fixtures are new."

"Are you a liar! You painted it. What then, you should

invest in new fixtures? Listen, if you don't mind, I'd like to see how you fixed up the back of the store."

"I can't show you."

"Why not?"

"I can't and that's all." Pinchus glared. It was his store now.

"Pinchus, you do your own candling?"

"What then?"

"I thought—well, you know, I thought maybe you're too busy. I see all the time you've got customers. . . ." A tone of wheedling had crept into his voice. I could not understand it. "And as for me," my grandfather whined and smirked, "as for me, *auf die lange yor,* I'm not so busy these days. So I thought maybe if I could come in by you a few days a week . . . as a favor, you understand, I would candle for you. For whatever you think it's worth . . ." He helped himself to another apricot and sucked it hungrily.

"This is a business," said Pinchus sternly.

"I know, I know, I understand, excuse me," said grandfather, replacing the wet apricot on the counter. "Mr. Machliss, tell me, maybe you sell figs?"

"No figs."

"So I'll tell you what. I'll give you figs. Na!" he cried, thrusting out his fist, the thumb folded between the first and second finger; and, laughing and coughing, scuffled out of the store pulling me after him.

"Such a pig!" said he, catching his breath after we had hurried down the street. "Did you see how he looked at me? Feh! Just what he wanted, I should come and beg by him! Ptu!" he spat. "I gave him good. He'll never get over it!"

He clung to me, laughing and wheezing, demanding admiration, gratitude. Over and over again he recounted the incident in the store, as if I had not been present; and now one might think it had all been for my benefit—he had been defending me, my name and honor, paying him back on my account. His humiliation had become a triumph in which he invited me to share, a life's work, an achievement. But it had cost him an effort. A branch of veins stood out on his forehead under the rim of the derby, and in the folds of his throat, over the soiled collar, his blood pulsed, moving the skin.

We were turning back toward the house. I thought I should leave at once, or, at the latest, right after supper. I had had enough.

But grandfather said, "It may be a little late and we should go home soon—your grandmother must be all cooled off by now. But if you think we could spare another ten minutes, being we are going by, I'd like to drop in and see Reb Feldman. Do you remember him? I took you when you were a little boy."

While speaking of Feldman, he had acquired a new dignity and gentleness, mentioning his name with respect. Feldman, as I remembered, was a *melamed,* he gave Hebrew lessons. His pale, puffy face under a black beard came to mind. He wore rings on his fingers. I remembered that my grandfather had always stood in awe of him, considering it a great honor when Feldman paid him a visit.

We were received in solemnity at Feldman's house by a man of my grandfather's age. "Maslov, Reb Feldman is all right?" asked grandfather, at the door.

"Thank God he is better, you may come in." Maslov led us to the living room where several elderly men were sitting at a table. In a corner of the room, propped on a divan, sat Feldman, wearing a skullcap and a long white coat, like a butcher's apron, over his clothes. He acknowledged my grandfather briefly, pronouncing his name by way of greeting, and took my hand in his ringed hand, which was moist and soft.

"My grandson, my Harry's son, *auf lange yor*," explained grandfather.

"I remember him. *Bar-mitzvah?*"

"Last year, thanks to God."

He released my hand, motioning us to sit down. Maslov, who served him as an attendant, brought chairs to the table and a moment later returned with two glasses of tea. Grandfather drank carefully, taking small, quiet sips.

The table was placed so that Feldman, though lying on the divan, was still at its head. The other men, who were holding a discussion, directed their remarks to him, and he followed the argument, nodding, interrupting with a word or a phrase and passing judgment. He spoke quietly, rather hoarsely and with some difficulty, pausing with each word as though he were in pain. The men, who would raise their voices and mercilessly break in on one another, immediately fell silent when he spoke.

I remembered several of them from the synagogue to which I had occasionally gone with my grandfather, years before. One, I was sure he was called Berrl, had a large spherical growth beside his ear, which his beard did not cover. Another I remembered as Yeshua the cigar maker, a portly man with stained fingers. They all wore earlocks. It occurred to me now that these must be *Chassidim,* a religious sect of which I had heard my grandfather speak, men of extraordinary piety and enthusiasm.

I waited for some sign, some indication of their mysticism. But the discussion was progressing in orderly fashion, with questions, objections and repetitions, and words of judgment from Feldman. I tried to follow the argument, but there were too many Hebrew words for my understanding, and frequent references to what I gathered were Talmudic matters. My grandfather also seemed perplexed, though he participated in the discussion to the extent of nodding his head, vigorously—I could not say whether in agreement or dissent—and repeating a few words that fell his way, such as, "Of course, of course, what a question!"

In a corner of the room sat two men playing chess. I had not noticed them when I came in. Their light was poor and, as they bent over the board, they themselves seemed like nothing so much as chessmen, knights with narrow, pendulant faces, carved out of bone to which skin and hair still clung. They did not speak to each other, but occasionally one struck up a melody in which his partner joined, humming and intoning the syllables, "aie, dai, dai, dai, dai—yam, bim, bom." Together they would nod over the melody, sharing and extending it, turning their hands in and out at the wrist, their elbows planted before them on the table. During pauses in the discussion one could hear them, and the melody also seemed to be issuing in an undertone from the remote and ponderous Feldman, as well as the men at our table, a slight weaving rhythm catching their heads.

Grandfather and I had finished our tea and were about to leave, when Reb Feldman drew himself up and began to speak. As I say, I was unable to understand him, but it seemed to me that he, the master and judge, was summing up for his disciples, giving them his wisdom and his truth. He now spoke more clearly and rapidly, emphasizing his words with sharp gestures of his hands. And while he spoke, his expression relaxed and a shrewd sweetness came over him and he no longer seemed to be in pain. The others sat forward in their chairs, listening intently, following each word as if it held a treasure and nodding with understanding and enlightenment. My grandfather, too, was nodding, and like

[93]

the others, he was muttering under his breath, "True, how true, amen!"

Feldman had finished speaking, but the men still sat motionless, watching him reverently, as if he had clarified a mystery before their eyes. The melody was heard again, coming softly from the corner, and it grew louder, sweeping across the room, and suddenly one of the chess players sprang up, clapped his hands and, followed by the other, began to dance. The men at the table also sprang up and joined the dance, holding their arms above their heads, clapping hands, turning and weaving on bent knees. Feldman lay back, his eyes half shut, a smile on his face, and he snapped out a rhythm with his ringed fingers.

Later, when we came to take our leave, I could see that my grandfather was transformed into a new person. A look of completeness lay on his face, an expression of gratitude as if for the ecstatic understanding to which Feldman had led him. Though unable to understand, I had shared the experience of that ecstasy, and I, too, felt grateful for it.

We were sitting down to dinner when the bell rang and Willy came up the stairs. I ran out to greet him, and it was not until I had nearly thrown myself at him, that I realized we were estranged.

His visit was unexpected. The table had only been set for three and grandfather, who let him in, did not at first recognize him, and had a difficult time establishing his identity for grandmother.

"Willy. Don't you remember him? The Seder. He's the one who sang. Martha Vogel, *olav hasholem*, her husband."

"Martha's husband? Oh, how is Martha?"

"Fool, you. Didn't I say *'olav hasholem'*? She's dead."

"Oh, I thought it was a different Martha. So who is he?"

"It's no use," said grandfather. "When she gets mixed up, it's hopeless."

"Oh, now I know!" exclaimed grandmother. "He's the one who cracks nuts with his teeth. Why didn't you say he was at the Seder?"

I now suspected she had been pretending.

"Well, I'll have to set another place." She got up, at once resuming her familiar attitude of resignation, and scuffled into the kitchen. She was a far more complicated soul than grandfather.

Willy made no objection to the dinner invitation; in fact, he drew up a chair and sat down at the table as if he had come for that very purpose—as, most likely, he had.

My grandfather, meanwhile, was in a quandary. Willy had brought a jug of wine, and the old man seemed at a loss to know what to do with it. He stood at the table, holding the jug by the ear, and I could tell he was debating whether to use it. It was obvious that he would have to serve wine. But should he serve the wine Willy had brought, or pour from his own stock—that is, the wine others had brought before Willy? At last he clapped the jug down on the table and unscrewed the cap, calling to my grandmother to bring glasses. I believe he had thought it out as follows: "I know what I've got. Some of it is not so wonderful, but on the whole, it's good wine. What this is, I don't know. It may be very good, the best yet. On the other hand, it may be *pisschachts*. If I open it to taste it, we'll have to use it. But if I don't open it, he may be insulted. So, we'll just have to take a chance."

For once, the prospect of a drink did not appeal to me. I was hurt. If Willy, who had been to grandfather's only once before, was quick enough to understand what was required of him, to know that he would be expected to bring a gift, the most acceptable, of course, being wine, then why shouldn't he have been able to understand me? Shouldn't it have occurred to him, that night when we left Minna and walked down to the lake, that what he had to say would shock me, and, even granting me a maturity beyond my years, upset me severely? . . . I had not seen him since then. We had been avoiding each other.

And we were still doing so, even though we sat opposite each other at the table and Willy winked at me and directed his jokes at me, and I winked back and laughed. We were no longer free with each other. Willy was embarrassed. He had not expected to find me here. I noticed that he ate rapidly and—what was rare for him—did not finish his food. Since he was the more uneasy of the two of us, I exploited my advantage, staring at him throughout the dinner, watching how he cut meat, how he chewed, used his napkin, drank water, extending my observations to the minutest point and with a growing satisfaction which the realization that this might be cruel served only to increase. Several times he glanced back and my stare broke. "What have you got against me, kid?" he seemed to say. Actually, what was I complaining of? For if he had lied to me that night, pretending that Minna suited him, would I have been better off? And if, later, I discovered that he had lied, wouldn't I have been all the more angry? For then I would have been offended by the fact that he had treated me as a child. And yet, I felt he had no right to assume innocence. He knew what I held against him, and first now, in his effort to humor me and pretend ignorance of the issue between us, he was treating me as a child, which made me even angrier.

I had a sip of Willy's wine and found it brackish. But it was just the thing for grandfather, to judge by the amount he drank—unless his enthusiasm may be ascribed to his thinking of the better wine he saved by drinking this. But as any wine would, it set his tongue wagging. He related the incident in the store, presenting it now in unrecognizably heroic proportions, and Willy laughed and called it a good one, and was content to hear it twice over. I was disappointed in my grandfather for yieldng so soon to his weaknesses. I still remembered the scene at Feldman's house. Why were people incapable of remaining fixed to the best moments of their lives?

I withdrew myself, as I had done coming down in the elevated, and continued to stare at Willy as from a great distance. I had noticed an improvement in his table manners. Despite his rather hurried chewing, he had a greater command over himself. He did not slouch so much; he used his napkin frequently and kept one hand in his lap. All of which, since he had no reason for being on good behavior at my grandfather's where the example was all to the contrary, led me to wondering. Furthermore, he was wearing a new suit, or an old one in very good condition which I had never seen before—brown with a tie to match. For once he had it right.

Only a few weeks ago, this improvement would have delighted me. Now it only made me feel uneasy. This was no natural or gradual change; nor was there anything in Willy's character to call forth such changes without reason. A reason I had once supplied myself in the form of Minna. But Minna was, evidently, not for him. What then? It hurt me that there should be reasons for Willy's behavior which I would not— and need not—know. His good suit and his good manners cut me rudely. I was no longer his concern.

Our uneasiness still persisted after supper when we went into the living room and Willy and my grandfather lighted cigars. He would have to speak with me, show me that his interest had not died, invent an excuse for failing to call me during these last few weeks, and find other soothing lies, though both of us knew the truth.

"How's it been going, kid?" Willy asked at last.

It was going all right. I avoided his eyes.

"Having vacation now?"

I was having vacation.

"Swell, eh? Lucky kid. We ought to get together one of these days. Why haven't you called me?"

I had been hoping he would avoid this question. It was unfair. I too could have asked it, but had restrained myself. I stammered some excuse, making out that it was entirely my fault that we had not seen each other.

He smiled at me, strangely, evidently understanding my embarrassment. I felt he wanted to speak to me about the evening at Minna's, perhaps even apologize for what he had said. But at the same time I could sense his reluctance, as if it were now impossible for him ever to mention her name to me again.

Suddenly it struck me that he might have been back to see her. This possibility, while it set off a train of complicated and, ultimately, perhaps even unpleasant consequences, at the outset, nevertheless afforded me great pleasure, for I had at least hit upon the answer to an immediate question. I thought, "That's why he looks so nice!"

"Have you found a job?" I asked, thereby testing and trying to extend what I already believed.

"Why, as a matter of fact, I have . . . sort of," he replied in extraordinary caution, evidently wanting to know exactly what I meant. "Just the other day," he went on, with more of his customary self-confidence, "just the other day a fellow named Jimson came up to me and said, 'Harpsmith, you're one man I want to work for me.' 'What's your deal?' said I. 'It's a square deal, here's my card,' says he. 'You come on

[98]

down to my office and we'll talk about it there.' Just like a shot, kid. I'm going down to see him tomorrow."

I was convinced. Gathering my courage, I asked, "Have you seen her?" My asking was already an answer. I thought, "If he had not seen her, he would have asked me first."

"Her? . . ." Willy pretended his memory had failed. "Oh, of course, you mean what's-her-name." He laughed. "No, no I ain't seen her." He added a moment later, "Say, you know, maybe I had the wrong slant on her. Don't take what I said too seriously—I sometimes go off half-cocked. . . . You know, I might sort of like to see her again. . . ."

This settled it for me. He was lying. It had evidently been troubling him and he wanted to retract. And what better reason could he have for regretting his words than the fact that he was actually seeing Minna? As for his half-hearted willingness to see her again—this was cover-up, should I learn, on my own account, that he had returned.

He left soon afterward. We exchanged lame promises to meet in the near future. He said his good-bye rather boisterously to my grandfather, calling him old-timer, and asking, in mock innocence, how many times a year the Seder came around; and thanked my grandmother profusely for the meal, kissing her cheek. I stood at the door, beside my grandfather, seeing him go, and I thought, apropos of his visit, which was otherwise unexplained, "Fine tricks! Sponging off a sponge. . . ."

They go to sleep early. My grandmother made the bed for me in the back room off the kitchen, brought me another slice of bread and chicken fat and kissed me good night. My grandfather came in in his underwear (long, winter) and his straw slippers and twisted my ear. It grew quiet in the house. They were in the front bedroom. In an hour or so they would begin to make their rounds, going at frequent intervals to the toilet. Until then they would have their only sound sleep.

I sat back on the bed eating the slice of bread and fat. I felt embittered toward Willy. Since I was convinced that he was now seeing Minna—against everything he had led me to expect—I could only believe that what he had told me that night on the rocks was nothing but malice. He had known what effect his words would produce—the very one he wanted. By shocking me, he thought he would drive me away and thus have Minna to himself, unencumbered by a curious and persistent little boy who knew nothing of such matters, and yet understood too much.

This satisfied my bitterness, my estrangement; nevertheless, I could feel that the account was short. To justify the hatred I could now sense rising against him, I should have had to know more, to feel more than conviction, to have the very truth, cold and complete in my hands. And here was a curious thing. Much as Willy's statement had shocked me, and my own anger had sought to dispose of it, I still found in it something admirable, and I knew I was not yet done wondering over the words which, seemingly in all sincerity, he had entrusted to me. For as I hated him for it, I was also drawn to him. It was not enough to account for his words by thinking that Willy wanted me out of the way. I would also have to have the truth. And while, at one moment, I had been satisfied to think that I knew enough, now I felt that my bewilderment was first beginning. Even if Willy had lied about Minna, how had he come about his lie, a lie that seemed so wild and fantastic to me, and yet held such a compelling attraction to belief? Much as I detested it, I could not help feeling that it represented a triumph of human intelligence and that his gift, whether for truth or falsehood, was a gift of the purest insight.

I, too, would have to know the truth. By whatever means, whatever penetration, by instincts not yet awakened in me, or by a common knowledge not yet accumulated, I, too, would bring myself into reality, knowing and understanding and seeing as clearly as a man could see.

For, as at Feldman's house, when I had seen a moment of understanding pass before a group of old men and had felt that this represented what was best in their lives and in Jewish life, so I now felt that possession of such understanding would be the very best of my own life, and knowing the truth, itself a kind of ecstasy.

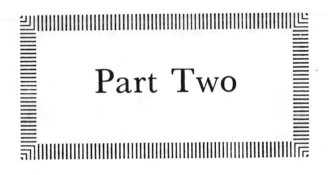

Part Two

Chapter 9

When I came home on the following Friday I found my stepmother depressed. The house showed it. Although it was not actually dirty or upset, it lacked some of its usual exuberant perfection. Our house was her personal instrument and it told her humor.

She was in the kitchen, cooking. It was past four o'clock; she was at least an hour late with her work and had not yet had her bath. Her tub. Something was wrong—which, I must admit, I was pleased to discover. Not that I bore her ill, or took pleasure in the fact that she was suffering; but the existence of distress, and therefore of an immediate mystery, served me as a stimulant. Here was something to be known.

I had often observed that around all my mistakes in judgment there lay an area of truth. It was therefore impossible not to know the truth. For no matter how wildly I might go guessing wrong, I would still instinctively be right, and the truth would be with me, exerting its influence. To know the truth it was only necessary to yield. Therefore, yielding to conjecture, to premonitions of domestic mishap—the mere awareness of which I now took to be a sign of wisdom—I began to question my stepmother: what was wrong, was she not well, or was something else troubling her? That is, was she worried, had she received bad news, had something happened in the family, or was it simply the housework piling up? Her answers were evasive, and yet I felt she was not annoyed with me. She seemed to welcome my questions, and while she would not answer, she would wait patiently until I should come upon the truth.

And so I went ahead, feeling my insight grow with each

guess. "You lost your purse and a lot of money. . . . Robbers broke into the house . . . A fight with the neighbors . . . Something happened to pa?"

"What kind of nonsense is this? Tell me better, how are your grandparents?"

"Something happened to the bathtub?"

"Now stop it! Nothing happened. Everything is all right. How did you enjoy your visit?" My stepmother could not understand my motive. Had I suddenly decided to become a mountain climber and therefore gone about chopping footholds in the walls to practice scaling, she would not have thought me engaged in a more senseless and destructive activity. Yet she still wanted me to know what was troubling her and was disappointed that I should, apparently, desire only to abuse the opportunity.

It was not so easy a matter to yield to the truth. I felt the complexity of things. I would dream of a simple world, of simple motives and emotions; but the world I knew was so complex that no knowledge was without a trace of disappointment. For my pleasure lay only in anticipating, in wondering whether I could foretell that which, when it occurred, would leave me feeling both surprised and cheated. Still it was a delight to know anything. And so I can remember the great pleasure I felt when I learned—through a close guess and my stepmother's subsequent confirmation—that she had been quarreling with my father, and the week I had spent away from home had been one of sheer misery for her.

She put down the ladle, wiped her hands on her apron and began recounting her troubles with a sad and long-suffering demeanor that did not fully conceal her eagerness; and while she was openly pitying herself, she tried also to impart, through force of habit, an impersonal air to her words, as if the story did not really concern her, hoping thereby to exonerate my father.

I had been gone only two days when my father began to complain of my absence. Why had I gone? At her suggestion. Ah, and why did she suggest I leave? Because I was only lying around the house, blue and depressed, and she thought a change might do me good. Besides, why shouldn't I keep in touch with Jewish surroundings? Oh, so, said my father. And what was I blue about? And isn't this a Jewish home? She didn't know why I was blue. She thought I needed a change—you know, young boys have moods and you can't always tell why. And of course this was a Jewish home, but still the grandparents are, after all, old folks, and there's no comparison.

Now my father was also a man of complexities and her explanations did not satisfy him. He pointed out, as the first undesirable possibility, that I might really not have gone to my grandparents at all—or, granted that I had been there (for hadn't I called up every day and hadn't she spoken with me and with the old folks as well?), still, I would call only in the morning, and who knows where I would spend the rest of the day? A very fine thing, incidentally, that I should call only mornings when my father was away at work. Now, if my stepmother had only used her head she could have seen that in sending me off to my grandparents she was really turning me loose to do as I liked—that is, to run around with my cousin and my aunt, a fine pair of friends for a boy like me.

"But Harry," she had objected, "you knew the boy was going. I told you so the night before he left. Why didn't you say something then?"

To which he had replied, "Did I know he would go to those two bums?"

When she had finished her account, had done telling me how my father had sulked and brooded, sulked and raged and grown in bitterness with each day—my stepmother began peeling the potatoes for our supper. The peelings rose over her knife, drooped and fell in chains, forming a pattern on the sink.

Now, said stepmother, she knew that father disliked Willy and Minna. It was not her business to know why, although she had an idea. As for herself, of course, she liked Willy very much, thought he was a fine person, but if my father thought otherwise, let him think what he please, she wouldn't argue with him. When it came to Minna, however, she had nothing to say. She had never met her. But judging from what she had heard, perhaps Minna wasn't such a fine woman, and maybe I should not see her.

I demanded to know what she had heard.

She gave it thought, weighing it as she would a potato in her hand. She continued her peeling, laying out several fresh long strips on the sink. "I haven't heard anything. . . . Well, you know how people talk. But it's not right to pay attention. You should never listen to gossip, Bernie. She's your mother's sister, after all. Still in all, the family is against her, and since they know her, maybe they know what they're talking about."

"But they're wrong!" I protested. "They're all wrong. Why do they all hate her?"

"Who says they hate her? Nobody hates her."

"Father hates her."

". . . Well, maybe he has reason to. After all, she did try to take you away from him."

"Take me away? I don't believe it!"

"You can't remember. You were too young at the time."

"But how can you remember? You didn't even know us then."

"No, but I found out."

"That she tried to take me away?"

"That she really did take you away. She kidnaped you!" solemnly declared my stepmother, giving her words a superstitious intensity. She had finished peeling the potatoes and was now jabbing out the eyes. "She took you away and kept you for more than a week! Your father had to call the police to get you back."

"I don't believe it. Why would she do that?"

"She's a strange woman, very hard to get along with," replied my stepmother in all earnestness, as if she were entrusting me with the fruits of her own observation. "I can't answer for her. But I think it's because your father wouldn't marry her. Do you hear what I say? As soon as your mother died, maybe no more than a month later, she was already making your father a proposition—if he would marry her, she would bring you up. Just like that! Your father naturally said no. So she takes you and runs off!"

"But she told me pa chased her out! And she never said anything about taking me."

"Naturally not. Chased her out? It's a wonder he didn't! She would have deserved it, Bernie. Your mother was her own sister, think of that. And not even dead a month yet! Some women, I tell you—even if she is your aunt—they're just the limit. Imagine, who would do a thing like that! Why, it's even against religion. Jewish law wouldn't allow it."

"I can't believe it," I replied. "I don't mean to call you a liar—but I know her, I know she wouldn't do anything like that." I realized that I was questioning my father's word rather than hers and, to conceal this implication, I repeated, "I just can't believe it."

[109]

"You don't understand certain things yet," she replied, making reference to my age in a manner that did not offend me, for she assumed an attitude, not of greater knowledge, but of greater faith. "But think of it. She would leave a man all alone when he needs help most and run away with his five-year-old child just because he wouldn't do what he knew was wrong. And who is she that everybody has to run to marry her? Some women, I tell you, can be so low, absolutely without respect, without consideration, selfish, cold, without feeling, not a bit of shame, just me, me, me all the time, all the time take, grab, destroy!"

There was a poetry in everything she did, a rhythm of adequacy and purpose that made the common objects of the house suit her deepest emotions. Now with these words, in which, as it were, she was presenting a vision of evil, she set the pot of potatoes down upon the stove, and in the flame she lit there was the very vision itself, bright blue and intense, a fire piped out of hell.

It would have been easy enough for me to accept this vision—it conformed to my forebodings, the omens I had had of the truth. And yet I could not bear to hear anyone speak ill of Minna. Besides, my stepmother was always too willing to incriminate. Whether Minna had left the family of her own accord or had been driven away by my father was immaterial to her—sufficient the fact that she was gone.

Because I had already found my own reasons to suspect her, quite apart from the family's, I felt I should remain loyal to Minna no matter what she had done. It occurred to me, however, that my stepmother was pledged to her own loyalty, and that while she had only a vague and biased notion of Minna, which she knew to be unfair, she would continue to accept it as the truth because my father demanded it.

"What you say about her is just what pa told you, isn't it?" I asked.

"Bernard, would your father lie?"

Though no more than his second wife, was she not more my father's child than I? She gave him her obedience, completely surrendering that private and independent perception which should have told her—as it told me—that it was certainly conceivable for my father to lie. Again I felt—as I so frequently did when I stood in the presence of my elders—that I was morally inferior, incapable of equaling them in faithfulness. Even my resolve to remain loyal to Minna had been made with half a heart, for I now realized that I could still believe evil of her, and not only would my own suspicions not vanish, but they would grow under the increment of Willy's and my stepmother's words. The very best that I could do for Minna would be to regard these suspicions as elements in an unfolding and still inconclusive account. Why, then, should my stepmother be incapable of feeling a divided emotion; what made her so much the better person that she should be unable to liberate herself, if only for a moment, from the obligations of loyalty?

"I don't say he's lying," I replied. "But maybe he hasn't told you everything. Maybe he doesn't know the whole truth any more than we do."

"I can see she's been putting ideas into your head," persisted my stepmother, indicating her disapproval by turning her back and giving her attention momentarily to the stove. "You would never have said that about your father before."

"But I'm not saying anything. All I mean is nobody is perfect."

"No, Bernard, you don't have to tell me what you mean. I can see what's been going on in your mind. No sir, it's not right." She shook her head, reproachfully.

[111]

But poetry at this point had failed her. When she took up a fork and began testing the potatoes, it was an awkward gesture conveying no more than the meanest significance— the emotion that she expended in bondage to the house and not what she drew in return. At such times she could appear the loneliest of women. When I refused to support her in admiration of my father, when I allowed so much as a hint of my disaffection to appear, she felt herself a stranger, perhaps even a hired woman working for a strange man, her love for whom was not only unappreciated but even unwelcome, and for his son who would never become her son. The withdrawing of my support was equivalent to abolishing her role. She would be checked in the very act of serving as heart and center of the family, and her devotion to its rituals, her preservation of its human warmth and its delicate and intimate structure, would be destroyed.

"At least you can try to be nice," she continued, no longer attempting to conceal the resentment in her voice. "You don't have to provoke him. If he doesn't want you to see that aunt of yours, then you shouldn't see her. That's the least you can do, and you can do it for me. Who do you think has to suffer when you disobey him, who do you think gets the blame?"

"But it's still not true what he says about her. And I'm going to find out the truth!" Avoiding her appeal for sympathy, I stared at her, holding my eyes set and my lips firm, an expression I had practised in the mirror, by which I meant to show her, and myself, that I would not be thwarted, and that if I had failed in my effort to yield to the truth, I would now make the truth yield to me.

My stepmother sighed dispiritedly. "Don't be such a fool, Bernard. Stop looking like a monkey and behave yourself.

At least for the next week you should behave yourself. . . . I bet you don't even know what next Saturday is."

"Next Saturday?"

"A week from tomorrow . . . I thought so. It's your father's birthday. Ah, what a fine son you are! I'm planning a surprise party for him. The whole family's coming. So be nice! For a whole week be nice!

"Aie, it's late!" she cried, and rushed off to finish her housework.

The next day I went downtown. I had worked out a course of action and invested it with secrecy and great importance. The plan—it hardly amounted to one—consisted simply in going to Minna's dress shop. I would stand outside the door, or perhaps across the street and look on, unobserved, while Minna went about her work. Thereby, I told myself, I would be able to make a fresh start, begin with the woman in her own surroundings into which I had never entered, and where neither loyalty nor disappointment would influence the judgment I should form. Since I had last seen her, nearly a month ago, she had become almost a grotesque image. I could not accept what Willy and my stepmother had told me. But no more than half a belief is necessary for full suspicion, and suspicion had distorted her in my eyes, had replaced the woman I admired by the very figure, capable of evil, who, while she was not the true Minna, nevertheless answered to every account I had heard of her. To see her therefore was both a means of determining whether these stories were true—and whether Minna was real.

It amuses me now to recall the extent to which I indulged myself. Despite the importance of my undertaking, I gave it all the accessories of play, converting it into a sort of detective work, determining to go to Minna's shop by a roundabout route and even scrutinizing the card she had given me as if it might provide some valuable clue in addition to her address. I remembered the club to which I had belonged when I was in seventh grade, the Secret Star Society, or S.S.S., the meetings we had held under password and drawn shades in a member's basement, how we had skimped and saved for a toy microscope and had obtained samples of chicken blood and compared it with our own, through the lens. In childhood we had courted danger and the sense of it, enacting a myth of risk and blood without recognizing that it was myth, aware only of the greater pleasure, the heightened consciousness of life that these measures afforded us. And now I was re-enacting the myth. More closely than I realized, my present life was connected with the past.

Minna did not have a shop of her own. The name printed on the card she had given me proved to be that of a firm with offices on the sixth floor of a building in the garment district on the outskirts of the Loop. I did not go up.

It was a clear afternoon, not very hot, the street was full. I remained in a doorway, opposite the entrance to Minna's building, deposited there by the momentum that had been carrying me, imagination thwarted and unconsumed. I had so confidently looked forward to an adventure that I was unprepared for this interruption of my activity. With the same alertness and excitement with which I had set out on my undertaking I began watching the passersby: shipping clerks pushing racks hung with garments, wheeling wagons piled high with cardboard boxes; delivery boys with caps on their heads and parcels and envelopes under their arms; men in straw hats carrying briefcases; women coming in and out of drugstores and restaurants, some of them cool, slender, with that tense delicacy I admired in Minna, others slovenly and warm, sweat on their upper lips or in semicircles under their arms. I noticed each person, my attention fastening upon an expression, a gesture, a trait, as though in this profusion of experience all knowledge were already contained, and I had only to discover some minute and insignificant part of it to be led to that knowledge of Minna which was my special object. If I had set out to look for clues, it now seemed to me that there was nothing that was not a clue. The whole world was involved in my particular quest, just as I was involved with the world. All these people here on the street seemed to be part of me, and I was part of them; and as my desire for knowledge that would serve a specific end expanded until it became a desire for knowledge in itself, so I too, expanding, dissolved and lost myself until I seemed no longer to exist in my own awareness. And yet I felt myself alone, an object among objects, life among lives, and the world—the very appearance of which asserted its intimate relationship to myself—was broken up into an unaccountable multiplicity without connection, just as bits of colored glass distributed at random in a kaleidoscope have no more in common than the external pattern that falls to them by chance.

It did not occur to me that it might be ridiculous to stand staring and entranced on a busy street. I did, however, realize that the rest of the world had nothing better on its mind than the immediate business of delivering a package, keeping an appointment, buying a dress; and this made me value my own occupation all the more highly. But my immediate business had, in large measure, been forgotten, or rather, growing larger and vaguer, had encompassed more than its original scope. And while I wondered over the diversity of the world as I watched the faces going by, knowing that no two were alike and that no two would ever be alike, I imagined that this fact imposed an extraordinary condition on life. Whatever happened to me, since it would always be different from what happened to another, and never exactly duplicated anywhere in time, had to happen; it was necessary because it was different. God, in whose existence I had profoundly believed as a child, again seemed to me a being I could believe in, at least on this basis. The world was absolutely endless and complex: this was God, the imagination that kept on creating differences, face from face and life from life.

And yet, why was there so wide a gulf between person and person; differences so great that to breach them one would have to cross the world itself? Why, now, on the street, should one man be a Negro, another have freckles on his nose, a third, a yellow moustache? And if there were some reason for having a yellow moustache, need a man limp? And if limping did, somehow, fit into the scheme of things, must a lame man with a yellow moustache limp with his right foot—why not his left? And suppose God knew the reason why, did that mean that the cane the lame man carried had to have precisely those little whorls and knobs and no others? For that matter, why was I what I was, instead of being the shipping clerk, not much older than myself, who had just gone by, pushing a wooden bin? And how could I strike up an acquaintance with him, supposing I were so inclined, without having to labor, so much harder than he at his bin, to push away the differences between us? Nevertheless, people did get to know one another with ease, it seemed a simple thing. But how in God's name was it possible?

Or the Negro, who was now quite a way down the street.

why was he a Negro and I a Jew? Why not the other way around? Or both of us Negroes, or both Jews? There was something between us that neither of us might grasp, some understanding of which we had only the dimmest impression; who knew what this was, or what the design was into which we had been cast? The connections between things were too fine to be discovered. I remembered the strings, invisible in the sunlight, that related the kites to the park below, where my father and I had walked; I thought of the relationship, invisible yet inseparable, that made us father and son.

Or, think for a moment, what was it like to be a Negro? I could only imagine myself to be obsessed if I were one; I should go about thinking, "I am black, I am black." Everything would remind me of it: the cover of the loose-leaf notebook I carried to school, and if it snowed on the way, snow, and therefore rain too; a chance word heard in the streetcar—"I fell off the step ladder and my side is black and blue"; any color named, or the word "color" spoken, the sight of the pavement, of a cocoanut or an eggplant in the grocer's window, a black dog, or a white dog, the strong sun in summer—everything would remind me of it. I should constantly be thinking, "I am a Negro, I am black." And yet, here we were, walking about in the street and no one gave thought to it, no one inquired, no one imagined what the differences were between men.

But I knew. I was discovering it now, and yet I had always known it, always known the remoteness of reality, the distance that separated us from the truth. I had never been without the realization that an empty space, which one might never hope to fill, stretched between person and person, between ignorance and knowledge, between one hand and the other, condemning all to loneliness. And, without ever having been able clearly to estimate it, feeling the weight of it and haunted by its presence, I had always carried it with me as a token, both secret and obvious, of my own existence. For as a Jew, I was acquainted, as perhaps a Negro might be, with the alien and the divided aspect of life that passed from sight at the open approach, but lingered, available to thought, ready to reveal itself to anyone who would inquire softly. I had come to know a certain homelessness in the world, and took it for granted as a part of nature; had seen in the family, and myself acquired, a sense of sadness from which both assurance and violence had forever vanished. We had accepted it unconsciously and without self-pity, as one might accept a sentence that had been passed generations ago, whose terms were still binding though its occasion had long been forgotten. The world is not entirely yours; and our reply is: very well then, not entirely. There were moments, however, when this minor world was more than universe enough; times such as when grandfather would be raised to nobility, or when the family, gathered of a holiday, would distil so rare and joyful a spirit that all the assurance which had been lacking would rush back in flood, and one could feel the presence of God in it, and one could cry, "This is reality, truth, beauty, freedom! What has the rest of the world to compare?" But then, this too would vanish, and I would ask, "What am I?" For as a Negro might ponder his outer body, asking himself why it should differ from other men's when inwardly he felt his common humanity, so I would consider my skin, my eyes, my hair, and wonder why I should feel an inner difference when outwardly I was the same as other men . . .

I had nearly fallen into a trance from which I awoke when

I saw Minna come out of the building across the street, accompanied by a man.

Before I had time to make sure it was she or see if I could recognize her companion, I was already pursuing them. Allowing them to get ahead of me so I would not pass through Minna's field of vision, I crossed the street and followed at a distance. After I had stayed with them for a block, I gathered courage and, cutting through the crowd on the sidewalk, I came up closer and fell in step. I was not near enough to hear their conversation; but the fact that they were speaking to each other and that Minna held his arm seemed so significant, and I am sure I must have imagined their conversation so vividly, that to my mind, at the time, their relationship was already defined and fixed.

Minna's companion was not much taller than she, but since he was about twice as broad, wore sneakers and a sweatshirt and had, in general, the outline of a sack of sand, he appeared actually the shorter of the two. He was bareheaded and bald; his scalp curved down over his head and around a fringe of graying, reddish hair like the flap of a baseball. Minna was holding his arm rather disdainfully, I thought, or at least with no more than a stale or condescending affection. He waddled as he walked; Minna, though keeping in step with him, was unaffected by his motion and held herself erect. Despite my resolution to let nothing escape me, I do not remember how she appeared that afternoon in the street.

I saw Minna wave to someone coming toward her and quicken her step, breaking away from her companion and leaving him a few paces behind. (Even before I had recognized the newcomer I felt a pleasant excitement at the thought that both men, competing with each other, had called by mischance on the same day to take her home from work.) It was Willy who, as he had been coming our way, saw me and pointed to me while he was greeting Minna. She turned around before I was able to run away.

I had to pretend surprise and find some reason for my presence. I don't know which of us was the most embarrassed, but there were differences in the quality of our embarrassment which I could not help noticing. I held the best claim to coincidence, which I at once presented, laughing aloud, in a feigned delight, through which my discomfort probably manifested itself, that we should all meet by accident. Minna, however, had Willy and the other man to account for; and as for Willy he seemed the most seriously disturbed of us all. I was certain that I had given myself away and that Minna knew I had been following her. But Willy was the one who reddened and stammered, and Minna—though I should not have thought it possible—was evidently ashamed before me and felt herself compromised.

I was not introduced to Minna's friend. The four of us walked down the block together, Willy keeping his hand on my head and Minna making the conversation necessary to relieve our strain, in the course of which she even asked why I had not been to see her and expressed an eagerness, which I knew was false, to have me visit her soon. As I had feared, the sight of Minna established nothing, disproved nothing. Her white skin was as delicate, her expression as tense and as fresh as ever; there was no sign, no blemish by which I might confirm my suspicions, no indication of evil, of the wickedness and selfishness that my stepmother had warned me against—nor could I even draw the general assurance that the woman now before me, no matter what I might think of her, was in any way related to the one existing in my imagination. She was forever herself, self-contained, engulfed in a privacy which I had only to stand before her to perceive. Neither I, nor Willy, nor any stranger would ever know her or leave so much as a mark upon her.

Still, there was Willy and the man beside him. Had either of them, perhaps, established that final insight which led, where I might never go, beyond mere truth? I could not make out the stranger. He had a humble and patient look about him that could as well have been an expression of peace and gratitude developed through intimacy, as, simply, his awareness of his place in the world, determined by age alone. (I judged he was in his fifties.) And Willy, how far forward had his initial burst of confidence carried him? Or had it, rather, undergone retreat, forcing him to renounce his insight and call it mistaken? As with Minna, I could learn nothing by looking at him. His embarrassment may have been no more than superficial, and I had, besides, no way of knowing whether I or the stranger was the cause of it. Profound embarrassment would have conveyed more; and yet, my impressions, even if I were certain that Willy was not pretending, would still have remained confused, for if it might please me to know that Willy was suffering, I should, at the same time, out of jealousy rather than sympathy, regret to think that he had cause to suffer, and fear that the depth of his emotion indicated the depth of his relationship with Minna.

But in spite of embarrassment, he was giving himself airs. First, there was his hand, which he had now removed from my head and placed on my shoulder—in all fatherliness and affection, and yet as if to restrain me. And his smile, which may have been entirely for my benefit, expressing a claim to innocence and guilelessness, as if to assure me that though I saw him together with Minna I should think nothing of it, for he—artless, awkward, and foolish—what chance would he have with her?—his smile, nevertheless, was not the one I was familiar with, not the one he would usually put on to flatter me. It seemed to me that while he had chosen to disarm me, he could not forego a boast, and his smile, which had now grown to a grin, mocked me and hinted at conquest. I could see him saying, "This here woman is your own aunt. Now, think of that, my lad!"

We parted at the corner. Minna shook hands with her friend, brushed a speck of dirt from the sleeve of his sweater and kissed him perfunctorily, saying, "Be good, Fred." She did not again invite me to visit her. Willy winked at me, nodded to Fred, and offered his arm, bent jauntily at the elbow, to Minna. They left us, Minna holding Willy's arm closely—if not in affection, at least with a certain pride, as if to say that here was the proper figure of a man with whom one might enjoy being seen in the street. How I hated him— hated them both!

Fred stood with his hands in his pockets, his stomach thrust out, watching them go. There was neither jealousy nor resentment in his expression. He remained placid and motionless until they were out of sight; then turned to me and said, "I don't suppose you remember me."

"Do I know you?"

"You might remember a man named Mason? I would come around from time to time to see your aunt." He said this with an ironic undertone, as if to indicate that coming around from time to time to see Minna had been his occupation for years. I felt at once that I understood him.

"You were this high." Carefully measuring out my height he brought his hand down to his thigh. His hand was small and dimpled at the knuckles and covered with light hair. "About four years old."

"I'm sorry, I don't remember."

"Try. I took you for boat rides. . . ."

"No, I'm sorry."

"A fine one! Whenever I wanted to go for a walk with your aunt, she'd insist we drag you along. You spoiled many an evening, young man—and now, you don't even remember!"

He had a way of goggling and twitching while he spoke, which was either unpleasant or comical—one would have to know him better to decide. The effort of speaking set his whole body in motion, made him shift his weight from one sneakered foot to the other, kept his eyes going, blinking and sliding from corner to corner—eyes covered with a bluish film that darkened the eyeball—and caused little bubbles to appear at the edges of his mouth and around his glossy lips. He had round, puffy cheeks that seemed to have been put on upside down, for they were fullest at the jaw, where they should have tapered off, and gave his face an elongated, drooping outline. His cheeks, moreover, were of the sort one would expect to be rosy—his figure, his gestures demanded it, as they demanded the simple, light-hearted accessories of merriment; but his cheeks were sallow and rather glum. I found myself striving to revise his appearance in accordance with my expectations of the comical. In so doing, I experienced the astonishment that comes over us when we realize, for the first time, that puppies, whom we have always seen frisking and rolling, are in reality the saddest of creatures, with eyes that are painful to look at.

"Maybe you would always come when it was dark," I suggested, fearing that he may have been wounded by my failure to remember him.

"Ah, so you know a thing or two! Of course I would come when it was dark. . . . Here," he exclaimed, scratching his bald head, "this—it was thick in those days, fine head of hair,

[123]

as good as your own. Your father, does he still have hair? Growing thin on top? Oh, gray, you say. It'll all fall out. So will yours. And that fellow . . . Willy . . . him too—ha, ha, ha, ha—" He suddenly stopped laughing—his laughter, having no momentum, came to a dead stop—frowned, and demanded, "What is he, your uncle?"

"My cousin."

"Of course, stupid of me. What do you say, would you like a soda? Ah, it's been such a long time—and your father, is he still in the hardware business? Such a long, long time. You were no bigger than this!"

He spoke rapidly, disconnectedly, saying whatever came into his head—or at least trying to create the impression that he spoke spontaneously and completely without motive. Thus in asking me if Willy was my uncle—he surely knew that he was not—he may have wanted to show me that he was no man to take heed of details and that such matters as uncles and cousins were nothing but irrelevant obstacles to the free flow of thought. He may also, however, have chosen this as a means of expressing dislike for Willy—as the fact that he had suddenly drawn back his laughter and frowned would indicate—and of increasing my responsibility for Willy by making me his nephew. This made me rather apprehensive of him, but I felt I need not fear him; and although everything he did seemed contrary to the expectations he aroused, I thought he should be a relatively easy man to understand. I had concluded that he was one of Minna's oldest friends—though, again, he was hardly the person I should have expected to find in this capacity—and while he gabbled on, throwing together present and past, it occurred to me that if I could only keep him going. I should have a treasure, a mine of information to draw upon.

"Maybe I do remember you," I suggested. "You seem a bit more familiar now."

But suddenly he seemed to take a dislike to me. He shook his head violently, setting his cheeks atremble, screwed up his face in an expression of disgust and looked away.

"Mr. Mason . . ."

"Ah, can you believe it? You? Did I say you spoiled my evenings? Look what you've done now! Him . . . Willy . . . You brought him around, didn't you? You fixed it, you little cockroach! You're always crossing me up!" He seized me by the shoulder.

I drew away in fright and tried to squirm loose, when I saw that he was laughing again.

"Scared you? Serves you right! Never mind, doesn't mean a thing. I've seen lots of them come and go. . . . He's not the first and not the last. But good old Fred—that's me, good old Fred—is here to stay. . . . What happened to that soda I promised you?"

We went into a drugstore and sat opposite each other in a booth off the fountain. Mason was the first to order, which he did with an alacrity that made me think the soda he had promised me was really a promise to himself. "Now we'll see what the young man wants," he said to the waitress who was taking our orders. "Perhaps a glass of milk, or—ah, I know what's good for him, a bowl of milk and toast. Consumptive little fellow, fatten him up." He would not let me give my order until he had succeeded in making the waitress laugh. Then, while we waited, he wanted to know if I thought her attractive and insisted that I tell him what my idea of a pretty girl was. "Pick out the prettiest girl in this store. Go ahead, now. I want to see you do it!" And at once changed the subject and began telling me that the drugstore business was

[125]

a very profitable one and that he regretted not having gone into it when he had had the opportunity. But business was bad for the character and he warned me against it. "Young boys of fifteen and sixteen going into business. It's a crime!" Thus, teasing me, and even teasing himself, assuming an attitude of utter vulgarity in everything he said as if to show that he, who could so readily stoop to the vulgar, was certainly above it—until the sodas came. He finished his off in no time, ending with a loud sucking on the straws, then began playing with the straws, bending and unravelling them. I judged he drank some five or six sodas a day; I was convinced—why, I do not know—that he had a passion for sweets, and that he derived more than an ordinary gratification from them, a gratification rather in the nature of solace. But as I sat confined with him in the booth, I began to notice an odor of alcohol, faint but disagreeable, the odor that might come from a man who drank not heavily but constantly. He belched, pleased with himself.

I was aware of my own restraint, the compulsions that kept me tidy; I felt enclosed in a set of stays, a fervent but rigid little boy, nervous, fastidious, plagued by a sense of order and propriety, devoted, like stepmother, to cleanliness, but with none of her physical pleasure in its ritual. Why, even my passion for understanding was a kind of lust, an itch. Here I was, sitting erect over an unfinished cherry soda, deposited at this table—by what, a sense of wrong, of injustice? No. A sense of dirt, of disorder—embarked on an endless inner housekeeping with no Sabbath in view, a perpetual scratching that prolonged the itch, accompanied by an elderly simpleton, a man of devotion and rancid humility whose rambling and belching and slopping over turned my disgust, not against him, but—so degraded was I—against myself. Let it be, say good-by to him, and to Minna and Willy

[126]

and to the secret sweet hopes turned sour and known, the revulsion of discovered motives, no longer a mystery. Let it be, close up, go away to pleasure in some innocent thing, without fear or complexity, and without fascination. Fascination had evil in it, the horror of the inner life. . . .

But instead I was urging him on, turning his conversation to my uses. "Tell me more about those days."

"Well, what is there to say? Women began cutting their hair short, there weren't many radios—and I think the gas-driven tractor was first becoming popular."

"No, I'm serious. I mean about my family."

"What do you want to know? You should know your own family better than I."

"But I've forgotten. I was so young then. I'd like to see if I can remember anything."

"Some other time. Shouldn't you be getting home now? You'll be late for supper."

"I can stay out as long as I like."

"So? Then you're quite a little man. But of course you're fibbing. Your father, as I remember, is punctual, and when he says 'Be home at suppertime,' he means suppertime. No? Better run along."

"But it's perfectly all right. I can explain that I ran into you."

"Well now, that's a different story. Now you've got something! I must say, you'll make a fine lawyer. What do you want to be when you grow up?"

"I haven't thought about it," I replied, incapable of concealing my resentment.

"Now, now, don't get excited, I'm joking, he, he! You're a fine boy, believe me, I wish I had a son. . . . But sonny boy, why do you want to know so much? Ha? Why do you have to mix in everywhere? Tend to your studies, enjoy life, visit

[127]

your friends, get acquainted with nice girls—you don't even know what a pretty girl looks like! Enjoy life, see?"

But I saw I had succeeded. He was eager to talk about the family; teasing me, he had whetted his own appetite.

"All right, sonny, I know you're impatient. You're curious, you want to know. I'll talk—I'll sing, as they say. But one thing, don't think I'm taken in. It's not just that you want to know—you want to know *something*. I know how little minds work. There's something you're driving at, because— because you're really not any more interested in your family than the top of this table!" He slapped it as he spoke. "So don't imagine you're smart. Agreed?"

"Agreed."

"Ahha. But I'll fool you—I'll talk about myself! He, he—" He halted his laughter as abruptly as before. "I was a handsome fellow, I kept a stable full of horses, I had my own private soda fountain, and I used to play the mandolin— this is true, I did play the mandolin. I was a very fine player. Played everything, pinochle with your father, horse with you —I was the horse and you used to ride me. You didn't like piggy-back either. Had me get down on my hands and knees . . . I played dominoes with your mother—a very fine woman, your mother. A pity, a shame that she died so young. Do you remember her?"

"Not very well," I replied uneasily. It always made me uncomfortable to hear her spoken of.

"I have an excellent photograph of her that I could let you see."

"There's one at home. . . . What did you play with Minna?"

"Ha, ha, ha—of course, that's where your interests lie. But isn't that a question, now? What would you call it? Let's say, paradox. We used to play paradox."

"How do you play that? Do you mean you would see who could say the most paradoxical things?"

"No, not exactly. We had a different way of playing. . . ." He blinked and rolled his eyes, as if to advise me of a hidden significance in his words. "There's no harm in telling you, I suppose, that I've known your aunt for a great number of years—oh, a very long time. I met her when she first came to this country—in fact we're both from the same town. I came across a few years earlier. So we're old friends, you see. That's the paradox."

"I don't understand."

"Ahha, you don't understand. You understand too much! You want me to tell on auntie, don't you? She intrigues you, she mystifies you, a regular little wonder woman! You're another one of those poor fish. I should live to see this, yet! To see the day when I am jealous of a baby I held on my lap, that wet my lap too, I don't mind telling you, make we-we all over the place. I am very very jealous of you. That's a nice paradox, no? I'm a specialist in paradoxes. Why, it's a prophecy: 'And the child that wets their seats shall unseat them.' You see, I went to night school.

"Oh, but see here, you want information. Well, she was an old-fashioned girl, would you believe it? She had all the old ways about her, worse than your mother. For a while she wouldn't even learn to speak English. She called it a bad language, and said it wasn't necessary. I remember the first time she tasted ice cream, the greatest American invention. She spit it out! She said 'Feh! This is for human beings?' Say, finish your soda. . . . Even such a wonderful thing as moving pictures—you needed a horse to drag her into one. She was a good, sweet, unspoiled girl, a hard-working dressmaker, religious as the holy devil, prayed all day long and wouldn't even do so much as carry a handkerchief on Saturday or answer the telephone. It could ring itself blue in the face, but she would say that when you picked up the receiver a little light went on in the main office—and a good woman wouldn't light a light on Saturday. That's the kind of woman she was. . . . Now me, I'm no saint, but when I see a pretty, homey little type, well . . . you understand. Only thing is, you know, your aunt didn't go on living with the family. And after your mother died, she . . . she changed, let's say. No more religion, and she learned to speak English soon enough and so on and so forth. So I think fine, that's all right with me. Why should she go on living with your father and with you? Why shouldn't she be free? Ah, but here's the paradox —I was better off in the old days! Ha ha—"

"What happened when she left? Where did she go?"

"Someday," he replied, "you'll be old enough to understand what this means. So I'm telling you now."

"But what happened then?" I repeated. "Where did she live?"

"Then? Ha, we must now draw the curtain of discretion." This, apparently, was a favorite phrase, and he seemed to puff on his words as if to enjoy their flavor.

"But why did she go away?"

"The curtain, young man, the curtain!"

"Tell me," I persisted, "did she take me with her?"

"Take you?"

"Did she kidnap me?"

"Kidnap you! Feh, ooh, what an ugly streak! Childish imagination. The next thing, you're an Indian prince and you fetch a ransom in gold. I don't like you any more."

"I'm serious, Mr. Mason."

"I'll Mr. Mason you in a minute. Call me Fred."

"Fred."

"Say it again."

"Fred."

"Doesn't sound right. Better keep your distance, brat!"

"Please, seriously . . ."

"Why of course not! Kidnap you yet! Wasn't it bad enough she had to drag you everywhere?"

"But that's what I heard . . ."

"You heard? From whom?"

"My stepmother."

"Your stepmother? Foo, I'll die! Where did she pick it up? Oh, sure, from your father, of course. Your father . . ."

"Then it's not true!"

"Ho, what a man your father is. Look, dear little boy, do me a great favor. I want you to tell me everything that you heard, everything! It'll give me such pleasure—I'm just malicious enough. Tell me the whole lie and then I'll tell you the whole truth."

"Well, I always wanted to know why the family hated Minna, why they never mentioned her name, or invited her to the house, or to a party, why they never wanted me to see her. So when I was talking to my stepmother she told me that after my mother died, just about three or four weeks after that, Minna told my father that she would leave him unless he married her. And he didn't want to, because it was against the law, my stepmother said, so Minna, just to be mean, ran away from him and took me with her, kidnaped me. And my mother was her own sister, too!"

"So. So that's it! Well, what do you know about that!"

"I'm just telling you what my stepmother told me."

"Yes, I know. Stop being such an angel."

"You're not angry at me?"

"Oh, no, no. Why should I be?"

"Then why did you make a face?"

"Because you're such a dear little boy."

"But—well . . ."

"Well what?"

"Aren't you going to tell me now? You said you would tell me what really happened."

"Master Miller," replied Fred, shaking his finger, squinting his eyelids together and wrinkling the loose, paunchy skin, *"Memento mori,* it says in the back of Webster. Have respect for the dead!"

"But—"

"Bargaining across a grave? And your own mother's, too!"

He sat with his hands folded about the soda glass, his cheeks sagging, his expression stern and reproachful. I knew he was insincere; I would have raised the same charge and accused him of bargaining with me, were it not that I felt guilty. The embarrassment that always came over me at the mention of my mother's name now made me think that I had perhaps been willing to use her as a term in a bargain. But it was guilt enough that I had forgotten her, and could speak of her coldly without having her image appear before me, without wondering who she was and what she was, and how life would have been different, had she lived, and how I should have been a different person. I had consented to her death by never having imagined her alive.

In the aisle, near our booth, stood a wire display case loaded with hot-water bottles, rubber syringes, knives, boxes of cotton, toy bunnies and ducks, articles of childhood, sickness and death. She died, I had been told, of pneumonia.

"You see, Master Bernard, you weren't brought up according to Webster. You don't know what right is, and you don't care. You wouldn't steal, you probably wouldn't lie very much, but when it comes to being really honest you're miles away. Young people nowadays—ah, but what's the use?"

[132]

I kept still, hoping his digressions would carry him back to the point.

"A fine way to spend an afternoon, impressing a young boy! Don't you despise me for it?"

"Mr. Mason, may I ask you to tell me about Minna?" I broke in, aware that I was not urging him to talk about my mother. "She is my aunt, it does concern me."

"I beg your pardon. I shouldn't annoy you. I see you want information, not enlightenment. Ah, what's happened to the intelligentsia? In Russia a boy of your age would have despised facts. He would be interested in theories. He would drink tea, play chess, argue politics, philosophy. America!

"Well, now, see here young man. Never bargain with me. I'm generous. I do things for people out of the goodness of my own heart, not because they'll give me something in return. Take your cousin Willy, for example. I can get him a job as a waiter in my own little night club, the Garter Belt. Why? Will it do me any good? Well, he needs a job. He's hanging around your aunt, the latest attraction. So, I fix him up. Right in the place where she goes, so he can see her at night. Wait on her table, sit down and talk to her when I'm not looking. Fine, eh? Nobody has to ask me twice. But what do I get out of it? Nothing. But that's my nature. So don't bargain with me.

"Only thing is, a big heart gets tired, too. Yes, yes, my boy. So if your cousin Willy . . . But I've seen it happen so many times already, poor boys, they don't understand her. The kind of woman that you take her to be—you're wrong about her, she, too, is wrong, she doesn't understand herself." (Although addressing his words to me, he was now speaking to himself, examining his own understanding.) "You think she's full of life, that she's enjoying herself, that she has lots of men because she's an attractive and interesting woman—

[133]

that's what she thinks, too—but it's not so at all. That's just a disguise. Not that she hates men, but if she wants them it's only to help her hide away. I say she's changed, but has she really? She's still waiting to be taken back. Much as she hates your father, and much as she looks upon you as a pain in the neck, don't you think that if she herself was capable of it, if she wasn't so set in keeping up appearances and making believe they're real, if it wasn't too late already—and if I may say so, if it weren't for me—don't you think she would go back? The family, her own people, after all, that's life! She's still the same girl, even if she's stopped praying twenty times a day. But she doesn't know it, she doesn't know! So she's got a new religion, of being independent, of pretending that she doesn't care about anything. But I'm not fooled by it, even if she is. By God, you can't get away from the truth—there's no make-believe in here!" With a thump and a flourish he brought his small, dimpled hand down against his chest.

The extravagance of the gesture had startled him. He was ashamed to have employed it before me. Now he regretted his words, and, as if to cancel them out, settled back into the irony of his self-depreciating pride. "So, do you think I have to be afraid of anyone? I know too much, even if I am nothing more than a decoy, a rubber duck. Quack! quack! quack!—But if your cousin Willy gets too smart and gives off too many quacks . . . well, if I give him a job I can fire him, no? After all, a rubber duck has to have some pride, too!"

"A rubber duck?" I asked.

"Oh, of course, you don't understand what I'm talking about. Let me tell you, it's a pleasure to find something these days that a little boy can't understand."

I had, however, understood perfectly—or at least to the extent that I was able to assimilate his words to my emotions;

and I was disappointed. I felt myself inclined to protest against his suggestion that there never really had been a sharp break between Minna and the family, and that, despite her estrangement, she was still one of us. I thought it a poor account, the more so as my own imagination, which had been unable to explain anything, was nevertheless richer inasmuch as it involved a belief in mysteries that satisfied my understanding at the same time that they baffled it. Moreover, I had begun to resent Mason and to dislike him thoroughly, and even though I may have resented his knowledge of my early life more than I resented his intimacy with Minna, I found it revolting to associate her with him. The possibility that, on greater acquaintance, I might find him enjoyable had vanished; he was merely disgusting. And yet an alternative remained—if he was no longer comical, he might still prove pathetic. The folds of his sweater sagged at his breast, suggesting loose flesh everywhere; his eyes were blinking and sliding, but whether in slyness or restlessness, pain perhaps, I had not yet determined. But however I might resolve his wilfully complex image—was this to be the analogue of Minna? He made her appear a petty, wretched creature. For if Mason, the man she had tormented more than any other—more than Willy, more than myself—and to whom, therefore, she was the most deeply attached, truly contained her measure; if he, who loved her steadily and hopelessly, who had made a career of his self-mocking devotion, was also her closest parallel, then their attachment could have persisted so long only because their natures had grown identical.

We had been silent for a time. Mason had destroyed his straws, unwound them completely and torn them to bits. He sat with one knee hooked over the edge of the booth, his foot swinging slowly, the white laces of his sneaker trailing

[135]

back and forth. He looked out at the people in the drugstore with an expression of unconscious contempt. The waitress who had served us passed our table several times, and Mason smiled at her, insisting that she recognize him.

I would prefer to find no trace of him in Minna. The story itself, the original undertaking I had set out upon, no longer interested me, and rather than hear it to the end only to have my disappointment confirmed, I would prefer to remain in ignorance.

But he resumed it. "Listen. This isn't the whole story, and I know you want to hear the rest of it. I'll tell you. But first there's something I want you to promise me."

"I don't think I can promise you anything," I replied, surprised that my resolution had come so quickly, and that I had had the courage to show my contempt.

He had stiffened, not in response to my audacity, which he ignored, but, rather, with the urgency and embarrassment of a sudden desperation. "Look here, you see your aunt every now and then, don't you? And your cousin . . . Well, now, I just want you to keep your eyes open. You know what I mean. . . ."

I arose. "I'm going home now," I said.

"Going home? Ha ha ha—" he grabbed my arm and pulled me over to his side, holding me against the booth. "Oh, are you smart! No, no, I'll really tell you now. You don't have to use any tricks."

"Please! I want to go." I tried to pull myself away.

"Now, now, you hurt me. Sit down, come on, we'll have another soda." He continued to hold me by the arm, as I showed no intention of complying.

"But really, I must go, Mr. Mason." I looked at the clock above the soda fountain to emphasize my anxiety. It was late, after seven.

"My boy, you're going to listen to me. You wanted to hear this, you were dying to get it out of me—but it concerns me more than you. Me! Do you hear?" He was full of anger now, but also rather bewildered by it, as if he himself were at a loss to know which, in the interplay of his attitudes, was the shifting and which the genuine emotion. "You're going to hear it if I have to hold you down. I'm going to tell you the truth about your father!"

People had begun to notice us. The waitress came up, glancing back at the manager of the store, and asked if there was anything else we wanted. Mason no longer tried to make her smile. "Nothing. We're leaving right away." She hurriedly wrote out our check and retreated, watching us.

"That man," he continued, still holding me by the arm, "someone in your damned family ought to know the truth about him! You have a wonderful aunt, do you hear me? She is a wonderful sweet girl!" With his free hand he pounded the table.

I was ready to believe that the soda had made him drunk; I was frightened, but nevertheless I smiled at the thought. He had drawn me over and was holding up his face toward mine; his eyes seemed to be revolving about the pupil, the smell of alcohol had become more pungent, as if the heat of his excitement were releasing the fumes. But now I saw pride in him. He was defending his wretchedness in Minna's name, justifying a humiliation that he had made a life's work.

"Your father . . . can you understand a thing like this? You're too young. But I want you to know that Minna was very much devoted to you, very much. She would have spent her life raising you, she would have asked nothing in return. But your father could not stand to see such absolute devotion—there are natures like that. It drove him mad. He couldn't accept it—so the only thing he could do was destroy

[137]

it. Right at the start when you, you little brat, needed a mother most, he said to her, lay off. He wouldn't let her come near you. Don't do this, don't do that—the kid'll be all right. Don't worry about him, don't fuss, don't trouble yourself—above all, *don't be so devoted.*

"And then what does he do? Ask her to marry him? Oh no, not on your life! That's not the way it went. He was going to break her devotion by stealing some of it for himself. Now do you see what I mean?"

"Mr. Mason, please, I don't want to hear any more!"

"You're going to hear this! Every time she'd put her arm around you or kiss you—ah-ha! there he'd be, wanting a kiss himself. He was so sad, you understand, so heartbroken on account of his poor dead wife, baloney. And the first thing you know—either she shows some pity or out she goes. Pity! Do you understand? Of all the low, mean, filthy tricks. He wanted her to be his mistress!"

He held me pinned to the table.

"That's how it all began. You can imagine what effect it had on a girl like her. But that's not it—it isn't so much the fact that he dared to touch her, but that he would dare to destroy what was so good in her. . . .

"Naturally, when she wouldn't agree, he kicked her out into the street! Oh, sure, he lied about it. It was easy to give her a bad name. Sure—she isn't living at the house any more. Why not? Well, she ran off. She was an indecent woman, a bad influence on the child. She's this, that, and the other thing. Sure, she even tried to steal you. Why not? Who'd know the difference? He lied his way out of it. But he's responsible for everything, for every single thing she's had to suffer. She suffered, innocently, do you hear? When he kicked her out into the street, God knows what would have happened to her if she hadn't come to me. Do you understand? Do you understand!"

He sprang up, his face flushed and sweating, his cheeks trembling, his lips spilling over. He threw down a half dollar piece, shoved it, together with the check, over to the side of the table and pulled me away. "You come with me! To Minna's, you must come! Tell her everything you told me!"

He dragged me after him, colliding with the customers who were coming in at the door.

There are no simple emotions. I should think that my feelings toward my father would have been fixed for all time. But there is no simplicity in what we feel and no perfection in what we do. We are bound to lose ourselves.

For Willy was there, lounging on the couch, in shirt sleeves, his collar unbuttoned, a cigar in one hand, a drink in the other. And Mason, fidgeting and perspiring at my side, was throwing his own influence upon me. I felt myself again dissolving, as I had on the crowded street, divided and drawn off into others. What, under such circumstances, committed but exposed, can a single emotion encompass?

Moreover, Minna was wearing pajamas; seeing which, I was embarrassed. True, she was now more fully dressed than usual. Her arms were lost in wide sleeves that billowed out at the shoulder and wrist; her throat was covered by a short, buttoned collar, figured with embroidery; an embroidered sash was drawn across her waist and her full trousers left not even her ankles exposed, revealing no more than the toes of her red slippers. Thus attired, she looked more like a mujik than a woman. And yet, as I realized that she was, after all, wearing pajamas, I began to blush.

It was no concern of mine that Minna wore pajamas. But

that she should wear them in Willy's presence . . . Certainly, I could have been mistaken in regarding this as a sign of their intimacy. But conviction is the source of prudishness, and it is easier to believe than not to believe.

Soon a complicated play began, introduced by Mason, an incomparable mimic, who, to my further discomfort, took over my position of embarrassment and enlarged upon it, perspiring, so it seemed, at will. "There is something young Bernard simply must tell you," he declared, meanwhile wringing his hands in violent apology for the intrusion. "You *will* excuse me? He virtually dragged me here. I don't know where such a little boy gets all that strength." This was addressed to Willy, obsequiously. Fred contorted his face into an exaggerated expression of envy, so pronounced, he could only have intended to present the actual envy he was feeling disguised as a jest; he ended by pinching Willy's arm, in brotherly fashion, as if to say, "You wouldn't for a moment suppose that I *was* jealous of you?"

Willy could not forego exhibiting his pleasure in Mason's obsequiousnesss. He leaned back on the couch with his arms folded behind his head and on his lips was the bashful grin that I had begun to find hateful.

A curious jealousy seized me too. (Just as Mason was imitating me, so I imitated him. He had lodged himself; I felt I should never be able to shake off his influence.) I was jealous of Mason because Willy, who was embarrassed yet pleased by our intrusion, saw fit to express his pride only to him; I should at least have wanted Willy to gloat at me. I, too, fell upon Willy, pinching him, imitating Mason's grunts of envy. But I overdid it. For no sooner had I pinched him, than I found him so loathsome, I could no longer stop, and I began to beat him with my fists, at first, lightly, and then falling full length upon him and pounding his body, each blow of greater force, meanwhile laughing hysterically as though, while carried away, I had still wanted to make a pretense at an innocent joke. Fred and Minna pulled me away, aided by Willy, who had begun to defend himself. They brought me back to the armchair and made me sit down; Minna forced me to drink from her glass, and a moment later Mason snatched the glass away crying, "No, no, he'll choke!" and began to tug at my tie and collar.

"What's got into him?" demanded Minna, when they had succeeded in calming me.

"It's all on account of you," replied Mason. "Young and old—you drive them crazy." He sat down on the arm of the chair.

"Here, leave the poor kid alone," said Willy, pulling him off. "Let him breathe." He knelt in front of me, cutting off more air than Mason had, and looked at me in great concern as if he were again recognizing the obligation to father me, which, in the pursuit of his own pleasure, he had conveniently forgotten. But as I, enjoying his sympathy, was determining to force it to whatever length I could, Minna pulled him aside. "Don't pamper him. He'll be all right."

"Sure, leave him alone," said Mason, siding with her. "Just let him get it off his chest, and he'll be all right."

"Get what off his chest? What's going on here?" cried Minna.

"Go ahead now, tell her," Mason urged me. "He'll tell you in a moment—all by himself without any help. He's a big boy—"

"He's a nuisance—it's no business of mine! Fred, have you been telling him anything? Why can't you keep your mouth shut? What is he staring at?"

"He's staring at you. He's dying to know all about you. Don't you see you fascinate him? You're his mystery woman!"

[141]

"Oh keep still! You get to be more of a pig each day!" cried Minna.

"Dry up, Mason!"

"He tells me to dry up! I'm your best friend, like a dog, and he tells me to dry up! Woof, woof! Why, for your own self-respect, my dear, you shouldn't let him insult me."

"Oh, do dry up!" cried Minna. "I want to know what the kid has to say."

"Ah, well then, to the point. Kid, talk!"

I could not talk. My father, pajamas, Willy, Minna, Mason, hysteria, my own and theirs, ran together in my mind. They stood over me looking down like figures in a nightmare, symbols of a massive, unknowable guilt, bloating, soaking up an atmosphere of evil. They were three separate and distinct monsters who had merged into one, and I felt them re-enter me, from whom they had issued like jinns from an un-stoppered bottle. It was my fever—call it curiosity, call it knowledge—that had created them, giving them face and flesh, endowing each with a distinctive means of torment—one of coldness, the other of kindness, the third, between the two, of an ugliness that comprised both. . . .

I could hear Mason recounting what had passed between us in the drugstore, embellishing it with a snicker, a timorous giggle here and there while Minna interrupted him with outcries and Willy, holding her in, was begging her to con-trol herself. Again like an image in a nightmare—for I could not tell whether she moved independently or whether I was controlling her in some obscure and helpless fashion—Minna was menacing me, terrifying me with that peculiar threat she always exerted—the threat of her inner life. She seemed to have grown vulgar and obtuse and physically heavy with anger. Hatred or shame had made something hideous out of her. This was not she, capable of losing herself, of cursing,

[142]

of crying, "The bastard! He'll pay for this, the bastard!" Rather, it was the figure, unnerved of its free will, conforming itself to my own depravity. I was shouting and swearing through her, moving her about the room, just as I was putting Mason through his paces, making him hop about her in a sucking mud and hold to the sleeve of her pajamas while he emptied sewers and drains that I had unclotted; and so, also, I had put aside the remnant of my own cleanliness in Willy, after striking him dumb and agoggle, uselessly bland.

"It's a lie! Stop it! He's lying!" I cried, springing out of the chair and grabbing Mason, trying to pull him away from Minna. "It's all a lie!" And suddenly I was defending my father, putting all my strength, in love and in fear, to the preservation of his name. "Pa never said anything like that! He's making it up, he's lying, I never told him a thing about the family. Pa never, never said anything about you to any one!"

"What! Then why did you come tearing in here?" demanded Minna.

"I didn't want to come here. Honestly, I didn't. Mr. Mason made me come. . . ."

"I should live so," said Mason. "Small as he is, he dragged me here."

"Now wait," said Willy, "just a minute, see here, this has gone far enough—"

"What do you want here?" cried Minna, taking me up by the collar and bringing me so close to her red and distorted face that I could feel her breath. "What the hell do you come snooping around for? Who sends you here? Can't you leave me alone? Alone! Tell your God damned family to leave me alone!"

[143]

"I only came to borrow some money . . . honest, that's all—"

"Money!" She pushed me away.

"It's my father's birthday next Saturday. He'll be forty years old and we're going to have a surprise party for him. . . ." My words sounded idiotic and inconsequent to my own ears. "I wanted to borrow some money so I could buy him a present—"

"Present! I'll give you presents!" cried Minna, rushing at me and dragging Mason after her. "Get out of here! Get out! Get out!"

I ran to the door. It seemed to me I was grinning as I looked back at the disheveled and transformed Minna, at Mason who had broken into a coughing fit and was doubled up, still holding her sleeve, and at Willy, pale and smarting, unprepared for so much violence. Get out? Impossible. We were all toppling at the pitch of an even greater involvement, ready to fall in upon one another. . . .

Chapter 10

My stepmother was getting on with her preparations for the party. She spent hours on the telephone, in conference with various members of the family, drawing up lists and issuing invitations, calling the butcher, the grocer, the delicatessen store. In consequence of which, she rather neglected her housework, and as the day approached, she found herself farther behind with her routine than she would have been, had she neglected it completely. "There's so much to be done!" she would cry. "Believe you me, I'll never do a thing like this again!"

And consider. She had no mere party to prepare, but a surprise party, so that her preparations, to their greater difficulty, had to remain unobserved. Thus, when she began washing the white woodwork and the window sills in the living room, it occurred to her that my father would notice their extraordinary cleanliness and know that something was under way. The woodwork was already half-done. To stop now would be to leave a glaring contrast between the washed and unwashed areas. To go ahead would also be to create contrast—between the woodwork and the dirty walls. It was therefore necessary to clean the walls as well—which could only be done by using a gummy preparation, obtainable at the paint store, guaranteed to remove dirt from wallpaper; it betrayed, however, an unadvertised affinity for removing wallpaper from walls. Even with my help, cleaning the walls took nearly an entire day. Now the floors could also stand a good scrubbing. But she would not repeat her mistake; they must be left for the very last. Still, her instinct drove her to floors, and so, over my protests and with my help, she rolled up the rugs and washed the areas that the rugs had covered, leaving the margins for a later day. "It's all right, it's all right, I know what I'm doing. Dirt gathers even when you don't see it. It's all right, the floors needed a washing anyway."

There were other details—buying additional glasses and plates and finding a place to hide them; testing the centerboards, which would be used to extend the table, and borrowing a board from a neighbor when it was found that one of ours had warped. An order for chicken had to be put in at the butcher's and revised several times with her growing estimate of the family's capacity for food. Then, telephone consultations over presents—stepmother protesting, in all cases, that no presents were necessary, and finally conceding the point, while urging moderation, especially upon the poorer members of the family, and calling extravagance a crime.

All this, and more, was accomplished in one week, during which time she was not on speaking terms with my father. He had caught a minor flaw in her secrecy, having observed that his winter coat and one of his winter suits were missing from the clothes closet. This bore directly upon the party. Stepmother had removed his coat and suit to the basement, hiding them in a trunk, along with other articles whose absence he did not notice, to make room for the treasures she was laying into the house. Why need it be any concern of hers, father had argued, whether the suit hung in the closet or at the tailor's? (She told him she had put it in storage with the tailor.) What was the idea—to create work for herself? But moths might get at the suit. Moths? A fine how-do-you-do! Didn't she keep the suit in a moth bag? But it was his best suit, he had only had it a year. Well, and the coat, which he had had five years? The coat, she replied, was already in such poor condition—although it was three, and not five years—that it didn't pay to take any chances. Besides, it needed a new lining. That, he declared, it certainly did not need. The lining would wear forever—it was pure gold and sheet iron. "Quick, go get it back from the tailor before he monkeys with it!" "It's too late, Harry, he's already put in the lining." "Ah, what a shame! How much did he charge?" "Five dollars." "Five dollars? A scandal! Five dollars thrown away like mud! Do you think money grows on trees? Maybe you don't know how business has been falling off all season? Sure, sure, go give it to the tailor. As long as you can find a way to spend money. Never mind, now, bring the coat and suit right back into the house. You should pay storage on the garments yet? Bring them back!" This she could not do at once since the coat, in its original metal lining, had not yet been to the tailor shop, where it would now be necessary to bring it for alteration. The result was a quarrel that passed from clothes to general household economy and ended with a reduction in her allowance and a demand for an itemized weekly account. They remained sullen and stony until the night of the party. Meanwhile, stepmother went about her preparations, her scrubbing and shopping and conferring, with an instinctive largesse and magnitude, a martyr's happiness, delighted by the opportunity to prove what a good woman she was.

The wonder is that I too took my father's birthday party as an occasion for a sort of martyrdom. The more he became an image of evil in my eyes, the more I wished him good. I had defended him before Minna; now I defended him before myself. This was no simple matter of excusing a wrong. There were no excuses; I condemned him. And yet, by that condemnation I exalted him.

I was not accustomed to the working of contraries. I was puzzled, but nevertheless pleased. I saw that I was looking forward to the event with the greatest excitement, that I was wishing the party success, and my father, happiness. I pitched in with my share about the house, ran errands, phoned relatives, helped make a stir. And if this enabled me to demonstrate the nobility of my character—why, so much to the good. But I could not tell if it represented a triumph or a defeat of my personal feelings.

Even after dinner on the night of the party, the preparations were still going on. In the interests of surprise, it had been arranged that my stepmother was to get my father out of the house to enable the guests to arrive. I was to stay and receive them.

Thus, when the dishes were washed, my stepmother, with a skill that astonished me (how could so loyal a woman be so well practiced in deception?), began to maneuver my father into the position where he would, of his own accord, suggest that they go out for the evening. She hadn't the least advantage, for although it was Saturday night, they were still angry with each other.

She was doing her hair in the bathroom; the door was open, so that my father might see her. He passed by, looked in, said nothing and went on to the living room, where he turned on the radio and spread out the evening paper. She was not discouraged. I saw a mischievous smile playing about her lips when I came into the bathroom in response to her call.

"You shouldn't have come so soon. You should have let me call you twice," she whispered.

"I'm sorry. . . ."

"That's all right. It'll work out anyway. Now go get me my hairpins."

"But you've got them." I pointed to the red box on the washstand.

"Oh. So bring anything. Bring me the hand mirror. Only take it around through the living room, so he should see you." She gave my hand a squeeze. There was happiness in her expression, a trace of exhaustion, which she would soon conceal, and none of the anxiety she had been suffering.

I brought her the hand mirror by the roundabout way she had recommended. My father had looked up. I was now sure that she would succeed, and I went back to my room, leaving the door open, and listened to the following conversation.

"Why are you getting all dolled up? Are you going somewhere?"

"No place in particular. I thought maybe you would like to go somewhere."

"I go somewhere? Just like that? Where should I go?"

"Maybe to a movie."

"What's the matter you've got movies on your mind? Why all of a sudden a movie?"

"It's Saturday."

"So if it's Saturday? All week long you were in the dumps. Just because it's Saturday you have to be happy? . . . Go away, Bessie, you'll get me full of powder!"

"Harry, what is today?"

"You just got through saying it's Saturday."

"But it's your birthday!"

"I know it's my birthday. What of it?"

"I never saw such a man! All week you were crabby because you thought I'd forget. Then, when I remind you, you say, 'What of it?' "

"But what am I, a little boy, that I have to make a fuss over my birthday? I can just as well stay home."

"Well, that's too bad if you want to stay home. I hope you don't mind if I go out. I have a right to celebrate your birthday."

"Where do you think you're going?"

"I'll treat myself to something special. It's not every day that you get to be forty years old."

"Forty! Ho, ho, a fine forty!"

"Not forty?"

"I'll never see forty again."

"What are you saying! You're forty! I should live so! Do you think I'd lose track?" There was a note of anxiety in her voice.

"Forty! I'm at least forty-five. I'm going on fifty. I'm an old man. I've got one foot in the grave!"

She had scored her victory. This was his method of conceding, and concealing, defeat. Thereafter, it was simply a matter of hurrying him through his shaving and dressing and getting him out of the house in time.

Before they left, my father came up to me, festive and shining, and observed that since, contrary to his wishes, he was forced to celebrate his birthday, the entire family might as well be in on it. Would I therefore like to come along with them to the movies? He was careful not to urge me too strongly. (He had to maintain his indifference toward all things affecting his personal life. It was his habit to conceal his pleasures in a perfunctory asceticism.) So it was not difficult for me to plead a headache and beg to be excused. My refusal, however, did not fail to hurt him.

And another matter. In asking me to accompany them, he had given the word "movies" a somewhat too indifferent inflection. It was plain to me that he was disappointed. Not that he gave a care about his birthday, you understand, but if stepmother would insist on a celebration, well then, couldn't it have been something the least bit better?

The family arrived in branches and in clusters, the order of their appearance revealing the inner structure of the tribal hierarchy. First came the foremost Millers, grandfather and grandmother. And even here order prevailed, grandfather reaching our door a full flight in advance of his wife. After producing a ring like a trumpet call, the loudest and the longest that had yet been played on our bell, he had clambered up at a speed he could hardly afford, wheezing and puffing, and not once helping the old woman.

I greeted them, I welcomed them, I offered them the

[150]

pleasure of the house. Grandfather let himself be greeted and welcomed and received. He pinched my cheeks and soon established himself with the grace of a king on a royal progress, at home in every corner of his realm. But grandmother minced and mumbled, nearly tripping with timidity as she came into the living room, where she took, not the soft chair to which I led her, but the hard one, wooden and straight-backed, standing beside it.

Grandfather went about the room, taking it in with great, but critical enthusiasm, the absorption of a connoisseur. Pictures, which were to be looked at, he found it more to his liking to touch, running his sleeve over the glass and putting his finger to the frames. And was not fully satisfied. "Why do they hang so low? They hit you right in the eye. You've got woodwork, so hang them from the woodwork." He peered behind one of the pictures to see how it was hanging on the wall, and replaced it carefully, but withheld his approval. Now the embroidered velvet spread which lay on the end table, a texture he might very well have enjoyed to feel, he rather preferred to sniff, bringing his nose down close to the surface. But it was the grand piano, on which he had long since set his heart, that truly fascinated him. He did not much care for the keys, merely lifting the cover to see if they were there. The body and the strings, however, made him melt away. He ran his nail over the harp, strumming back and forth, and took up a most minute inspection of the wood, its grain and polish, caressing it gently, then pressing his fingers down until it squeaked. "A fine piece furniture," he said to me, his words restrained, but his tone unmistakably that of material rapture.

While grandfather set out to review, room by room, the rest of his son's domain, grandmother rose and stole into the kitchen, settling herself in a chair by the stove, where, with the table before her and the sink at her side, she might feel herself less out of place.

Next to arrive were the Greenbergs, uncle Joe and aunt Chiah Gitel, or Anita Gertrude, as she was called in English, together with their daughter Essie. Uncle Joe—but once I have mentioned that he had a wen on his forehead, there will not be much more to say. Chiah Gitel–Anita Gertrude, however, was a power, the Greenberg family all in a piece. She was both matriarch and patriarch, her own man and wife. On her cheek stood a furious mole, in which grew a forest of hairs; her head was a fortress, her bosom, a mountainside. She set about inspecting the preparations for the party, looking into the ice box, counting glasses and plates; which done, she attached herself to grandmother and showered her with questions that sounded like commands. Uncle Joe attached himself to grandfather and waited to be spoken to. Cousin Essie attached herself to me.

She was my age, a matter of some two weeks separating our birthdays. Essie was a round girl, thoroughly devoted to roundness, as if on principle. She wore round silver-rimmed glasses over her round eyes, a round skirt—of some stiff material which had incorporated into itself the properties of a hoop—and a brace on her teeth. Nevertheless, she was pretty, in the way of the family, having to endure a privation of natural resources. Her pigtails had recently been put up in braids; she wore make-up, a discreet layer of powder and rouge applied, no doubt, under her mother's most exacting supervision, and, on her mouth, the thinnest smear of lipstick, which, used so sparingly, served rather to emphasize the paleness of her lips. Essie had not yet learned properly to govern the movements of her body, and was therefore always schooling her awkwardness to a striving for grace. Thus, she would take the prettiest, firmest, gliding step forward; but her arms, momentarily neglected, would hang down heavily, as if dragging chains. Or, she would advance an arm, correctly curved at the elbow, her little finger curling like the stem of a leaf; but her ankles, while she was engaged elsewhere, would buckle to either side of her high heels. Then, too, she would occasionally become conscious of her breasts, which were now growing full, and would furtively look down at her bodice; one moment she would slouch, and the next, stand erect with her shoulders thrown back and her spine curving in so sharply, you feared it might snap under her. (I should add that I was fully as embarrassed as she, never daring to look directly at her bosom, and all the more ashamed when she detected my covert glance.) But already she had her mother's air of dispatch and authority; her eyes had the young girl's naïve liveliness, but in their depths you could see the clubwoman's stare.

I say she attached herself to me. More accurately, she presented herself like a summons. "Bernard, how have you been?" said Essie, pronouncing the word "bean."

Although she had crossed the entire length of the room, she found it necessary to express a general and deep-seated disinclination toward me. "Isn't the summer unbearable in the city?" she asked, down the length of her nose. "I don't know what I should do without the lake. Next week I shall go to a summer camp. What's the idea of this shindig, Bernard?"

"It's my father's party."

"Oh, really. Dear me."

She fluttered her eyelids and let her lips part with ennui, thereby displaying her brace as well as her boredom. Essie was not ashamed of her brace. Her mother had imposed it on her in a fit of absolutism—perhaps because Essie resem-

[153]

bled her father—and she wore it in defiance. (Her teeth would have done well enough without straightening.) It was shortly to be removed, after having served only to make Essie hate boys.

Other members of the family arrived. There were soon enough men in the house for a poker game. I was sent for cards and chips. My grandfather shuffled and dealt, and they began to play. As more men arrived they took a hand in the game. The women assembled in the living room, or crowded themselves into the kitchen where they examined my step-mother's housekeeping, peeking in on her linens and her pots and pans. There was now a proper atmosphere of whispering and laughter, of shirt sleeves and cigars and gleaming, pink and golden baldness.

Disengaging myself from Essie, I stayed at the men's table in the dining room, watching them play. My grandfather was winning; Joe Greenberg, losing heavily; the others, slapping their cards down on the table-pad, nudging one another, sighing over their hands, calling themselves ruined for life.

They had entered that free and jovial mood, characteristic of all large families, in which an illusion of love, of undying, unalterable warmth is created, such that one would think, these people are all good, pure, gentle, devoted, affectionate, incapable of a single cold word, of a single selfish thought. They live for one another, they enjoy one another; these gatherings inspire their best—why, their only real moments. See, there, Joe Greenberg pounds his fist against his fore-head in a mock agony of ruination—he does so only because he knows it will please my grandfather. And grandfather rakes in the chips, clucking his tongue and cackling—again because this is what the others expect of him and he would not think of pleasing himself without first pleasing the com-pany. It is all illusion—but though you know it is illusion, you think that these men are lords in mankind, for that is what you feel so clearly; whereas, what you know for a fact— that they are not so good, or so clever, sweet, kind, gentle, or unspoiled—becomes a shallow, inappropriate abstraction, and you go on thinking that your own family is the only one of its kind in all the wide open world.

The same spirit had come over the women. Their talk flowed from the other rooms, rapid and sweet, with runs of laughter, a squeaking and squealing. And while they may have begun in a lower, less generous key, detailing, no doubt, the various faults of my stepmother's housekeeping and thus passing on to her character and the character of her husband, to say nothing of my own, still, they too were creating for themselves the illusion of perfection which spreads charity over all domestic things.

Essie had been with my younger cousins who were incapable of conversation and wanted only to play. She detached herself and slowly, by imperceptible degrees, made her way back to me, and just as carefully drew me away from the table, going about it as if there were any number of better things she could easily find to do, and were merely acting out a condescending role to favor me with her company.

I had been assigned to the look-out in the sun parlor, the windows of which commanded a view of both sides of the street. Essie went in with me as the time drew near, and we sat on the window seat, waiting for a sign of my father. We were at the front of the house. Behind us, set off by partly drawn curtains and a row of rubber plants, were the women in the living room, where the lights, which could not be seen from the street, were blazing. The sound of their conversation threw a screen around our silence; from the rooms beyond them came the men's voices; running in and out, the

[155]

younger cousins' piping. The whole family had arrived. You felt them in every corner of the house, pervading the atmosphere with a common clatter. At such times, when they are all packed in, the house becomes a ship; you can feel it rocking under you; you think it has taken on an independent motion, torn itself free from its foundations, leaped forth over the trees in the street with a spray of leaves, hitting the family's course. Where they go, you go, no longer thinking of your own course; for if you were to leap overboard or cut loose and cast yourself adrift, there would be only the sea around you and, unable to survive without them, you would drown.

Essie did not share my mood. She sat beside me on the window seat, swinging her legs and humming to herself. From time to time she would yawn and mutter, "Oh dear," at the last extreme of boredom.

"Bernard, don't you ever get tired of all this?" she asked.

"Tired of what?"

"All this family stuff. Uncles and aunts. Doesn't it ever give you a pain?"

I found it necessary to agree. "It bores me."

"Oh the hell it does. You lap it up."

I did not answer.

"When are they going to show up?"

"Soon. Any minute now."

"I wish they'd make it snappy and get it over with. I gave up a dance tonight."

She began humming again. "Look," she broke off, "don't you think they could see us up here? All that light from the living room."

"It's dark enough. It doesn't show on the street."

"Oh, you may as well do it right." She got up and drew

the curtains across the arch, shutting off the living room. Now our only light came from a street lamp. I could see the rims of her glasses against the window.

"Aren't you nervous, sitting in the dark?" she asked.

"Why should I be nervous?"

"But you are. I bet you're afraid those old hens will know we're sitting together."

"No, I'm not. I'm just anxious for them to come." I could see her lips curling again, and the wide golden grin of her brace.

"I don't see how you can stand it," said Essie. "Don't you ever want to break away?"

"Sure I do," I replied, conscious of a lack in myself.

"My eye. You love the family."

She made me seem timid and bound, lacking in a proper restlessness. My desire to leave the family—it had never occurred to me as such—had merely taken the form, through Willy and Minna, of a further dependence on others, an exchange of families. For a moment, feeling myself vulnerable, and not realizing that she was more tightly bound than I, I envied her independence.

"Go on, you're a mama's boy. Now, honestly, don't you want to get away? You're a boy. It ought to be easy for you."

"Sure I can get away," I replied, realizing that she was actually envying me and wanting me to assume that attitude of personal freedom which she herself was incapable of sustaining. "As a matter of fact—but don't tell any one—I've been planning to go away soon."

"Will you! Where will you go?"

"I'll get a room on the North side and live by myself."

"Oh, that's dull. Can't you go to another city? That's what I'm going to do. I'm going to go to New York. I have my things packed now. Mother doesn't even suspect. I'm just going to walk out one night, and that's the last she'll see of me. You'd never do that."

"How do you know?"

"I just know."

Essie moved closer to me and our arms touched. She did not draw away. Afraid to show I was aware that she had drawn closer to me, and yet, nervous and embarrassed, I leaned back against the window without breaking the contact.

"You're a sissy. You're the dullest little mama's boy. Have you ever gone out on a date?"

"Sure, lots of them."

"Go on, you don't know any girls."

"Oh, don't I? I've got a girl."

"What's her name?"

"I'll tell you her initial. It's M."

"You're making that up."

"I don't have to make anything up, the way you do. You don't have any boy friends."

"Look who's talking. I bet you don't even know how to dance. Get up and we'll go in there and dance."

"No, I've got to stay on the look-out."

"I wish they'd hurry up and come. This is getting so dull."

"I think they are coming!" I said, looking out the window.

"Where?"

"On the other side of the street. At the corner."

She leaned over me, her cheek brushing mine, her hair falling against my face.

"I don't see anything."

"Right over there. That's them! They're coming!" I called out.

"Shh!" said Essie, turning on me and throwing her lips against mine. I could feel the brace under her kiss.

"Oh, are you a baby!" said Essie. She pushed me away from her and ran out crying, "They're here! They're here!"

It was a genuine surprise. The family had hidden and kept still in the darkened house. I heard my father say, "The boy must have gone to sleep," while he fumbled about in the dark. He turned on the light in the living room and conjured up the whole family. Out they leaped, pouring out of closets, crawling from under the piano, from under tables, from behind chairs, crying, "Surprise! Surprise! Surprise!"

They crowded around him, they shook his hand, pounded his shoulders. The women kissed him, and kissed their own husbands and one another's husbands. The illusions maintained themselves. It was a love feast, an exaltation of the family—and even if these kisses, like Essie's behind the curtain, had something of a cold, metal taste, the unpleasant touch of everything domestic, still it was a surprise, an excellent surprise, not only to my father, but to the entire family, each discovering how deeply he could participate in illusion.

My stepmother, aided by the other women, with grandmother doing more than she could successfully manage and therefore getting in the way, set out food and drink on the table—corned beef and pickles, salmon salad, herring, tongue, cherry pop for the youngsters, mild wine for the women, strong wine and whisky for the men. We stuffed ourselves, got up from the table to dance—or merely to wander grinning about the house and shout "Hoo! Haa!"—came back and drank, got up to dance, to wander and to shout again. My father was in glory, his face flushed and full, the hollows filled out, his eyes bright, not only with excitement, but with the peace that came from knowing that this evening was his, and none could compare with him.

But even in his abandonment there was something of the self-conscious quality of a man who had never completely trusted himself, and whose pleasures were, therefore, mixed. I had to see him in a frenzy of good humor, all restraints as far away as he could cast them, to recognize the ultimate restraints of his nature, the severe, unbalanced, brooding weight, the burden of violence that he never released. Several times he lifted me off my feet to set me on his shoulders, or seizing me by the arm, sent me whirling round and round with him before the company, always crying out, "This is my boy!" or, "This is my son!" as if it needed clarification. And yet I saw him hopelessly remote from me, cut off by his own complexity, isolated, as on a rocky place, that I could only approach through steep, winding paths, forever in danger of bruising myself or losing the way, never, perhaps, to reach it. All he wanted was simplicity—a simple relationship with me, with stepmother, with the family—the reality of contact. This he went begging after, always silently reproaching me that it should be necessary for him to descend to me, to seek me out. But how could I come to him? It was his unhappiness that made him inaccessible. And his unhappiness was too shrewd to be overcome. If he knew human nature to be at all corrupt, he would be suspicious even of its purest motives. Sons deceive their fathers; therefore, he suspected a constant thievery. Wives are often disloyal; he therefore demanded of my stepmother, precisely because she was a loyal woman, an austerity which, if it never led to betrayal, might well have encouraged the temptation. He was a man of ideals who knew too well what was going on in the world. And thus, whenever excel-

lence came within his grasp—some good which would overcome not only the disappointment he felt in the world, but
the deeper disappointment in himself—he would fling himself after it, pursuing it as other men pursue revenge.

And so I understood his abandonment. The fury with
which he ate and danced, the gaiety of his singing, the bright
color of his cheeks—all this, since he could not allow the
world its natural imperfection (a truly abandoned man,
furthermore, would have lost his restraint even to the point
of admitting that he took some offense at being startled out
of his wits by a conglomeration of the family); all this was
the mark of his obligation to overwhelm happiness and force
a full reality upon a moment that owed its joy to illusion. . . .

The coffee cups were empty; of the cakes there were now
only flakes of icing and crumbs. We sat at the table, no longer
to eat. The rest of the night was to be spent peacefully,
drawn out with quiet conversation, a song or two. Most of
the lights were turned off, the smoke was yellow in the room;
all the foreheads that had glared with sweat had taken on
the tone of thought, ivory and dim, appropriate to abstract
emotion. Even Chiah Gitel–Anita Gertrude's voice was
nearly a whisper, and when the women laughed, there was
no longer such a tinkling and cascading. We sang, somewhat
off key, drowsily. Even Essie was singing—and letting me
see that she sang, and, what's more, that she knew the Yiddish words. Her eyes, which had been full of scorn, were
friendly; she had not kissed me in vain, for, having done so,
she could now imagine that I loved her, and that it was I
who had led her behind the curtain, and could even admire
my bravery. And when I looked at her as if to say, "Well,
why don't you get up and leave?" she seemed to answer, "Not
now. Never." Grandfather was blinking peacefully and smiling into his beard—a smile of no content, without mischief or

design, utterly vacant and mild. Grandmother, at the other end of the table, had quietly fallen asleep, her humiliations forgotten. She had asked, earlier in the evening, "What is the occasion for this party?" turning her vindictiveness, when the celebration was at its height, crankily upon herself. Now she slept, forgiving the world. We, too, were lulling ourselves, soothing one another's wakefulness. The ship sped on, hardly seeming to move.

It was at this point that the bell rang and my aunt Minna appeared at the door.

She strode right in, pushing aside my stepmother, who, seeing a stranger, had tried to detain her. "Happy birthday, Harry!" cried Minna, before she had even seen my father, and proceeded to the table in the dining room to seek him out.

None of the family recognized her; and as my father was sitting with his back to the door, he did not know it was she until she stood beside him at the table. Several of the men rose to offer her a chair—in response to which gesture Minna smiled with more graciousness than she could muster when intending no sarcasm. Altogether, she was very charming and amiable—the fright I was suffering did not prevent me from observing this—and although she was overcome with timidity as she realized the extent of her daring and was seized with a nervous trembling, she was nevertheless proud, defiantly proud of herself, and therefore self-confident and even calm; and while she was enacting a desperate role—it had all so obviously been planned in advance!—the strain of her impudence had heightened all her natural qualities, so that she now seemed more herself than when behaving in a casual and unpremeditated manner.

"Many happy returns, Harry. Let me wish you the very best of everything," said Minna.

My father, rising, had knocked over his chair. He had turned pale, and he, too, was trembling, although his unpremeditated anger, while stronger, at the same time appeared to be a less convincing emotion than Minna's. Suffering shock (more than actual anger), he was not quite himself; besides, the night's deep peace, not yet fully broken, still told on him, and, as he was first now coming into full awareness of the significance and danger of Minna's presence, he was like a man who had suddenly been waked from a sound sleep.

"Don't tell me you don't recognize me, Harry!" exclaimed Minna. "I'm his sister-in-law," she said, turning to the family. "Why, I know all of you! Hello, grandpa! And you're the Greenbergs!—there's Essie—how she's grown—good for her! Hello everybody! My dear, we've never met." She turned to my stepmother. "But I've heard so much about you. Bernard always raves about his home—and to think, I'd never been in it! Not in your day, dearie. Bernard, come here. You haven't said hello. Don't you recognize me in your own house?" And when I remain rooted in my seat, she added, "He's such a bashful child. Takes right after his father. There, there, Harry." And patted his cheek.

"The nerve . . . who told you to—" began my father.

"Won't you sit down?" said my stepmother, pleasantly, instinctively selecting the most tactful defense against Minna.

Minna complied, sitting down next to my father. Her eyes were extraordinarily bright, and her face flushed; it occurred to me that she might have been drinking. I observed, however, that she had excellent control over herself. She responded to my stepmother's courteous antagonism with a courtesy of her own, smiling sweetly and at once raising the

[163]

conflict onto a subtle plane, above the violence which my father would have imposed on it.

My stepmother hovered over her, armed with a smile. "You should have come earlier—we were having such a nice time. I'm sorry the food's all gone now. But there must still be some coffee. Bernie, go into the kitchen and pour your aunt a cup of coffee. No, wait, maybe she likes tea better. . . ." (She would not let her out of her sight for a moment.)

"Don't fret over me, sweetheart," said Minna. "I do all my drinking the hard way, don't I, Harry? Besides, I didn't come for a spread. I've just come to wish Harry a happy birthday. Happy birthday, Harry! I mean it, Harry, honestly I do! I want you to be so, so happy. . . . He doesn't believe me. He thinks I only want to do him in. He's so suspicious— like a woman. Isn't he, honey? He must give you an awful time. By the way, what's your name? Isn't it Bessie? Am I right? I've only known you as Bernard's stepmother, and I'm sure you don't deserve to be called that. You're just like a mother to him—"

"Wouldn't you like some—"

"Oh, no, nothing, nothing, please. I just want to be by my Harry. Or should I say, your Harry? Dear, how he's changed! I'd never recognize him. . . . Oh, he's so moody!" And she threw her arms around his neck.

My father sprang up, pushing Minna away. "Get out of here!" he cried, pointing to the door. "Get out of this house!"

"Oh, he doesn't like me any more," said Minna, in a small voice. "You know, he used to, my dear. I was such a fool. I should never have refused him. He was so, so handsome in those days."

"Get out!" cried my father, and would have thrown her out of the house; but the men, fearing violence, had crowded around him and were holding him back. They wanted to avert violence; but there was something under way which it would be a pity to end so soon. Thus, they tried to pacify my father, and urged both him and Minna to sit down—not, however, to keep still. It was obvious that while the family had by now recognized her—with this recognition came, of course, the awareness of the role she had reputedly played in our life; an awareness so largely influenced by my father's efforts as to consist, almost entirely, in the false legend he had constructed—they were, however, unwilling to waste an opportunity for scandal, and while they had at once turned against her, believing every evil with which my father had damned her, and perhaps, adding a few of their own invention, they were, nevertheless, taking her side.

But grandfather was more interested to assert his authority over the family than to enjoy a scene, and, rallying his strength, drawing himself up in all his shabby patriarchy, he began to denounce her, in Yiddish, calling her "a devil and a plague, an evil woman, an abandoned creature, a black soul, a streetwalker, a whore, a disgrace to women and a temptation to men, and altogether unfit to remain for one moment in a Jewish home. . . ."

But before grandfather could check the family's appetite for scandal and turn her out of the house, Minna, no longer playing a role—in fact, screaming at the top of her lungs (it made her seem one of us)—began to denounce my father, declaring that "this fine man, oh, such a fine man!" had assaulted her.

"Get out! Get the hell out of here!" he cried, and broke away, rushing at her. But my stepmother had already sprung at Minna and, pulling her by the hair, tearing and clawing, had pushed her to the door.

I had been numb with fear and guilt. I cannot say whether I was moved by a sense of the injustice my father had committed against Minna, or whether I was afraid to remain and face the consequences of her intrusion for which, I knew, my father would hold me responsible—but I cried, "Wait, wait, I'm coming, too!" and ran after her when she was already on the stairs. The house was in an uproar.

Part Three

Chapter 11

I did not stay long at Minna's, perhaps four weeks in all, but that period has remained one of the most clearly remembered and at once the most confused of my life. Days run together as I try to distinguish them or stand apart, one unrelated to the other. The most certain, but also the most trivial conclusion I can reach in looking back is that I was miserable, and that I did not realize it at once.

I felt I had done something daring; and even if what had been done was not my doing, its daring and rashness were mine. For I found myself away from home, the tie that had held me suddenly broken—and could I say that this was not my desire? And yet leaving home, especially under such circumstances, appeared to be an act not entirely of the will—or an act so deeply of the will that it was incommensurate with my own conscious desire. I thought of it as an accident, although a necessary one; an accident which I had somehow contrived.

But I was not to blame, I told myself. It was no fault of mine, though I had mentioned my father's party in her presence, that Minna had chosen that night to appear at our house in the very role of abductor which family legend had assigned to her. I felt that my responsibility in the event was negligible since, strictly speaking, I was no longer myself. My life had been interrupted, a great change had occurred and my identity was overthrown. Moreover, I did not really believe in the change. Because I had not yet been ready to leave home, I still continued to think, even after I was living with Minna, that it was impossible for me to leave. Something would intercede for me, revoke the change and restore me to my former condition—a condition, incidentally, which

[169]

I took to be freer than the present because, while living at home, I had always dreamed of my liberty.

But the fact was that I had run after Minna, and so into a new existence. At the moment of leaving the house it had seemed that there was nothing else to do. But I did not know what had led me to accompany her any more than I knew what had made her come after me. I assumed, of course, that she had come after me—otherwise, why had she come at all? It was so clear to me that Minna's intrusion into the party could have had no other consequence, that I was certain it had had no other cause. In this I was mistaken, as I saw from the look of astonishment that entered her dull rage when she saw me following her down the stairs. And so when we rode to her house, Minna sitting opposite me on the L train but not saying a word; straightening her hair when her anger had subsided, taking out her compact and powdering her face and noticing a scratch on her cheek where my step-mother had hit out at her and going over it several times until she had concealed it—but not once noticing me. And so when we entered her house and found Willy there, asleep on the couch, and a pile of records at the side of the phonograph, the last record gone dead on the turntable and the machine humming to itself. She woke him and he sprang up expressing what I thought was feigned delight and surprise to see me, and wanting to know what I was doing there. Minna refused to explain. She ordered us down to the basement, where there was a cot on which I was to sleep. We climbed down the back stairs and groped in the dark, touching the damp rough walls until we found the light switch, then poked among washtubs, discarded lamps, tin cans full of nails, rusting tools, stirring up dust, and at last saw the cot folded in a corner of a shed under a pile of boxes and mattresses, and I was obliged to crawl after it, Willy being too big to squeeze through the stripped frame of a buggy that barred the way. And all the while that we were overturning the basement and trying not to make noise, and pulling the cot up the stairs, bumping at every turn, Willy kept nagging me, wanting to know how and why I had come, his resentment not very well concealed. I told him nothing.

Minna had us put up the cot in the kitchen in the narrow space between the table and the sink; then left me alone, closing the door, and taking Willy with her into the other room, in which I could hear them quarreling. He was demanding to be told what I was doing away from home, and she was evasive and sullen and apparently drunk all over again. I undressed, feeling unclean. I was sweating from exhaustion. I went to the sink to wash under the tap, but saw a roach scurrying across the drainboard and drew back, nauseated. The moment of nausea was in the nature of a perception and the kitchen suddenly became for me a room of utter disorder, the paint flaking over the sink, the wall behind the stove streaked with dirt and grease. I could feel crowding into the room the long row of predecessors who had scraped toast and boiled coffee in the morning, and the lodgers yet to come, pressing in to prepare midnight sandwiches, and the kitchen receiving them, violated but indifferent, squalid, peeling, darkening, incapacitated at the very heart of home. I thought of our own kitchen as I turned off the light. It shocked me to see Minna enveloped in this atmosphere, and as I was wondering why I had never before been aware of its sordidness I felt a pang of guilt, as if I had abandoned her at the moment of coming to live here, and had secretly joined my family in seeing her as she truly was.

I had difficulty falling asleep. Their voices reached me from the front room, still quarreling; and when they were silent and the slit of light had vanished from the threshold my father's face appeared before me, ashen and hurt over the ruined party table.

That first day, if it were to serve only as an example of the violent contrasts of my moods, would show what confusion had befallen me. Whatever I felt, I also felt the opposite; and all in great self-consciousness so that I was constantly asking myself whether it might not be better, more proper, almost, as it were, more righteous, to feel something else again. Thus, when I awoke in guilt I thought, should I feel guilty? Later, when guilt gave way to disappointment, I thought, I do not feel guilty at all, I have done nothing; I am merely disappointed—with myself, with Minna, with the sudden turning stale of an adventure—but do I have the right to my disappointment, do I have a right to expect anything? And before long, of all misplaced emotions, what should I feel but happiness and the exciting desire to embrace each new fact of the new existence, observe the particular changes that I imagined to have occurred in me and the whole fresh aspect of life—until I was bored and pained and finally chastened, concluding that I did not understand what was happening to me, and that I no longer counted for anything in the new existence I had entered, being now submerged in a larger life which was free but vacuous, and loveless and indifferent when it was not actually hostile.

I awoke thinking of my father, aware that I had just been dreaming of him. I did not remember my dream, but I was sure (and relieved by the knowledge) that it did not refer to the night before; it went back to an earlier event, now forgotten, a lesser, more innocent transgression. I dressed, and since Minna and Willy were not yet up—the sound of their breathing, still profound at the late morning hour, was coming through the door—I went out on the back porch to while away the time. The sun was high and strong. Flies had entered through holes in the screen and were circling the garbage can that stood open and unemptied at the head of the stairs, or crawling on the rim, pausing to rub their legs together and preen their wings, their bodies a bright green in the sunlight.

I looked out over the cluster of roofs and small, neatly assembled back yards. Few people were about, it was still time for Church or late breakfast. A dog sat chained in a nearby yard, suffering his masters' boredom. It was the dead heart of Sunday, the spoiled morning lengthening across the day. A block away the factories began, the water tanks and the idle smokestacks, and a strip of a railyard was visible to the left, this, too, lying dead. Straight out over the brick landscape lay home, another drab rectangle in its little space, and there, too, ran the alternating rows of alleys and streets, wooden fences and plots of clipped grass, stretching out to a horizon of chimneys. But indulging myself, I endowed home and the old neighborhood with the quality of my loneliness, as if I had been away years instead of hours, and thus what I desired became desirable: the sound of the balloon vendor's horn, boys hawking papers in the street, and within the house, the sound of coffee in the percolator and the smell of it, the three of us at the breakfast table, my stepmother's clean apron and my father's undershirt—everything acquired an infinity of goodness. I stood looking out over the factories and alleys, the houses and fences, feeling immeasurable self-pity and wondering that I should ever have imagined desirable the position in which I now found myself.

So when I wrote a letter to my father that morning, stating that I was at Minna's and did not intend to return, it is quite possible that I wrote not to relieve him of anxiety, but to furnish him with my address that he might come to take me home.

The letter increased my misery. First, because I felt myself continuing the dishonesty I had always shown toward him. I made no reference to what had happened, merely setting forth my decision to remain with Minna. Because I felt so great a need to apologize, and therefore to believe in my guilt, I thought that my letter was unforgivably arrogant and that it would anger my father. While I was writing, a blot of ink fell from the pen, but I did not take another sheet of paper. I let the blot remain, feeling it might somehow soften my letter. I finished with a rather childish scrawl and spelled my name out in capitals.

Moreover, the very writing of the letter was a degrading experience. Minna and Willy were still asleep when I decided to write, and since paper, envelopes, stamps and pen were in their room, I was obliged to steal in. I lost all trust in myself, not knowing what my real motive was, and, to prove that I was beyond suspicion, I kept my eyes averted from the bed as I stole into the room on tiptoe. I stepped carefully among their scattered clothes and made my way to the desk in the corner of the room, listening for any interruption of their breathing. I found the stationery without difficulty, but on the way out, precisely because I had been anxious to avoid doing so, I looked directly at the bed. They were lying in heavy, indelicate sleep, Minna sprawled out and Willy with his back turned, one arm flung across her body; both of them uncovered and naked. When I sat down to write I felt that my conscientious desire to communicate with my father had masked an unclean impulse.

It was from this that I drew my next emotion, which was shame. I felt it as I went out to mail the letter and when I returned; as I sulked about the kitchen and back porch waiting for Willy and Minna to wake up, and also at break-fast, when I did not even dare look at them, for fear they would read my shame. My very presence in the house was ugly and perverse.

How, then, shall I account for the happiness which suc-ceeded it? I had gone out for a walk and had been circling about in the neighborhood, inspecting the houses and streets, the shop windows, the men and women along upper Michigan Avenue, the trees and grass and bushes in the park near the lake when I suddenly felt convinced that I had never been so free in all my life. What had home to compare with this? How dreary it had been, each day as predictable as the next.

At this very moment father would be lying on the couch in his stocking feet, asleep, snoring lightly; stepmother would have begun to read the Sunday paper (her first opportunity since morning) and fallen asleep over it, nodding in the armchair; soon she would wake, and wake father and beg him to go for a walk with her. They would walk in the park, he, half a step in advance of her; they would sit on a bench by the water and watch the boats. ("I don't see how some people get all that energy at the end of the week," she would say. He would reply, "Some energy! What's there to pushing a boat around?" Thus she would offer, and he would decline, to go for a boat ride.) They would return home and have supper ("A light snack, it's such a relief to have just a snack on Sundays"). After supper they would go down for another walk. All of Sunday they slept fitfully, at odd moments, or walked the streets in search of rest.

I felt their emptiness, their loneliness. Now I was free, liberated from dullness, from the pattern of days. Here was freedom, open and full, and a yearning to know myself, an adventure which, only the night before, when Essie had mocked me, I should never have dared to embark upon. And yet though I thought of home, could still feel myself tied to that existence, and see deep into its essential sadness, I could not help observing how happy I was.

When I returned from my walk I was at last presented with a proper vision of the life I would be leading at Minna's and the emotion which would make up my dominant response. Willy and Minna had not waited with dinner, and I found them at the table, well along with the meal. No place had been set for me.

"I'm sorry I'm late." I washed, drew a chair up to the table and sat down next to Willy.

"You're not going to eat off the tablecloth, are you?" said Minna. "Go get yourself a plate. And a knife and fork."

"Where?"

"Don't be so helpless. Right in front of your nose, on the drainboard. See?"

"I don't see a fork," I replied from the sink. "A knife and spoon, but no fork."

"There should be a fork. There are more than two."

"I'll find it," said Willy, beginning to rise.

"Sit still. He can find it himself. Use the spoon if you're so blind. There are more than two forks."

There was no fork in sight. I returned to the table with a plate and spoon. The "tablecloth" to which Minna had referred was a strip of checkered oilcloth that did not quite reach to my edge of the table. A few scoops of salmon remained in a dish; beside it a loaf of bread and a squeezed lemon.

"I didn't feel like cooking supper," said Minna, seeing that there was not enough for me. "There are still some beans on the stove."

Willy hastily swallowed his last piece of salami and eggs

and winked at me and nudged me with his knee. "Pot luck, kid. You're roughing it now."

"I don't want any beans," I replied, helping myself to the remains of the salmon. "I'm not hungry."

"I'll make coffee soon," said Minna.

"I'll make it now," said Willy, springing up and giving me a playful tap on the head. He went to the sink and began to wash the coffee pot, and was at once absolved of the injustice he felt he had done me.

Minna busied herself with finishing the salami and eggs and did not look up from her plate. "Where was I?" she asked when Willy returned to the table.

"You were saying something about Mason. It's not worth repeating."

"Oh, yes. But this is really good."

"I don't think he's funny," said Willy, making an obvious effort to look bored.

"But this is about a goat, the time he kept a goat in his apartment. He had to ride it out on the street for a lodge initiation."

"Oh, what's a goat! When I was a boy there were goats all over the place. My old man used to keep a—"

"You're jealous of him!" cried Minna. She laughed and wagged her finger in his face.

"Jealous of that old— Say—" Willy put on an expression of utter scorn, aware, however, that by so responding he merely increased her delight in teasing him. He glowered, angry and unskilled.

"Oh but he is so *funny,*" she insisted, giving the word a very broad accent as if, in recalling the early days, she had unconsciously slipped back into the foreign accent which she had since learned to correct. "I think you're a snob. A prole-tarian snob."

"Cut it out!"

"See, look how offended he is. No sense of humor, that's the first sign of a snob." Her amusement was animated with a sense of power over him, the pleasure of tripping him up at will. I gathered from the quality of Willy's resentment that they had often quarreled about Mason; that Minna used him as a perfect foil against Willy.

Willy drew up the corners of his mouth in a futile expression of disgust, resigning himself to her mockery. I wondered what had happened that she should now triumph over him so readily.

"What about the goat?" I asked. "Did he really ride it down the street?"

"I'll tell you some other time," said Minna, turning to me, and, the better to tease Willy, taking full account of my presence for the first time that day. "When your cousin Willy isn't around. He just can't stand to hear about Fred."

"She's trying to buffalo me with this goat business," said Willy, also turning to me on the inspiration that I could be put to use. It went much better now; he made several variations on his pun and felt he had righted himself, and soon abandoned altogether the premise of moral superiority with which he had justified his discomfiture.

I had spooned up my supper and remaining hungry, had gone to the stove and begun to eat the cold beans right out of the pot. Minna and Willy did not notice me even when I protested my neglect by scraping the pot with the spoon. The coffee boiled over while I was at the stove, and at this point Willy rose, but when he saw that I had turned off the flame he resumed his seat and at once forgot about me. I returned to the table and gloomily played with a few crumbs.

At least outwardly, my aunt and my cousin were getting

along quite well. Willy had begun to tell stories about his childhood and youth, his days aboard ship, his experiences as a semiprofessional ballplayer and a fruit peddler—the stories, as usual, would become inextricably entangled with one another—and Minna, though she had already heard most of the anecdotes, was listening intently and watching the expression that played over his face, quite unaware of her own. From time to time she laughed and interrupted him to make a point of her own, but he cut back in to the point of his narrative and rambled on, enjoying the look of her eyes as she turned patient and submissive. They were happy with each other, after all. He was now quite relaxed with her and his gestures and his voice had lost that insistent, inquisitive, mistrustful quality which he had shown the night before. Evidently, she had satisfied him so far as my presence in the house was concerned; had told him the truth, whatever that was, or a plausible, convenient lie. He was no longer questioning me; my presence he now took for granted and he could relax also before me, feeling in me no threat, no link to the disquietude that Minna's motives aroused in him. But if so, his calmness could mean only that he was no longer aware of me. I simply did not exist in his eyes or in hers. They would exist only for each other, accepting me as a quiet, irrelevant unreality, an undesirable background of their lives, which could easily be ignored.

And yet something incomplete remained in that completeness in each other which they had declared for themselves. Perhaps my presence was still effective, if only to make them somewhat shy and reserved, hesitant and rather uncertain with each other. They had not accepted me, for, after all, how could they? I would always remain for Willy evidence of the irrational, an impulse to vengeance that Minna had never fully stifled, the vestige of a life that set her off from him. And for Minna, too, I would persist as an omen, even if it were unrecognized, of the capacity for bitterness in her life, a sign of that rage and hysteria, the mad but purposeful hatred she had evinced toward my father. It would always prevail over her ease, the free, sensual pleasure she might find in Willy's company, or the sense of pleasure she derived simply in leading her life as she chose, within that freedom that she thought fully hers. She could not help hating me; so long as I remained with her, I would constitute a disproof of her existence.

Was I, I asked myself, really the worst off, the most neglected, the most "unreal" of us three? With what was perhaps an excess of presumption I took my presence to be the criterion of their life; they could not accept me, or believe that my existence was natural to them, as did my parents, and therefore they did not really accept each other. Yes, they got along quite well, they lived easy and irresponsible lives—had made coffee and forgotten to drink it, had had supper out of cans, and were remaining at the table, far into the evening, because to rise would have necessitated their washing the dishes, clearing off the oilcloth, cleaning up the kitchen; and because the coffee cups were still full of this morning's dregs, or for a better reason, they had got a bottle of whisky out of the cupboard and were drinking out of glasses that needed no washing, purified by the absolution they dispensed. But this was the whole of their existence, not a drunken fragment accidentally cast into view, but a reality, fully revealed. This was the level of acceptance and meaning in each other to which they had finally sunk, abandoing all principle of resistance. Of course they would get along, if only because quarreling was now impossible; there might be words, angry words, just as there was now laughter and an occasional kiss, but they would proceed from the same open, unquestioning mouth, made sterile and impersonal by drink. Each would forget himself, forget the point at which he differed from and questioned the other. They might awaken later, and Willy would remember that there had been some ground other than mere childish jealousy for disapproving of Minna, something in her life which he had set himself to reform with the force and worth of his personality; and Minna would recall that she had reason other than woman's mischief to tease him, that her teasing was a protest against something stupid and obdurate and unjustifiable in his relationship to her, that there was an insult and an injustice in the very premise from which he accepted her. They would both remember and collect themselves and fall apart, their false unity evaporating with the fumes that had inspired it. Then there might be real quarreling and an approach to real intimacy, but not before.

No, it was not I who was the intruder. Each of them had intruded upon the other. I watched them drinking together, Minna with her arms folded on the oilcloth and her head resting on her arms, looking up at Willy, and he with his chair swung around, leaning over her, smiling his perpetually wide, blurred, forgetful grin, both of them now completely oblivious of me and, in the most essential sense, also of each other. What were *they* doing here? Why were they living together, why had each let the other in? To violate privacy, because they had no use for it? To end an old loneliness, or establish a new one? What had they to bring to their living together, when what they wanted was apparently as loveless as the present hour, forgotten in the very moments of its creation; when each, out of a fear of contact, touched nothing in the other; when all they wanted was the protection of each other's sleep, for waking would at once bring criticism and exposure, tension and hostility, a moral vindictiveness from which they would both suffer. What utter contempt they had for each other while they sat and drank, their eyes blurring over with smiles, their hands meeting on the table, their lips smearing each other. . . . Or was I again the intruder, understanding nothing, seeing in them only the outer image of my own shame, and was this all—neither contempt nor forgetfulness, but humanly all one could ask? . . .

"I want soda," said Minna, and got up and went unsteadily to the ice box. She peered in and kept repeating the word under her breath, "Soda, soda, soda," until it hurt me to hear it. "Here it is, green bottle." She pulled out the bottle and held it up; and laughed as if she were still at the level of her former conscious, controlled cleverness and her present babbling still constituted an assault on Willy, a superior mode of contempt.

"You open it!" she declared, standing with her legs spread and leaning back against the box. "I'm too good to you. Do something for your keep." And then she flew into a rage, as if suddenly remembering, while drunk, the poise she had abandoned and, ashamed of letting herself down, were striving to regain herself at his expense. "Lazy good-for-nothing long-eared jackass!" she screamed, mixing up his typical expletives with her own. "You snob, you idiot, you rural half-wit, you wormy old carcass of a skunk!"

He rocked in his chair, laughing, then sprang up and embraced her and pulled the bottle out of her hands. "You cold hunk of pickerel," he replied, thinking her cleverness more than adequately countered. He pulled off the cork with a bottle opener and caught the overflow on his shoes. He hugged the glasses, the whisky and the soda bottles against his chest, much as he had embraced her a moment before, and pushed her into the other room.

[182]

I remained at the kitchen table. I could hear them drinking in the other room, laughing, whispering, teasing each other, thrashing on the couch. I knew they were waiting for me to go to sleep, but again they were taking no account of me, finding, perhaps, an element of stimulation and self-contempt in my presence. I sat paralyzed at the table, trying not to hear them.

Later, Minna came out to shut the door. She looked into the kitchen, saw me and paused for a moment as if the sight of me had shocked her back into a sense of propriety—and it seemed to me that in that moment her sympathy went out to me, releasing a sudden tenderness which, seeing me as a child, would have expressed compassion and shame. But in the same instant her shame inverted itself and then, to show that she was in no way inhibited by my presence she laughed and said, "Be a good boy and wash the dishes," and withdrew, shutting the door.

I drew the cot out from under the sink and undressed and crept into it, pulling the sheet over my head the better not to hear them, and concentrated on falling asleep. But I could hear them in the other room where, thinking I was already asleep, or knowing perhaps that I was not, but feeling that my presence added a touch of spice to their relationship, they had begun to make love. I lay with my eyes shut tight, trying to blot out the dark kitchen with the unwashed dishes and the table naked at the edge of the oilcloth, trying to lose myself in the sound of the dripping faucet, but I could hear them and I could imagine them in the bed, naked as I had seen them in the morning. An image of horror persisted in my excitement, as if their act had become, not one of love, but of devastation, something brutal, intent, among the sighs that I heard, upon pain, pain only, the ultimate, devouring satisfaction.

[183]

Chapter 12

It rained the next night, as I have good reason to remember. The house was damp and chilly; after supper, Minna suggested that we have a fire. I can still see Willy cracking boards over his knee and piling them in the grate over torn newspaper. I was sent down to the basement to steal some coal, and when I came up with a full bucket the fire was blazing. There was no other light in the room; the fire sent out a cheerful orange flickering that fell on Minna and Willy as they sat on the couch looking on, and there was a harmony between them, a warmth and a natural liveliness cast over them which, particularly after the events of the day before, I would never have suspected that they could achieve.

Willy carefully put on the coal, informing us that this was a skilled operation and that it was not many who could start a coal fire in an open grate and keep it going. The evening was in his hands.

He had drawn from the fire an immediate satisfaction, as if he, too, had been kindled. Then it was merely a matter of his lighting a cigar, crossing his legs and clasping his hands behind his head before he became (with our consent) the perfect image of domestic contentment, a man's comfort in his own home.

He had that quality, appearing as laziness in daytime, which becomes at night the inborn capacity for ease. It was something that my father, who was never idle for a moment, did not possess. And so, on my second night away from home, I felt that Willy was my father, or rather that his scope for fatherhood, consisting as it did not in mere providence and sternness, but in buoyancy of understanding, sympathy and warmth, was the first I had encountered that was capable of including me as a son. And now I was pleased to see Minna also expanding, almost beyond the resources of her nature, with a similar comfort and animal satisfaction, most human, which my virtuous stepmother had never shown. She leaned against Willy, one hand on his shoulder, the other in her hair, patting the strands as if to welcome the influence of the fire.

Slowly the wood fire dropped, its flame turning wan, leaving the glow of the coals under a blue fringe that tore itself free to escape into the air with which it was kin. The rain could be heard beating against the windows and the glass of the skylight; also drumming softer on the wooden porch. I could no longer see them distinctly; only another coal where Willy puffed on his cigar, and his face and Minna's appearing rosy for a moment and then again pale. I wondered that peace should descend so soon—upon the same scene, the same latent tension—after the night before.

It was natural that Willy begin to talk about himself out of remembered experience, the counterpart of the present ease. Minna, resting beside him, and I, sitting near the fireplace which I could reach with the poker, both expected it. A comment formed itself in my mind, which did not, however, cancel my consent and participation in the present scene: whether he was drunk or sober, struggling to maintain his pride or secure in the momentary inviolability of peace, all things reminded Willy of himself, the perpetual host and exemplar of experience.

He began with haphazard reminiscences, anything that came to mind. But perhaps my presence suggested a final theme; he fell to telling us how he had run away from home when he was fourteen. It was the natural age, he remarked, referring to me, and I could imagine him winking at me through the darkness. But at once he was absorbed in his own story. He had gone south and west, emerging after several weeks at a point near Memphis; covered some two hundred fifty miles, going one way and the other, and, once he had lit out, not knowing or much caring which way he went.

"But I'll never forget that first night away from home. I'd lit out early in the morning, before sun-up—it was in spring —and made tracks as fast as I could because I knew that my old man would be up in about an hour and I wanted to get away before anyone saw me. Especially him. I had a few shirts and a couple dollars that I'd stolen rolled up under my arm. I went through the woods, I didn't want to come out until I was far enough away from home. I knew my way pretty well, at least so I could keep going straight and not get lost and go around in a circle. Were you ever in the woods in spring?

"You know, when you walk through the woods, real thick virgin woods, it's like nothing else on earth. Every step you take resounds, the ground is soft and hollow. The leaves have been piling up year after year and rotting and decaying and fresh ones coming down every fall, and all that time the trees have been standing, some of the old ones torn down by lightning or wind and lying dead and some young ones choking their way up for breath. You begin to feel that you've been on earth for a mighty long time. You forget this was all here before you and that it'll stand long after you're deep down under it. You think you're so much a part of the world that even though there's all that rot around you, the ground going boom, boom, boom while you walk and the damp smell and the streaked, cracked rocks and everything crumbling from the winter—you never once think that what all this really is is death. It's there all right. When you read those old German fairy tales or any of the stories of people who've lived in the woods you realize how some of the worst cruelties, chopping a head off, eating someone alive, getting imprisoned in a tree or a rock, can appear so innocent and fantastic. It's the woods that do it. The shadows are full of monsters, but the spring leaves are coming up sticky and yellow, you see that the birds are back and you recognize their calls, you see them hopping around with twigs in their beaks, building nests, and then the wood flowers are shooting up. There's one especially, I forget what it's called. It's just a few inches high, and pale, not a spot of color in it. Just a slender stem and petals that you can almost see through; it's sickly looking, but it's the most beautiful thing, and it's growing right on the spot, say, where an Indian and his dog went by three or four centuries ago and the dog left a lump and shoveled a pile of leaves over it with his hind legs. . . ."

It occurred to me that Minna, from her childhood in the old country, must certainly have been acquainted with the woods as well as Willy. It was only I who had never set foot in a forest; my childhood seemed a poor and artificial thing, an unenlivened time that had been completely wasted.

"Well, I hit out on the road later in the day," went on Willy. "I had a rough idea where I was. I had taken enough grub along for a meal and I sat down and ate it and then I went and got a handout from a farmer, so you can see I'd worked up a fine appetite. Until then I hadn't seen a soul for twelve hours, but I wasn't lonely.

"Anyone I'd run into on the road—I was still pretty near home and I didn't want the word to get around that I'd been seen, just in case my old man set out to look for me—anyone I'd run into I'd give a false name and tell 'em that I was going over to see an aunt or a cousin. No matter what name I'd give, they'd all say they knew kin of mine—old Jed, or Bill Cooper, or Tom Stewart, and so on; they'd even point the way out to me—over the hill and then bear right, or go along until you reach the creek and turn off at the first barn. I never felt gayer in my life. I stretched out on a hill and rested a while in the afternoon and then went on and I knew I'd done the right thing to leave, to get away from my old man, and I wasn't going to come back. I knew I'd miss my mother and my brothers and sisters, but he was a mean old cuss; I thought there'd never been such a tyrant in all creation.

"I went on until it got dark and I was getting tired. I wasn't going to be afraid of spending the night out in the open; I was sure I could live like an Indian, and for that matter there was no need to stay out in the open. I was looking around to find me a nice barn for the night. But as I went on a ways I came to a small stream and I saw a boat tied up to the bank. I got in and shoved off and rowed for a while, and then I took in the oars and just drifted. Pretty soon, before I knew it, the stars were out, a wind was blowing and I was cold. And most of all—it was something I hadn't been looking for and never suspected it would hit me—I was lonely. Man, was I lonely!

"I wanted to row over to the bank and get ashore, and then I saw I'd dropped the oars overboard while I was dreaming up at the evening sky. It seemed to me that the stream had broadened—I couldn't see the bank anyway because there was no moon—and that I was drifting much faster now. I had no idea where I was, and by then I sure wanted to know. Just to know the name of the nearest farmer, who was probably miles away, or to know what township or county I was in, would have made me feel that I still had some contact with the world, something that could pull me ashore, that wouldn't let me disappear from the face of the earth. Some Indian, was I scared! Maybe a storm would come up and I'd be swamped, or maybe I'd run into a rapids, or drift out into the Mississippi and get mixed up with a steamer, or somehow a shot would find me in the middle of the night, just pick me out in the darkness and I'd go floating downstream with a bullet hole oozing blood. But worst of all was the loneliness. I remembered walking through the woods, the happiness I'd felt all day long, the berries I'd picked, the people I'd met—it all seemed so hopelessly far away and unreal, and yet most real to me as if it were the last thing on earth I'd have to remember. I thought of home and all my folks. Even my old man seemed good to me. Why did I have to run away? Well, I prayed some that night, and between praying I'd try to paddle the boat over to shore with my hands, but I never got anywhere and the current was running faster. I would have cried, too, but every time I felt tears coming up I swallowed hard. Lonely as I was, I wouldn't let myself cry because that was something I'd learned not to do in case someone might see me. See me? I had the feeling not only of being alone, but of being the only living creature left in the world.

"Every now and then the boat would hit a log and I'd get ready to dive clear and swim for shore, even though I was sure I could never make it. I tried calling for help, but all I got was the sound of my own voice and the echo, or a screech owl from away off in the distance. It was an awful night. Because while I was cold and hungry (but too scared to know it), while I was afraid of drowning and of death in general, it was the first time in my life I had *really* been afraid. Afraid in a way that had nothing to do with danger or being lost. Just plain fear in my bones, fear even in the wind, in the stars that were shining.

"I pulled through, as you can see." His cigar had gone out and he relit it, his face and Minna's flaring up in the match and then glowing with the first few vigorous puffs. "Bernie, put some more coal on. Easy now."

I carefully shook a few lumps of coal into the bed, watching for the blue flame to reappear. I felt Willy was guiding me, imparting his skill. Back in the armchair I was once again aware of the rain.

"What finally happened?" asked Minna.

"I fell asleep. God knows how. I woke up late in the morning with the sun shining into my eyes. The boat had drifted into a clump of reeds and was stuck there. I could not have gone far, and I don't know how I ever came to imagine that the stream had widened and deepened—it was no bigger than it had been at the start. A few yards down stream some kids were splashing and swimming around the bank. I made sure they saw me in my boat and then I undressed and dived in and swam up to them."

He spoke of the rest of his journey, how he had worked his way down to Memphis, gone hungry for days or stolen food, several times taking milk directly from a cow in pasture. He had been gone nearly a year; it was still winter when he returned, late one night, by the way he had gone, and the woods were still frozen. Almost a year had passed, but as he was going home his wandering seemed to him no more than an extension of the first day and he expected his father to beat him with an anger preserved from the morning of his departure. The family was asleep, but the old man, who always slept lightly, was awakened by the barking of the dogs and heard him outside the door. Maybe he understood the dogs were barking in welcome; he came to the door saying, "That you, boy?" and shook hands with him and led him to the stove where the fire was banked for the night. There were no blows, no questions asked. The old man looked him over, saw he had grown and was satisfied;

saw also that he was cold and threw some wood on the fire. Their meeting after nearly a year told Willy that from then on his father would respect him and regard him as a man. The rest of the family had jumped out of bed and his brothers and sisters, sleepy-eyed, were poking fun at him as if he had in fact left only that morning. He embraced his mother, but did not kiss her and did not cry, as he wanted to do, and did not let her make a fuss over him. He felt he no longer belonged to her in the old way. It surprised him to find, after a year's absence, that he should return not with his mother, not his brothers or his sisters, but with his father stamped in his heart and driven into his soul, to resemble above all else the man he had fled.

"I've been doing too much talkin'," said Willy, by way of announcing that his story was at an end.

Of all the stories I had heard Willy tell, it was this one which made the deepest impression upon me—perhaps because its theme suited me so well, expressing my own loneliness and reassuring me in my fear of my father. But I also felt that the story, and moreover the manner in which he had related it, established the theme of Willy's life. So he had lived and was now living; a life which was either idleness or adventure, impossible to distinguish the two. Such was his experience, and whether he sought it out or found it only in retrospect after its anxiety had passed, it was the whole meaning of his existence—necessary or accidental, colorful or dull, a natural thing in which there was always evidence of grace.

In the shift of attention to other things—to the rain and again to the fire—after Willy had spoken, I thought, half-turning to Minna, What about you? What sort of life have you led? It seemed to me that she would never be able to explain herself, never consciously understand or unconsciously reveal the single pattern or emotion or experience that had once entered and marked her life, determining its essence for all time. With her, the superseding moment canceled its predecessor, depriving her of that increment of mind with which one grows at last into a knowledge of himself. Minna, I felt certain, had no memory—each fresh experience destroyed her anew. If I were suddenly to ask, "What made you come to our house the other night?" she would be unable to answer. It had occurred; and while it had certainly had a meaning, the mere occurrence had obscured everything else. The act, its cause, its consequence, all floated like so much shaken sediment in the unclear medium of her malice. I thought of her leaning on Willy, as she did now, reflecting light from his match, acquiring peace and a sense of memory from his reminiscences, stealing, as it were, the shadow of his consciousness to constitute her own. Her life, which had always been a mystery to me, seemed even more a mystery to herself.

She had not once changed her position or the expression of indulgence with which, dark as it was, I was sure she was looking at Willy. "Oh, that's charming!" she exclaimed, when he had ended. "You tell such amusing stories. Tell me another." I could make out that she pushed him to the end of the couch and then threw herself into his lap. She was looking up at him—I was certain of this—with a self-satisfied smile, never once suspecting that she envied him.

"Well—" and he too suspected nothing, "there's the time in California that I set myself up as a psychologist."

"What do you know about psychology?"

"You'd be surprised. Now I wasn't an ordinary psychologist."

"Well, I shouldn't think so."

"I'll say you shouldn't. I was a dog psychologist."

"A what!"

I began to laugh, and missed some of the explanation that followed. As far as I could gather, Willy had rented an office in Los Angeles and put out a shingle advertising himself as a canine psychological consultant. He administered intelligence tests to dogs—by whatever method he neglected to say—charging fifteen dollars for his services.

"I printed a circular. If I remember it went something like this. 'YOUR DOG'—in large letters at the top—'HAS AN I. Q. WHAT IS IT? Have your dog's intelligence tested by a famous expert. Thirty years' experience, endorsed by leading dog clinics. Special attention given to the problems of neurotic dogs.' That was some racket, let me tell you."

"I don't like that story," said Minna, who hadn't laughed once.

"It's no story. It's true."

"I know. But I don't like it." She sat up. "It's so dark here. Bernard, turn on the light."

Contrariety, contradiction; nothing escaped. We blinked at one another, Willy with a look, still undisturbed, of infinite self-esteem, very much as I had imagined it in the dark. Minna was cross, peace dispelled, one emotion superseded by the next.

"What's the matter, what's eating you?" said Willy, self-confidently yawning.

"I don't like such stories. It's a fine way to live."

"But that was years ago."

"You haven't changed much," said Minna.

Willy had a good laugh. "But you're the one who's supposed to be the nonconformist, who's supposed to dote on that sort of thing. You're coming apart at the seams."

"I don't care. I don't like it."

"So. I guess that's that. Bernie, suppose you run along to

[193]

bed now." He had turned to me as if to say, "We got her that time, didn't we?" and although he regretted the loss of the evening's mood, he was still sure he could regain it. He was kneeling by the fireplace as I went into the kitchen, and when I shut the door I could see him stirring the coals and once again snapping boards across his knee.

I lay in bed, hearing the rain on the roof over me and behind me on the porch and I imagined my cot had become a boat, cut loose and drifting; but I felt I was now incapable of fear. I felt grateful to Willy for having lent some of his own meaning and natural dignity to my life.

I could hear him talking to her in the same low, pleasant, drawling, self-assured voice and I knew he would prevail over her and not let her undermine his composure. It was remarkable that he should again have his strength—a Samson whose hair grew quickly. And it was all the more remarkable, thought I, that I could go to bed without feeling a trace of the ugliness which I had taken to be essential to their relationship.

I do not know how long I had been sound asleep. I awoke gradually, thinking at first that I was again responding to Willy and Minna, as if I lay in the same bed with them. I listened, sickening, but they were silent and, I judged, asleep. Then I thought it must have been mosquitoes that had wakened me, for I felt welts on my arms and face and I realized I had been scratching. I felt disappointment more than discomfort. It was impossible to remain content; happiness, like sleep, was meant only to be broken. I lay still, hoping the itch would abate, and expecting, meanwhile, to hear the mosquitoes whining in my ears. I heard only the rain pouring.

I could not control the itching of my arms, and at last I got out of bed and turned on the light. The gloomy kitchen

sprang back at me even before I could stop blinking. I
thought I should momentarily hear a stirring in their bed
and I waited for it, but they remained quiet.

The welts on my body were long and swollen, bleeding
at several places where my nails had dug in. Under a fold of
the sheet I saw a small, flat brown insect running. I crushed it
with my nail and for a long time sat staring at the bloody
mark and regretting the rain, which, I thought, had brought
on the bedbugs.

Chapter 13

The infested cot made me revise my private symbolism of
reference to Minna's life. Shocked by the discovery I forgot
extenuating circumstances such as, to begin with, the fact
that the cot had been brought up from the basement; that,
at least to my knowledge, it had never before been in her
apartment and could not have become infested there, and
that Minna was to be spared disgrace and not held responsible
for evidence of moral ruin—which, rather than poverty, I
took to be the cause of such uncleanness. The cot had descended shabbily from others' lives directly upon Minna, and
I could no longer dissociate her from even the most extrane-
ous symbols of decay. This evidence, this ruin, implicated her
in a history of spoliation. It did not matter that her own bed
was clean.

I thought, at first, that I should attribute my revulsion to
an outraged sense of decency. And yet, I told myself, if such
were the conditions of life, I should learn to accept them,
and perhaps even take a certain pleasure in the proof I

thereby gained that I was indeed engaged with life itself. I remembered that when I was a child and my father's shaving had first begun to fascinate me, I had once been alarmed to see a cut appear on his face and blood spread, coloring the lather. My father showed no pain, and went on calmly shaving. "Doesn't it hurt?" I had asked, ready to cry. He assured me that the pain was negligible, that the flow of blood would soon stop of its own accord, and that such trifles would not interfere with the pride and joy I myself should find in shaving when I grew older. Now then, here were the cuts of experience, and I should value them.

Moreover, I remembered scenes from that same childhood in which bedbugs had figured, not as symbolic episodes, but in their own flat, bloody and segmented bodies. These had appeared in my grandfather's house and created a comical scandal. For grandfather, instead of hiding his shame, had proclaimed it at a gathering of the family, and since every article of furniture in his possession had come from some other house, it was not himself but his relatives on whom he laid the fault. The bugs had been found in the iron bed in which he and grandmother slept. This bed, however, had been in the house for several years, and grandfather therefore preferred to trace the origin of the pest to some more recent acquisition, say, the soft chair donated by the Greenbergs, or the couch that some other member of the family had given him. His accusations brought on such outcries that it was finally agreed that the infestation had spread neither from couch nor chair, but from a rug, originating with Wolf Mabish, who did not belong to the family. Wolf, wife and children, had left that year for Palestine, disposing of their furniture. "They need him there?" grandfather observed. "*Eretz Israel* can't get along without bedbugs?" This had assuaged their pride, not only by sparing them shame, but by reducing Malbish, who had left as a hero, to proportions more suitable to the jealousy of my family, most of whom entertained a sentimental yearning for Palestine that grew stronger, but less practicable, with the years. But we were not to be spared the work of eradicating the pest. The Sunday paper, comics included, was spread on the bedroom floor and grandfather stood by giving orders while the bed was dismantled and candles were brought from the pantry. The women held the lighted candles to the coils of the spring; and I, assisted by the other children, peered along the seams of the mattress in search of "anything that crawled" —for so our parents had instructed us, taking pains to show that not only were we so unfamiliar with the insects as to need instruction, but that they, too, had so remote an acquaintance that their descriptions were necessarily vague. A few bugs fell scorched onto the newspapers; several others, escaping with their lives, ran for cracks in the floor, the children after them. It was a delightful afternoon. We children roamed, unreproved, over the entire house, poking into corners, under rugs, behind beds and chairs in search of crawling things. The women indulged a similar passion and, over grandmother's protests, which they met by arguing that the house was upset anyway, began to rearrange the furniture, seeing how it would be "if the lamp stood over there, or if the bookcase was brought over here, against this wall, and maybe the couch should be moved out of this room altogether." Then the children were sent to the store for smoked fish and rolls, and we sat among piles of bedding in the steaming kitchen around the table, which was now in a new position, all of us exalted. Grandmother, of course, did not share in the festivity. Her humiliation, if it had had no earlier origin, would have begun on that day. Why, the very candles that she blessed of a Friday night, there they were scorching bugs!

Having such a background in natural and domestic science, I was surprised to discover so tender a sense of decency in myself. I should have been inured; my experience should have enabled me to encounter anything crude with crudeness of my own. Bugs, very well, bugs. But I found myself reacting after the fashion of grandmother, for whom candles were sanctified; any connection between them and the bedbugs—which relationship only she was sensitive or humble enough to perceive—was unholy, unclean, sacrilegious. I too was capable of establishing connections: the beautiful with the ugly, the sacred, or at least, forbidden, with the disgust of a revolting thing. For the infestation of my cot had spread over all experience, so that when I came to ask if Minna and Willy loved each other, and what love itself could be, I found everything bearing the sign of corruption. I compared, and finally united, Minna's bed with my own, and there the hot noises that I needed only hear once to understand became linked with the burning I would feel, bitten, unable to sleep, lying alone on the tight cot, crawling with revulsion and desire.

A letter, meanwhile, had come from home, in reply to the one I had sent to my father. It was written by my stepmother, who contradicted herself. Father, she wrote, was too busy to answer me and had asked her to do so. For her part, she thought I had acted wrong, as I would see for myself if I wasn't too spoiled to admit it. The best thing for me to do would be to come right straight back home. I should stop all this nonsense, it was about time I began to act decent for a change. She had once heard that when I was a child a neighbor of ours had called me a *gilgul*. A *gilgul*, in case I didn't know, was a monster, an inhuman thing, the kind, God forbid, that might be born to a woman who was frightened by a cat while she was carrying. It was true, the way I was acting one might think I was a monster. It just wasn't right for a young boy to be so hard-hearted. But all the same, I couldn't live like an animal. All my things were at the house—shirts, socks, and underwear, for instance, which I would need no matter what had happened. I could call for these at any time, or she could mail them to me, whatever I liked best. Clothes, of course, weren't the important thing. There was something else that she would like to give me, I would know what she meant. Now she would like to help me in any way that she could, only I must remember that her hands were tied, she was only one person, and there was the rest of the family to take into consideration. My father, for instance, did not even know she was writing me this letter, and she needn't tell me what he would do if he found out. Was it right I should aggravate him so? And especially now, when Slutsky, the helper at the store, got into an automobile accident. It's a fine thing, I tell you, to raise children and devote your whole life to them, and then—for what, for what? Sometimes she was glad, real glad, she could cry with relief, that she had no children of her own. At least I should get all my socks and have a fresh change every day. She had darned all the socks that needed mending. Did I think my aunt Minna would darn socks for me? What was going to become of me, she didn't know, but, believe her, if I had been her son, things would have been much different.

I was surprised by the detachment I felt while reading her letter. She was right, I was becoming monstrously hard-hearted. My very guilt was crusty; soon it would harden completely, and I should be unable to feel anything. In place of guilt, I would bear with me only a sense of unfulfilled obligations—what these were, and what my duties and my sacrifices should have been, I would never know.

I accepted my indifference. It meant growing up; breaking away was inevitable, and no home could last. But beneath my indifference and my "hardening" there lingered a regret for what I had lost: I no longer recognized obligations that had existed for me, simply and indubitably, when I was a child. There were things only a child understood, and in passing from childhood, we acquired ignorance. It was therefore not with a sense of moral, but of intellectual failure, that I regarded my stepmother's letter.

Still, I could not help laughing at it. Stepmother had an ear for English, and her spelling was phonetic. She set down on paper exactly what she heard. Thus, the word, "what," in her passionate complaint against my ingratitude ("for what, for what?") occurred as "wot" and the immediately following sentence, while reading which I felt, not shame itself, but the obligation toward shame, stood thus: "Sometimes am I gled, real gled, I could cry with releef that I have no children of my own." In the next sentence, the word "socks" was spelled with an "x" to make it a perfect rhyme with "lox," which she saw every day, written in whitewash, on the window of the corner delicatessen store. I knew that I should not laugh; I even had no right to notice her mistakes, for noticing them would only amuse me. Suddenly I felt a great tenderness for her: for her simplicity, her piety, her confusion, her belief in stratagem, so naïve, that, unable to decide whether it were better to say that my father knew, or that he did not know she was writing to me, she had said both.

I had never loved her; but now that I felt myself emptied of all emotion, I knew that I was capable of loving her. When I went back home to pick up my things, I would make this clear to her. I saw myself kissing her, reverently, yet amused, in the fulness of an empty heart. There was something sweet in my guilt, something original in what I had learned, after forgetting everything. My stepmother, startled, would break out of my embrace and run from me, a pot in one hand, a jar of cold cream in the other. . . .

It was not to be. Though I had arranged with her over the phone to call for my things at home, when I arrived, I found a note fastened under the doorbell telling me that she had unexpectedly been called away, and that I would find a bundle waiting for me at the corner store. I knew she had lied; she did not want to see me. And the reason was the bulky parcel, as I realized on opening it, back at Minna's; for she had prepared it with such great care and love that, had I opened it in her presence, as I should certainly have done, arguing that I could get along with much less, I would have embarrassed her. But so long as she was not with me when I saw what the bundle contained, it would stand as a reminder of her devotion, and a silent reproach to my in-gratitude. For I found, not only an adequate supply of shirts, underwear, towels, handkerchiefs, and socks—darned, as she had said—but a jar of cherry preserves, a prayer shawl, and a pair of phylacteries. You have forsaken your father, I could hear her say; do not forsake your God. Remember that you are a Jew and will always remain one.

The incongruity of reverence and amusement was now so much the greater. For the prayer shawl and phylacteries evoked the image of my father; and while he prayed only on important holidays, and never put on phylacteries (a neglect in which I followed him; only my grandfather observed the letter of the law), still, this was the inheritance I had received from him. It was vacant of God, but it had the element, as of religious transmission, whereby we were united in feeling. I knew what fathers must feel when children break away;

when I should have children, I would feel the same. For fathers, deep in themselves, were still sons, and still remembered the love they had broken; and sons were forever preparing to enact, and regret, an unchanging transgression. We were united in generation as those might be in God, who had always spoken the same prayer.

Chapter 14

I had the days to myself, and my evenings were often solitary for Willy and Minna, as if to avoid me, would spend many hours away from the house, and when they stayed home, I would keep to myself as much as possible, which meant that I remained in the kitchen. There I lived, ate, and, fitfully, slept, cut off from the fireplace, the sloping ceiling and the books in the living room, where I had imagined the spirit of freedom was enshrined. The door between our two rooms would frequently be shut. I would sit at the kitchen table, on which there might be some fruit and a newspaper, or the book that I had taken, without permission, from Minna's shelves. I would read, munch grapes, or chew an apple until I felt the first touch of drowsiness; then I would pull out the cot from under the sink and retire, always hours before they did, and in the hope that I would have an undisturbed sleep.

It was not so much my solitude which oppressed me as the feeling that I was being punished—although I could not say what was the nature of my guilt, and I knew that, except in the most general sense, comparable to the grief one may feel over the universal sadness of life when no specific sorrow is kept in mind, there was in fact no guilt which I could be called upon to expiate. Certainly, I had done nothing wrong. I had been too dull a child and timid a boy ever to have committed a clear and positive misdeed. One of the boys who had been in my eighth-grade class, for example, had stolen money from our teacher's desk. Another, whom I remembered no longer except as a boy born to trouble, a stammerer with a spike of red hair cutting out of his head, had dipped a cat into a bucket of paint. Such was the stuff of conscience, that which in later life could be regretted; but it could also bring pleasure and amusement to the recollection. A life of petty sins, of a partial, even friendly, involvement with evil was a spectacle running its course in a constantly shifting moral scenery. But it was the great sins, the ones we committed deeply, which were either too clear or too dim to stand before our sight.

Such, I suspected, was the nature of the guilt that weighed upon me. Through guilt, as it had once through fear, my life continued to center in my father. I considered him one of those who had sinned deeply in their lives—what I knew of his relations with Minna, as well as my own instinctive feeling for his character, confirmed this. Thus I felt guilt not only in my own behalf; it was for his guilt, too, that I was being punished. I bore his guilt as I bore the equal burden of his love. I was his son, and bound to suffer. Because I had failed him and denied him, because I had been the agent through which his shame had confronted him, therefore I was now sitting alone in the kitchen, facing the shut door. But even more intolerable than the sense of punishment was the humiliation of the kitchen. Thus, the fruit which would lie in a bowl before me—Willy never failed to divide the night's supply of fruit into two equal portions so that I had for my own consumption as much as Minna and he

[203]

had between them. And yet, such largesse, so natural to him, always seemed an uneasy gesture, as if he thereby meant to compensate me for my having to eat my share in the kitchen. Moreover, the casual manner in which he dumped the fruit into the bowl, his attitude of reckless generosity and freedom was an obvious exaggeration and a downright lie. For while he may have been exercising no more than his native generosity, he never failed to remind me, by the awkwardness and constraint that came over him whenever our relationship, as in the act of giving and taking, approached its original intimacy, that he was no longer acting freely, but always, to a degree, as Minna's representative, interpreting her will, modifying it, striving to soften it, yet carrying out its provisions. So, when he put the fruit down before me, in such quantity, I should never have been able to eat it all in a single night, I was confronted with the fact that Minna did not approve of my helping myself at the refrigerator. This was his way—especially when he poured a glass of milk for me, always spilling a few drops (another gesture at private benevolence)—of removing temptation from my path; and also of reminding me that I was always being tempted.

He would come in from the front room about an hour after supper. Before opening the refrigerator to bring out the fruit, he would offer me the evening paper, which he and Minna would already have read. I always found it folded the same way—one section arranged so that the sports page was on the top; the other, with the comics given prominence. This was, evidently, a further attempt to prove his solicitude, though it should immediately have been obvious to him that I would resent his persistence in believing that I put sports and comics first in importance; and he might also have known that it would confirm me in my growing dislike for his mentality, his habit of apologizing for intelligence. While

I understood, I also resented his efforts to relieve my humiliation and break my fall from grace.

He would linger in the kitchen, as if at a loss to know how to detach himself. He would say a few abruptly cheerful words, then, just as abruptly, turn away, distracted and pre-occupied, often leaving the room without finishing his sentence. This was an affectation of absent-mindedness that enabled him to shut the kitchen door, as if he were locking me in inadvertently.

And yet my humiliation was also self-imposed. My banishment to the kitchen had begun when I realized that they might have a perfectly natural desire to be left alone. I had withdrawn voluntarily. But as soon as it was clear that they did not object to my exile, I began to resent it and to blame them for it, imagining myself degraded to the status of a servant, a slave, a cast-off and unwanted beggar whom they kept only for charity's sake. It was I who decreed that I should not set foot out of the kitchen.

Between kitchen and front room there was a door, and I had taken this door as my symbol. It shut me off, not only from Minna and Willy, but from access to myself, and imparted finality to my bitterness. Therefore, do not wonder that I lay in the infested cot. Willy, observing the bites on my forehead, remarked, one morning at the breakfast table, that I was breaking out in pimples. I said nothing; I bore his winkng at me. I had performed the absolute act of slamming a door in my own face.

Willy, meanwhile, was neither employed nor very seriously looking for a job. He would rise with Minna in the morning and come into the kitchen to put up the coffee, at the same time waking me. Sometimes the sound of water running from the tap would be enough to rouse me; other mornings, when I was sleeping soundly, or when I had suffered a particularly heavy raid—as I had begun to call the activity of the insects—on the night before and had thus lost sleep, it would take a resolute shaking with my name called loudly, or even a few drops of water which Willy would flick into my face, to get me out of bed. The sounder I slept, the greater would be his delight in waking me; and the more clearly would I realize, as I rose gummy-eyed and sour, how desperately I had taken to looking not only for rest, but for liberty, for solace and escape, in sleep.

Willy would dress quickly and come out of the bathroom with his hair sleeked down wet and his face shaved and powdered, giving off a scent of lotion. Invariably a fleck of shaving cream would be left to dry on his ear lobe. He would lower the flame under the percolator, drop bread into the toaster and go about setting the table, laying out cups and saucers and silverware, with a brisk, competent air, as if nothing he did, no matter how menial, could fail to afford him some sense of satisfaction. He was, to all appearances, a man with his day, to say nothing of his life, mapped out before him; who knew exactly what time and what motion to allow for each gesture. Then Minna would hurry out in her slip, one stocking, perhaps, sagging loose from its garter and the other awry and her mouth holding half a dozen hairpins. Distraught with haste, she would plunge into the armholes of her dress and begin to draw it on over her head, twisting and bending as if she were struggling to cast a great burden from her shoulders. Then her old dressmaker's habit of holding pins in her mouth would, more likely than not, get the better of her and obstruct the passage of her head through the neck of the dress. She would spit the pins out and then have to stoop to gather them from the floor, losing more time and patience and what little composure she had left. "I'm late, I've no time for breakfast!" she would cry, and Willy, holding her chair out, would reply, with the ironic majesty of a head waiter, "Everything's ready, this way please." He poured the coffee and handed her buttered toast, sugar and cream; and she rushed on, not thanking him, drank her coffee scalding hot and took no account of his conscientious management of the breakfast table. She would say, "You'd better hurry if you want to come with me." The look which accompanied her remark would make it clear, to the undoing of his pride, that if he could get about so well and do everything so skilfully, it was because his was the skill of idleness which had nothing better to do, no job to rush off to in the morning.

She remained at the table no more than two minutes and never indicated, while she gobbled her food, that it was of the least interest to her whether Willy could keep pace. It was she who was late and she who had to get off at once; the morning and everything pertaining to it was strictly her own concern. And so there was no conversation. Minna would not have allowed it. Once, when I asked Willy a question, she interrupted me—"Bernie, there's no time for questions!" —as if I had been speaking to her. But there was one compensation for haste and loss of dignity which she never neglected to draw. As she was about to leave, she always said, "Willy, are you coming with me?" Thus making it plain that he had no reason to do so. She resented the fact that he did not work, and did not permit him the illusion of having a purpose in life.

Several times, catching Willy alone for a moment, I asked him to take me along.

"Where do you want to go?"

"I'll go with you."

"But I'm going on business. I've got an appointment at nine-thirty and another at eleven. Sorry, kid."

"Can't I meet you later?"

"Not today, I'm afraid. I'm all taken up."

"But I don't like to hang around the house all day."

"That can't be helped, I'll be busy all week. You'll just have to wait until Sunday. Here, why don't you take in a movie?"

And he would give me a quarter, pat me on the head and, straightening his tie, go off to his day of affairs, running down the stairs after Minna.

You may be sure I did not believe him. In a way, I suppose, I pitied him for having to keep up pretenses. Minna was no more taken in than I was—and yet he outdid himself to make us both believe that he was on the trail of something big and important, which would more than amply repay all his effort.

I pictured him riding to work with Minna and describing his various plans for the day—provided that she would listen. First he had to stop off and see so and so in the lobby of a certain hotel. Why yes, in a hotel lobby. (He was so skilled in invention that I was sure he would remember to add a slightly inconsistent and therefore outstanding detail to give his story the authenticity of experience.) But that was not, strictly speaking, a business call. He was stopping off to see a certain Murphy (let us call him), the friend of a friend of his (of Johnson, let us say). Johnson had asked Willy if he wouldn't be so kind as to meet Murphy, who was a stranger in town, to give him a few leads and line him up to one situation or another; which Willy, of course, consented to do only as a favor to Johnson. This done, he would go to such and such a place and meet so and so and talk to him about whatever it was—and don't you worry, it was a big thing and it was coming across soon. I could see him talking in this way to Minna as he took her to the door of her job, and waving good-bye to her leisurely and expansively while she ran in, casting back a glance of irony and skepticism, full of the same suspicion that I, too, was entertaining: that Willy had come to her just in time to keep a roof over his head.

The rest of the day, I was sure, he spent idling. Perhaps he went "to see a man," applied somewhere, half-heartedly, for a job, or lingered in an employment office where he spread himself out on a bench, read his paper and puffed on his cigar and boasted to the unemployed beside him. But his chief activity—I needed no evidence to convince me— was keeping himself amused: a ball game one day and a movie the next, so long as he had money (with which, it was by now quite possible, Minna supplied him); the beach if it was hot, the library if it rained, or simply sitting on the breakwater at the lake or dozing in Grant Park and perhaps somewhere a game of cards or pool or a visit with cronies.

My own day wore heavy on my hands. After they left I would wash the dishes and make my bed, sometimes going over it carefully with a lighted candle to see if I could drive out the pest. I met with no success, not daring to bring the fire very near the canvas or the wooden frame of the cot. Some days I might also sweep out the kitchen and then tidy the front room and make the bed there. Because I was listless and inclined to go woolgathering, this would take up the entire morning; it would then be time for lunch, which would consist of left-overs from the night before, a remnant of beans or soup, etc.

My father, so long as I could remember, had always worried about me, claiming that one who had so few friends and cook so little interest in what he considered a boy's normal affairs would come to no good end. "You'll go crazy," he warned me. "If this keeps up much longer, in a few years you won't even have enough ambition to come in out of the rain. As it is, I don't think you'd care very much." He had great energy, as did the rest of the family, and since there was no one from whom I could have inherited my sluggishness, he regarded me as a case of regressive development.

I knew myself well enough not to share his fears. I had had many friends in my early days, and had my father cared to recall the number of times he had thought my misconduct justified a spanking, he would have been willing to concede that I was wild, and therefore normal, enough.

But certainly a kind of lassitude had set in. I had lost all my childish interests and not yet gained new ones, and the brief period of excitement I had known about a year earlier, when I had first begun to read books that were well over my head, was now entirely dissipated. What exaltation that had been! I remembered how I had read *First Principles*, all of a fall and winter, had gone over each page several times and copied whole sections in a notebook to force what sense and meaning I could out of the heavy text. I had also read Schopenhauer and Nietzsche and had gone about for days in a great wild excitement, feeling there was light in me, strength and courage, an infinite capacity and hunger to understand life. Also at that time I had become interested in astronomy, and I went many times at night to the park and walked over the snow on the fields until I came to a clearing and there stood, murmuring a Biblical passage that I had read on the flyleaf of an astronomy book:

> When I consider the Heavens, the work
> of Thy fingers, the moon and the stars
> which Thou hast ordained, what is Man

that Thou art mindful of him, or the
Son of Man that Thou visitest him?

Thus I would stand and stare at the constellations, or lie back in the snow to look up and let myself sink deep into the bank and let the snow creep down my collar and enter my sleeves and feel no cold; and I would think that there was danger that I might fall asleep and freeze to death, but I would feel no fear—only a sense of life and inner heat spending itself in radiation like the stars themselves, and, like them, joined to them, beyond life and incapable of death.

Sometimes I would take a friend with me and trace out the constellations for him—Orion, the Dipper, the Bull, the red star in Orion's shoulder and brightest Sirius flashing at his feet—and as my friend would grow cold and tug at my sleeve and threaten to duck my head in the snow unless I stopped all this nonsense and left with him, I would feel all the more clearly the excitement and enthusiasm that marked me off from him and from all others, and recognize in his ridicule, the price, but also the blessing, of being what I was.

Now, on a dull summer day, alone in a strange house, I could find nothing to turn to, nothing to call me out of myself, no energy, no strength, no comfort. Vaguely I thought of girls, regretting that I had made so few friends among them at school, and wishing I had some one to call on. I lay on the couch, letting the afternoon gather heavily upon me. Before long a girl whom I had seen several times in school and whose last name I did not even know was standing beside me, and I imagined myself kissing her and fondling her and feeling her body. But at once my reverie was broken by a sense of guilt and anxiety, and I rose from the couch, disgusted with myself and unable to shake off the thought, the fear, the growing terror of my father which had again come upon me.

I ran out of the house and down to the park. Sweating and exhausted I threw myself onto a bench near the tennis court. There young boys were playing, stripped to the waist, springing about on the clay, lively and happy and shouting at one another. My shirt was drenched; several recent bedbug bites, irritated by the sweat, resumed their itching. The blood pounded in my eyes and I felt a headache coming on. On top of a hill to my right, the shade of a cluster of trees and bushes, their branches bending in the wind, beckoned to me, but I remained in the sun.

Later I climbed the hill, looking up at the sky as I went. I thought of the winter constellations which now stood invisible overhead, and, in a sort of prayer, though I did not recognize it as such, I asked that my purity of heart be restored to me.

As I climbed up the hill I saw a man sitting back against a tree trunk, rather dejected, as I judged from the slouch of his shoulders, and apparently half asleep. I recognized Willy, and suddenly felt a great delight in thus encountering him. I circled about him, to come upon him directly and catch the full sight of his dejection (I was sure he was suffering like myself) before he could see me. I stole along a row of bushes and stepped out, confronting him. He looked up, saw me and smiled—not brightening, however, for he had not been downcast; he had been smiling to himself, and now he smiled at me. His eyes blinked against the sky, he was relaxed, at peace with the world, pleased with every phase of the Creation, the greatest of which was himself. "Well!" he declared, drawling the word out in a half yawn, "look who's here."

The stub of a burned out cigar was flattened in his mouth.

He had unbuttoned his collar and removed his tie; one end of it hung out of his pocket. He held out his hand to me and said, "Hoist me up and we'll go for a boat ride," and swung himself up lightly and gracefully and started down the hill, so much happier and freer, so much younger than I.

Nothing could touch him when he was feeling pleased with himself. Even when we came home and he set about making supper to have it ready when Minna returned from work, he was still at peace. He whistled and hummed and skipped about, in no way humiliated by the task he was performing. Just as I had once envied him for his understanding nature, I now envied his perfect, unruffled complacency in which not a single qualm 'appeared.

Chapter 15

One afternoon Willy came home early. There was a huge cone of green paper under his arm; undoing it, he thrust a bouquet of flowers under my nose, and himself assumed an expression of ecstasy, as if he were anticipating the delight that would surely seize me. They were roses, at least three dozen, of all varieties, red and pink and yellow and white, bunched together with fronds of fern.

I was aware of the insincerity with which I forced myself to exclaim, "How wonderful!"

"That's the nicest bunch of posies I've seen in a long time. Fetch a vase, or something, and we'll put 'em up real pretty."

"What's the occasion?" I asked.

"Occasion? No occasion." It hurt him that I should suggest a motive. When he gave a gift, it was pure giving, no strings attached. That was the sort of man he was.

"I hope Minna will like them."

"Sure she'll like them. Say, you don't get flowers like this every day! There's a stand at the L station—never mind where. Just look at 'em. Here, have another smell! You know, when I was a kid—"

He checked himself. I saw that he had prepared a story to go along with the flowers—an epic of his childhood, full of roses as high as your head, acre after acre—and, not wanting to take the edge off its extravagance, had stopped, to save it for Minna.

"Ain't they the beauties, though?"

"Maybe you ought to put them in several vases."

"Oh, no. It'd ruin the effect. This way it hits you right in the eye. See!"

He held them aloft, and, as he had enacted what he had hoped would be my response, he now tried to give the emotion of the flowers themselves, holding himself tall and full and blooming with excitement.

"Minna might like a smaller bunch better," I suggested.

"Go on, why spoil it?" He did not understand.

"I'd forgotten, there is no vase," I said, coming out of the pantry with a milk bottle.

He did not mind. I found him fluffing the petals and drawing the stems out, arranging the flowers by color, and engrossed in himself, convinced of the worth of his own principle, a man who thought in round terms, without fractions, the big, the simple, the complete. Admiring the flowers, he was admiring himself.

But I was right, Minna did not enjoy the huge bouquet. She tried, first, to ignore it, but it drew too heavily upon the eye and, after looking disapprovingly at the overflowing milk bottle, she asked, as I had asked, "Why the flowers?"

This was too much for poor Willy. He was surrounded by mean-spirited skeptics who examined his motives, rather than giving him the open admiration that he required.

"They must have cost at least three dollars," went on Minna.

"Oh, money!" He was insulted now. "God's sake, can't you ever stop counting pennies?"

"They're my pennies," brought out Minna. "You could stop spending them for me."

"There you go. Go ahead. Now start in, say it, start in on jobs again. I should have taken that stinking job in the grocery while I had the chance. I'd never get anything better anyway. Well, go ahead, I'm waiting!"

"You've said it already," replied Minna, smiling to find him so weak, and no doubt relieved that instead of condemning her ungratefulness, he had taken to defending himself. "But really, you mustn't put ideas into my head. I may take you up on it. May I point out that you really haven't done a thing to get a job? Do you expect to go on living off me?"

"That's right, I knew you wouldn't be able to resist!" he cried. "Now you've said it, you're happy, you've got in your cheap little dig!"

Even while he was provoking her and "putting into her head" the ideas that had been rankling in his own, he was mounting his dignity, and he now stood scornful and proud, aware that in tempting her to take advantage of his obvious vulnerability, he had sustained a triumph of righteousness. It told on him; he could not help dramatizing his emotion. He held his underlip curled in a petulant, sour, disappointed grimace, as if he had just then tasted something of life and rejected it. His facial wrinkles were also called into play,

[215]

further to delineate his vast disenchantment, and there were three deeply frowning lines in the fleshy plane of his forehead above the bridge of his nose, while the lines about his mouth were flattened and drawn down. (I saw his expression change suddenly, as if, while seized with his emotion, he had, in all naïveté, found a better face for it.) His eyes remained wide open and unblinking, their light blue wild with self-declaration.

"Don't stand so stiff, pretty boy, you'll crack," said Minna. Hers was the colder, more unassuming hostility, sufficient unto itself. She did not come forward, as he did; her emotion was content to be suggested, and rather complacent in its skill. The occasion was welcome; she enjoyed a quarrel. Again she was comparing herself with Willy, and was pleased that she was doing so well—never raising her voice, never giving way, controlling everything with subtle direction, an indication of weariness and indifference, the competence and mastery of habit. All weakness was suppressed and denied, as if she were herself convinced that she had never suffered or lost command of herself. To look at her expression, so sleek and clear, even good-natured in its condescension toward Willy, you would see in her not the vanity of the person, but of the sex—the woman's affectation of independence, of standing alone, complete in herself, and discarding the contemptible man. But for all that, she remained insecure—for if she was deliberately comparing herself to Willy, she was also unable to avoid the comparison. His full emotion, in all its naïve excess, made her envious, and while she met it with contempt, she was unable to crush it, and she must have felt guilty for wanting to crush it. Besides, she had not yet thanked him for the flowers.

"But what of the thing itself?" he seemed to be saying. "Not the money, not jobs, but the flowers, standing there in

that milk bottle?" This was his triumph, but he was unsatis-
fied and thwarted. The story he had meant to tell, the
extravagant personal narrative, remained untold, and it was
the accompanying emotion, rather than the gesture of giving,
that he had valued above everything else.

"Willy," she said, facing his reproach, "understand, I'm
glad you brought the flowers. Thank you, they're lovely, I'm
grateful to you. But—well, so many of them! I mean—it was
unnecessary, a few would have been enough. This is—oh, so
obvious!"

That was the point. She had let it out.

Minna left the house soon after without saying a word.
About an hour later, Mason rang the bell.

He burst into the house in a fury of apology, devoting all
his energy to establishing the reluctance with which he had
come. "I know I'm disturbing you. I am, don't deny it!" he
insisted, and so for several minutes, until he pulled up short,
blinking as if he had been surprised out of his wits, and
asked, "Why, where's Minna?"

"She's just gone out," said Willy, tonelessly. "I don't know
when she'll be back."

"She went out? Where did she go?"

"She didn't say. Are you going to wait for her?"

"How come you didn't go with her? Did she go for the
evening?"

"I tell you I don't know!" shouted Willy.

"Of course, of course. Well then—oh Bernard, ah, just the
one I want to see. I really came to see him, William, ha
ha. . . . You will excuse us? Come with me, young man."

He led me into the kitchen, shut the door, and put his
finger to his lips. "A secret, a very important secret," he
whispered. "Don't breathe a word, do you hear?" There was

again a faint smell, sweet and stale, of alcohol on his breath. "Do you know where Minna is?" he asked, bringing his face against mine. "Don't say a word. She's at my place, in my house—understand? She came over after she walked out on him and—ha ha . . ." Mason broke into a fit of laughter which, this time, he could not stop abruptly. He ended by coughing and choking, pounding himself on the chest.

"This is wonderful!" he went on, his face red and his eyes watering. "She's going to stay there all night and I—I'm going to stay here! Ha ha—I'm not even going to bother about business tonight. This is too good to miss!"

He sat down on a kitchen chair and rocked with silent, empty laughter, as if to show that he was beyond expressing his delight. Then sprang up, whispering, "Tell me, is he worried about her, does he miss her yet? Does he wonder where she went?"

"No, he hasn't said anything yet," I replied, joining in his malice.

"Well he will, he will! You just wait and see. All night— ha ha. . . . I'll enjoy every minute of it. Now don't spoil it. Let him find out tomorrow, or the next day. Don't say a word!"

"I won't. I promise you."

"That's the stuff. That's a fine, upstanding boy! Fact is, I'm going to sleep here! You sleep here in the kitchen, don't you? So—don't give up your bed—so, naturally, I'll have to sleep in there, with him. He'll love that! As long as he doesn't try to cut my throat during the night, everything will work out to satisfaction. Perfect! So, not a peep out of you— all right, let's go in. Oh, wait, and one more thing. Some day I really want to have a talk with you. An important talk, you understand. Is he"—he hated to mention Willy by name—"is he here during the day? No? Good, then I'll be over, in the afternoon. But not a word, now!"

Willy was standing at the window, looking out, his legs planted far apart, his arms folded behind his back—exactly the pose, I was startled to realize, that my father had always struck.

"Bernard and I have concluded our conference," announced Mason, "and we are now at your service."

I was afraid Willy would throw him out, but he didn't—why, I don't know. Perhaps he suspected Minna was spending the night in Mason's room, and therefore preferred not to let him out of his sight. His suspicion, however, would only augment his anxiety; and in the course of the night, as Mason had predicted, Willy began to worry about Minna, once even going out for nearly an hour to look for her. Mason, meanwhile, had established himself comfortably in the armchair, had taken off his shoes, lighted a cigar and spread out a newspaper, so that one would think he were the host and Willy the visitor. Every few minutes he found a new reason for prolonging his visit. First, it was terribly important that he see Minna—had Willy any notion where she was, did he know where he might reach her, could he say when she might come back? Then, when it had grown late, he intimated that he had, besides, locked himself out of his apartment and had no idea where he could get hold of the janitor, at that hour, to let him in. Finally, it was too late to go back; even if he had had a key it would have been too late, for, to tell the truth, he was afraid to go about at night. A man who carried money with him had to take a few elementary precautions, such as keeping himself well insured, or preferring a crowded to a deserted street at night, and, while he was on a crowded street, holding his hand in the same pocket with his wallet—he, personally, thought that the right front pants pocket was best, although some had other opinions—so that no pickpocket should lift it. "Let them club you and kick you and stab you—but hold on to that little leather pocketbook with your life!" Saying which, he drew forth his wallet, and began counting his money, asking Willy if there was anything he needed, and perhaps he could loan him ten or twenty, or any amount—no need to be ashamed, just tell him. Well, and how was the job situation? Rather tough going these days, he wouldn't be at all surprised; but he knew of a place that was opening up down the street, and they'd probably need a counterman, so, if Willy liked, he'd be glad to look into it. And come to think of it, they needed a new place. It was crowded here, especially with the kid staying, why there just wasn't room to turn around in, and as for the requirements of civilized and hospitable living, such as a place to put up a visitor—you never can tell, sometimes someone drops in—it was a real hardship the way they were stuck. And so on and so forth, his pleasure keeping pace with his inventions, and his courage rising as he came to have less and less need for it, seeing that he was succeeding in making a fool of Willy.

Willy took it all grimly, with little show of emotion. His anxiety over Minna had not decreased, but he forced himself to suppress it as he realized that it was the very thing Mason was seizing upon. At one point he put up resistance and tried to hit back, calling Mason lost and diseased, and crying, "God, man, don't you believe in anything?"; in reply to which Mason had shrugged his shoulders and answered, "Of course not," and then, in the next breath asserted that he did, and set out to demonstrate that one could both believe and not believe at the same time, and that the world was nowhere nearly as simple as Willy imagined it to be. For example, had he, Willy, ever been unfaithful to a woman

[220]

that he loved? Well now, since that was a delicate question, he wouldn't expect Willy to answer if he didn't choose to. But as for himself, Mason could say that he had, and that he had done so deliberately, and yet unintentionally. He had done it deliberately, as a means of proving his love to a certain woman. Never mind who. And yet he believed in fidelity; but at the same time, one must recognize that it requires little of a man to be faithful if he believes in fidelity —so, to prove his love, he had shown that he did not believe in fidelity. Now if one doesn't believe in being faithful, he can really set about showing what faithfulness means. But if he doesn't believe in fidelity, then infidelity can hardly be called an intentional thing. So it was both deliberate and unintentional, and he, Mason, could say that he both believed and did not believe in the same thing. Did Willy follow him? He would put it more simply: the only way one could really show that he believed in something was to believe in it, despite the fact that he did not believe in it. There. Willy was by now completely at sea. He replied, "That's a lot of bullshit. If you believe in something, you believe in it, and that's that!" I presume it was at this point that Willy really began to fear Mason; for if he had hitherto imagined that he understood him, he now had to admit to himself that he did not. It was impossible for him to understand Mason, there was nothing he might take hold of, no set of traits that he might single out and take up one at a time, each in its proper place. Mason came all in a piece of confusion, and there was no limit to him and no order, except insofar as chaos itself is a kind of order. Willy, incapable of understanding him, no longer knew what to do with Mason. He relapsed, for a while, into his former belligerency and threatened to pitch Mason "out on his ear." But Mason now had sufficient courage to withstand his threats, and he stuck to his sly complacency, never raising his voice, and never for a moment ceasing to be reasonable, demonstrating that there existed a higher hostility than violence, and that he, Mason, was master of it. Willy, finally, collapsed into a glum anxiety—irritable, nervous and beaten —in which he suffered a foretaste of defeat. It may well have seemed to him that Minna had no means of attack half so vicious as the armor with which she protected herself. He, Mason, the fat, disorderly sophist, was her hardened shield, behind which, if she chose, she could easily remain inviolable.

It ended more or less as Mason had said, with the two of them going to sleep, late, in the front room, each taking a half of Minna's bed. Willy, incapable of further struggle, had, however, won one concession, but a very small one, which served rather to emphasize than to diminish his defeat. He had shoved Mason's half of the bed into the farthest corner of the opposite wall. There was soon a sound of snoring, which, since Willy never snored, I knew to be Mason's. It was loud enough, I am sure, to have kept Willy up; exactly how Mason should have snored, it proved him the same man, awake or asleep. . . .

There was no sign of him in the morning. He had already left when Willy rose. I felt an uncertain pity for Willy, the result of a divided conscience. I had stood by and seen him demolished, myself having conspired to that end. Nevertheless, by what reason I did not yet know, I felt he had somehow, and at least in part, deserved it. It was not only that he had wounded me, or that he had all along contributed to my humiliation, so that I had had to turn against him the very bedbug bites from which I suffered. Beyond all this, I felt an utter lack of justification in the life we had been leading, which, in turn, seemed to justify the trouncing he had received.

We avoided each other, neither of us speaking, so that we should not have to mention Minna. We were sitting down to breakfast, which Willy had despondently prepared, setting out only two plates, when Minna whisked into the house, saying good morning.

She was as cheerful as she had ever been, absolutely in fine humor. "Good, breakfast is ready. But I really don't have time for anything, I'll be late for work."

Chapter 16

Childish and insignificant as that night's episode was, Willy's pride never recovered from the blow it had suffered. From thinking of Mason as a curiosity, a strange but unimportant creature who represented a strange but unimportant aspect of Minna's life, he came to regard him as a threat, a token of that contrariness in Minna which, he began to fear, he might never conquer. Now when Mason came to the house Willy would show his hostility either by keeping still and retreating into himself so that you couldn't get a word out of him, or else by an unusual boisterousness in which he sprang out of his chair, rushed about the room, shouted and argued and contradicted Mason and employed every means at his command to outdo him. And always with disastrous results; for when he sulked, Minna ignored him and when he was quarrelsome she sided with Mason.

Mason pretended to be unaware of Willy's jealousy. But it was too good an opportunity to let pass, and so, with alternating courage and cowardice, guiding himself by Willy's reaction and by the strength of the support he was receiving from Minna, he set about teasing and plaguing him, sneering and snickering—and drawing himself in by simulating a coughing spell whenever he feared Willy had felt too keenly the edge of his malice. His favorite device was to remove his shoes as soon as he entered the house. Mason would sink into a chair and groan and puff with exaggerated labor as he bent down to draw off his shoes. He fell back after pulling off each shoe, sighed with satisfaction, wiggled his toes and unstuck his socks from the soles of his feet. On one occasion he removed his socks entirely, but was obliged to pull them on again when he saw that Minna's approval did not extend so far.

Willy was defeated by these maneuvers. He had been in the habit of going about the apartment in his stocking feet, a privilege which he had obviously considered as belonging to the man of the house, and while Mason, in imitating him, did not lay claim to the same right but showed quite clearly that he knew himself to be a usurper, the effect on Willy was in no way diminished, and he gave up the privilege altogether. A similar maneuver and retreat was executed on hot nights when Mason took the liberty of removing his shirt. "Take off your shirt and be comfortable," he said to Willy in his most inviting tone and dodged into a coughing fit when Willy's expression turned sour. But Mason spent the evening in his undershirt, his fat chest and arms exposed, while Willy did not even roll up his sleeves.

But what gave Mason his greatest delight was to bestow the benefits of his generosity upon us. He came up at times with such great quantities of soda pop or beer that one could only think he had carefully calculated his extravagance. Somewhere he got the notion that I was fond of popcorn; and so, for days, I would have popcorn to burn. Under his urging I ate more than I had a taste for. I had never quite overcome my fear of Mason, and while I did not feel obliged to please him, there was no sense of proportion to govern my relationship to him, and consequently I succeeded in pleasing him beyond all measure. I was in fact taken sick with the stuff and vomited in his presence. He was delighted. "That's the idea!" he declared when I came choking and red-eyed out of the toilet. "Make room for more. Wipe your nose first, and then start on another box." He tore the cover off and thrust the box at me and broke into a paroxysm of laughter when I made a grimace and pushed the popcorn away. "Nothing suits me better," said he, when he had caught his breath, "than to see a young boy eat himself sick on candy, ice cream, popcorn, or malted milk. Too much of a good thing—that's the way to live! If something is good, how can there ever be enough of it?" The gestures and innuendoes that accompanied his statement, as well as the statement itself, all conspired to give it that sense of hidden meaning which characterized all his remarks. It took some time to learn that what Mason concealed was not the meaning of his observations, but the fact that they had no meaning.

Nevertheless, he continued to hint at the hidden and recondite almost as a mystic would who spelled out the invisible truth from the letters of the invisible world. (In his own fashion, I suppose, one might call him a mystic—a mystic who elevated not holiness but vulgarity to a fantastic principle.) And no matter how I had grown to suspect him and to believe I could see through him, his antics cast him into an illusory but persistent depth in which his character, and especially the largesse by which he loved to give expression to it (as on a day which I am about to describe)—his character, seen only dimly, appeared to be profound.

The three of us (Willy stayed home) took a boat across the lake, then a train to the sand dunes. Mason bought lunch for us on the boat and forced us to eat well beyond our limit. His generosity, as usual, was pointless, and, again, so calculated that it seemed to be a kind of parsimony. The lake trip alone, including fares, meals, tips, and flourishes cost him, as far as I could estimate, about twenty-five dollars. But as we entrained for the sand dunes he drew me aside and whispered, "If they ask you, remember, you're under twelve." And argued in vain with the ticket agent, trying to get me on for half fare.

He had been extremely talkative on the boat. On the train, however, he was silent, thus suggesting that the twenty cents or so that he had failed to save on my train fare were rankling him. He sat brooding by the window, cast a dispirited eye at the countryside, and confined himself to muttering "Robbers!" from time to time; whereas what was in fact troubling him was the conversation which he and Minna had held on the boat.

The day had begun gray and chilly. As we left shore and lost sight of the land we were engulfed in fog, a dull atmosphere the color of copper turned green that obliterated the horizon. Sky and water merged without distinction and the ships in the near distance seemed to hang in air. Plumes of smoke, the color and substance of the fog, lay motionless behind them. "Have faith in the press," said Mason. "It says fair and warm in the afternoon." Later the sun appeared; we had come in sight of the opposite shore. The lake sprang to life, the sky established itself, receding from the water. We saw the slopes of the sand hills standing out bright yellow along the shore, gently rounded and covered with knots of grass.

Most of the way across I had leaned against the rail, looking down at the water, creamy with froth as it sped by the side of the boat. Minna and Mason sat on deck chairs behind me.

I was lost in contemplation of the ship, the water, the waves, the throbbing of the engines, given over in a trance (it was my first trip by boat) to a study of the whole spectacle about me. But after some time had passed and the freshness of the experience had worn off, I found myself listening to Minna and Mason's conversation. I realized that I had been doing so longer than I had been aware, and when my attention turned consciously to their talk I already knew that they were discussing Willy.

"Did you think maybe we'd get into a fight if he came along?" I heard Mason say. "That he'd pick me up by the neck and throw me overboard? So you thought I'd be afraid? Do you really think I'm a coward? Minna, you know me better than that. A coward always gets into fights and loses. But I don't get into fights—and with me a man is licked even before he begins—that is, he gets discouraged, I'm not so easy to get hold of So tell me, maybe you thought I'd be jealous if you asked him to come along with us? But that's childish. Willy would think like that. You must have picked it up from him."

"But I tell you he didn't want to come. You shouldn't find it so hard to understand why."

"I do understand, but I'm disappointed, would you believe it? I wanted him to come."

"Sometimes I can't make you out. You know you hate him. You can't stand him any more than he can stand you."

"I should live so, it's not true! I hate Willy? I love him! Such a fine man—a head like a peanut and shoulders like an ox. I like nothing better than to see the two of you together. But look now, you weren't fishing for something a moment ago when you said I hate him, were you? After all, it would flatter you . . ."

[227]

"I certainly was not. I'm glad to hear that you love him. It makes everything so much simpler."

"Fine, everything's cozy. But you do think I'm jealous, don't you? Ah, women! How can I be jealous? A jealous man goes around imagining things. But what have I got left to imagine? Don't you think I know what's going on? You haven't once tried to hide a single thing from me. I would appreciate it, by the way, if you would try to hide something —at least once. It would be so considerate of you. But never mind. So what do you want me to do now, pretend that I don't know? Wait, let me tell you something—he's the one who hides the fact. He's ashamed of you, the way you are. He thinks, believe me, he thinks you're wicked—can you imagine that?—and he hates you for it. Just as you have a certain contempt for him, so he hates you. But the difference between you is that while you have contempt for him, you really respect him, you look up to him—that's what breaks my heart—while he, all he sees in you is a challenge. He wants to see if he can't change you. Such an idea yet, change you! Why, he doesn't know the first thing about you. That's just what a man like him would want to do—a man straight from the sticks, a prize lunkhead who never saw a civilized woman before in his life."

"But Fred, you just got through saying that you love him!"

"And so I do. But it's all right for me to love him—what I want to know is, why should you? What do you see in him? He's stupid, he's lazy, he's got a big grin. When you shake hands with him you can feel your bones break. Fine. But where's the bargain? Does that make him wonderful?"

I took a few steps along the rail, moving nearer to Minna and Fred, but keeping my head turned toward the water, as if some object dim in the fog, a gull or a ship, had caught my attention. I leaned over the rail, drew my head down and

[228]

my shoulders together to make myself inconspicuous. The conversation continued; they were paying no attention to me.

"I never thought I should have to defend my choice of friends," Minna was saying with some asperity. "I thought we settled that long ago."

"You settled it, my dear. What have I got to say in the matter?"

"Too bad. Don't feel so sorry for yourself. I don't see you dying of loneliness."

"Spoken like a modern woman. Aren't you the least bit afraid of me? Not the least bit?"

"Not the least," Minna answered, smiling (as I could tell by the sound of her voice) and apparently won over for a moment by his self-depreciating charm. "Not that much."

"Ah, what good does it do me that you're such an understanding woman? I need your understanding like a hole in the head. I wish you were stupid enough to be afraid of me—or at least to respect me a little."

"But I do respect you, Fred!"

"A lot of good it does. No, I tell you, with these modern women—you let them have their way so they think you're a coward."

"You protest too much. I will begin thinking you're a coward."

"Think what you like, I wouldn't care. As long as you don't get me mixed up with that brave man of yours. Do you know—sometimes you're so taken up with him, I half expect you to call me 'Willy'."

"Don't worry. There's not a chance."

"Boy, do you respect me! Just be careful you don't call him Fred or you'll really regret it."

"You fool, don't you know he's jealous of you?"

"Of me? Now isn't that something to be proud of! I can

[229]

see where you women with two men on your hands really have your problems."

"He's not 'on my hands'!"

"I don't care about *him*."

"You're not either, silly!"

"Saved by the bell! Don't you see, it's no fun to know everything. I've got to pretend there are still a few secrets left, so I was only trying to trap you. If you'd somehow let on that I was on your hands, I would have thrown you in the lake!"

"But Fred, you know it's not so! Even if I'd said it, it would only have been a slip of the tongue."

"I know, but what do you want me to do? If I know everything already, at least you should grant me the right to insist that you keep your story straight. Some men spy on their women—me, all I can do is listen! But really now—let's get back to the subject—what's so wonderful about that simple-minded specimen of yours?"

"Oh, he's not so simple-minded."

"Then he pretends to be, which is worse. How can you trust a man like that? He's capable of tormenting you to death—always, of course, in a naïve, simple way. No, I still don't see it."

"Fred, this is foolishness. Do you really want me to tell you?" There was a sudden tenderness in her voice, and I could imagine her taking his hand and pressing it to show her sincerity. I resisted the impulse to turn around and look at them.

Mason hesitated, not answering.

"Do you?" she asked again, still tender, with sympathy, even pitying him.

"I guess not."

"Thanks. I was sure you'd understand."

I could hear him sigh. He began to hum under his breath, an incongruously merry tune, then broke it off abruptly, as if he had decided to force the question, but still said nothing. When he spoke at last, he had returned to his familiarly sly, ironic, self-mocking tone, avoiding the danger of intimacy.

"I must be getting old. After all, he is a bit younger than me, eh? I suppose you know that I take a pill after each meal —but I wasn't going to let you know. I left them home today. If you hear me belching, you'll know that you're a cruel woman."

Again silence. My back was beginning to ache.

Suddenly he cried out, hurt, in anger, "Don't you understand what he is? He's an enemy! After all, our way of life . . . have you forgotten? Ah, how you've given in! I tell you, it breaks my heart when I hear you talking in words of one syllable. Tfoo! What's become of you? You've forgotten! You're so afraid! You're afraid that hillbilly will think you've got a thought in your head, an impulse, an idea. Afraid to open your mouth, to live, to insist on what you know to be right—"

"Fred, it can't go on being 1920 forever."

"That's cynicism, Minna. Right now, you're lower than Willy. Ugh, what he's been putting into your head! Look here, I don't give a damn how stupid he is, but don't you go taking pride in his stupidity. I won't stand for it—"

"Control yourself, please—"

"I won't have it! You used to stand for something! You used—"

"Fred, I'm getting impatient with you!"

"Ah, what's the use! We sit here like a pair of idiots. If you want to talk to me, be polite, be amusing—go ahead, say

[231]

it, that's what you mean! I can't even talk to you any more. A pair of strangers all of a sudden. 'I don't see you dying of loneliness.' That's what you said, didn't you? Don't deny it! A fine thing to say. 'I'm getting impatient with you.' God damn it, after all these years . . ."

She did not respond to his anger. After about a minute he spoke again, "Minna, please!" with the same quiet sincerity and tenderness that she had used to turn him away from inquiring into her relationship with Willy; only now he was claiming it for himself, demanding his due, asserting his older and more powerful right over her, and shocked, turned cold to find that he had lost it. It seemed to me that this must have been the first time in years that he had been able to assert, without slyness or mockery and with the full force of his unbroken attachment to her, his sense of pride and undiminished personal worth. But in his pleading with her he seemed to recognize his own fault for having so long submitted to an irony which he himself had made literal, and he withdrew his anger in resignation.

The conversation was at an end.

Instead of jumping up at once to prove my innocence, I continued to stare out at the horizon, which was gradually becoming defined through the mist. "Look at the sea gulls," I said at length. "I could watch them for hours." There was no answer. Minna was now staring out into space and Mason had already begun to brood.

He kept it up on the train, as I have said, and even the little comedy of the half fare and the rest of the extravagances and parsimonies in which he indulged himself all day were mechanical and obvious and lacking in that freshness of invention of which he was capable at his best.

Even so, it was worth seeing him in a bathing suit. We changed our clothes at the dunes and lay in the sand, the water proving too cold. Mason wore an old-fashioned suit with a long, flapping skirt that reached to his knees. His breasts were larger than Minna's, his stomach when he sat up, bunched itself into several fatty tires; half naked, he proved to be so much more obese than he seemed in his clothes as to suggest that all this time he had been wearing a corset. To see him thus, in a bathing suit, was to form the clearest definition of the comedies he had been performing. The suit was perfect for the comedian's role, a jester's costume which he may have bought with the very thought in mind. It was in fact nothing other than the type of suit worn by fat men in the slapsticks—a proof, if any were needed, and a belated insight that Mason, much as any high-school girl might do, drew the inspiration for his character from the movies.

He lay back in the sand and asked me to bury him. I heaped sand on his belly while he grunted in satisfaction. Soon his eyes were shut and he was fast asleep. He lay abandoned, surprisingly defenseless and sincere in sleep for one whose waking life was so contrived. Relieved of all special effort to maintain himself, of his gestures and inventions, he slept in infantile peace, his deep breathing naïve and innocent and, for all the world, an act of faith. I looked at Minna to see if our insight coincided. She was lying on her elbows and gazing out at the water, paying no attention to him. There was tension in her eyes which the sweep of the lake and the rhythm of its moderate waves did nothing to relieve. She seemed careful not to commit herself, not to allow even the most casual or unconscious expression to reveal what she really felt for the man beside her, and had somehow managed to convince herself that she had forgotten he was there. But there may have been a trace of disgust in her expression as if she, too, had recognized that in Mason

[233]

as he was naturally, there was something a little helpless and revolting.

He brought us one night to his saloon, The Garter Belt, where we bored ourselves miserably. Minna had been there many times before, and had come reluctantly. Willy was sulky and critical and I was ill at ease.

Mason, however, was in all his splendor. That is, he had doffed his sweater and sneakers for a white shirt, a black suit, and a pair of patent leather shoes. His shirt cuffs were too long, his collar too tight, the suit was too warm. But I tried my best to ignore him, not to respond, as I had been doing, with wonder at his deliberate incongruities.

It was a small place, "One thing to be thankful for," as Willy remarked in an undertone. The room had a low metal ceiling in which one could trace out through the overhanging strata of smoke a stamped pattern of vine leaves and curlicues —a sign that the room was of considerable age and that it once might have housed, say, a dry-goods store; I thought also of my grandfather's store which had had a similar ceiling. A number of tables were squeezed into the room, more than the space could comfortably hold. There were no clearly defined aisles. Lamps, made to resemble lanterns, were screwed to the walls and cast a dirty reddish light on the tables under them. The rest of the room, with the exception of a small bar in a corner, was quite dark.

The saloon was crowded with men, most of whom I thought were drunk. "Just some of the local tramps," explained Minna, when I asked who these people were.

"Bohemians," added Willy, contemptuously. "Near North Side riff-raff, most of them fags."

"What are fags?" I asked as Mason began to defend his clientèle.

"You'll do without knowing," said Minna.

"If he hangs around places like this much longer," said Willy, "he won't be able to help knowing."

"Oh, so now you don't want him to hang around," replied Minna, angrily. "You were the one who was so glad to have him, who was going to show him such a good time, who was so sure it would all be good for him. Now we're a bad influence on the poor boy. Now—"

"And what's the idea getting so high-hat on me?" broke in Mason. "This place used to be good enough for you, and it's still the same place. I expect all my customers to be treated with respect—"

"You and your customers! You're just a stuffy old bartender," said Minna.

"They're trash," said Willy, "scum of the Near North Side, and the place is a dump. Garter Belt!"

"He calls it a dump, Minna, a dump! Do you hear what he says?" cried Mason, his eyes rolling in a frenzy of mock rage. His anger had begun genuinely enough, and he had banged the table with his fist, but no sooner had he expressed his emotion than he found it necessary to detach himself from it.

"That's what it is exactly," said Minna. "A dump."

There was a piano a few feet away from our table. A woman was pounding the keys and tossing her head back as if to throw her voice over her shoulders. I became aware of her during the uncomfortable silence that followed the conversation. The piano, tinkling in the treble and booming in the bass, kept up a steady beat while she broke a syllable into minute parts and tossed each back over her shoulders with a separate jerk of her head. "Ba-a-a-a-a-a-a-a-a-a-a-a-by . . ." Her mouth was open to its fullest extent, as if she were sitting in a dentist's chair. Her eyes were beaded with mascara; the irises lay pale, curiously vacant and unmoving. I could see the powder standing out on the down of her cheeks.

"Well," said Mason, shrugging his shoulders and striking what he must have thought was a philosophical attitude, "I don't say, mind you, that this is the Ritz Bar or anything. But a decent place it is."

"Stop it, Fred, stop being ridiculous."

"All right, darling. But you know," he turned to Willy and drew a smile from some obscure source of pride, "at one time she used to be very much taken by the place. Very, very much—but say, let's have a drink. Waldo!" he called one of the waiters (whose name, I was sure, was not Waldo). "What'll it be?"

Minna ordered a whisky and soda.

"I'm not drinking," said Willy.

"William! I won't allow it," protested Mason.

"I don't care to."

"But something . . ."

"I'll drink," I volunteered.

"About you drinking I don't have to worry. You want me to be put in jail for serving liquor to minors? I'll let you lick my glass. William!"

"All right, beer."

"And the usual thing for me," said Mason to the waiter, who hesitated, thereby indicating that there was no "usual thing." Mason had to frown to make him understand that anything would do, so long as he didn't have to name it. "Oh yes, as I was saying, at one time Minna was—"

"Please!" said Minna.

"What's the matter, you want to deny it? She personally decided on the decorations of the place. She chose the colors, the tablecloths . . ." he waved his arm, drawing an arc about the smoke-filled room.

The pianist had disappeared and now a juke box was

blaring. Bands of red, green and violet light spun across the round glass belly of the machine, like the stripes of a barber pole.

"Fred," said Minna uncomfortably.

"Well, all right. Not is not. But you should have seen how she was then. Yes, yes. This was our first little venture, you might say."

The hint, however it was given, was not very graciously received. Minna, resenting any reference to her relationship with Mason, reddened, then made a wry face, as much at her own embarrassment as at Mason's indiscretion. Willy was plainly startled. He looked from Minna to Mason in silence, staring much as my father would when he demanded an explanation.

Our drinks came at this moment, which was just as well, for even Mason sensed that he had spoken too freely. He drained off his drink, welcoming the distraction; and the better to utilize the opportunity, he turned to me and said, "Youngster, you may stick your finger in my glass and suck it."

He recovered from his initial embarrassment well enough, only to create another. Once more recommending his place to us, he suggested to Willy that he come on as a bus boy. Again his words were not taken in very good faith, and to extricate himself from the new difficulty, Mason had to cover up by saying, "Oh, temporarily, temporarily, until you find something better. I just thought it might make things a little easier for you two." Then, realizing that this, far from being ingratiating, was but a further lapse, he went on to state that he was not really looking for help, he had enough on hand, if he wanted a bus boy he had only to hang a sign out the window. He had just thought that maybe Willy . . . But he saw that this was getting him nowhere; perspiring, squirming and fidgeting he had merely worked his way deeper into embarrassment.

"It's just my cockeyed ideas of economics," he explained. "That's why I take on men when I don't need them and lay them off when I do." He smiled rather weakly, in apology to Minna for talking about business. "I mean I work on the theory that what makes me no richer makes me no poorer. See here, Bernie!" he exclaimed, wiping his forehead with his sleeve. "We know how much Bernie likes popcorn. Well, if I gave him some now he'd throw it away—that is, ha, if he didn't throw it up first. Here, I don't have any popcorn, but I've got a mint. Do you like mints? Bernie, yes or no."

He pulled a roll of mints out of his coat pocket and thrust it at me.

"No, not very much."

"Fine. But let's say for a moment that you do. Suppose you do, so take one. Now what do you do? You put it in your mouth. Go ahead, put it in your mouth—just for a minute. So. Now if you liked it you'd eat it. But you don't like it. So throw it away. Go ahead, take it out of your mouth and throw it away. Throw it on the piano. Hit the girl on the neck before she has a chance to start singing—or wait till she starts and then throw it into her mouth. But throw it! There. All right, he's thrown it away. So what difference does it make to me whether he eats it or throws it away? Do you see what I mean?" he asked, blinking his eyes in great earnestness, as if here, finally, were truth and unequivocal meaning, a confession it had been necessary for him to make. "Does it make me any richer or poorer? Do you follow me?"

No one had followed him. Minna patted him on the wrist and said, "You're a very bright boy. But I think we'd better be getting on. It's late." She hadn't touched her drink.

"Wait, wait, how can you go now? You've just come! Just

[238]

a minute, please, relax. I won't talk any more. I'll do a juggling act. Bernie, would you like to see me juggle? At least finish your drink."

"The boy's getting sleepy," said Minna.

"I'm getting sleepy," said Willy. "Let's go."

Mason rose to see us to the door.

"Don't get up, please don't get up," insisted Minna, weary and impatient, and yet somehow resigned to him. "Maybe you'd better get behind the bar. In shirt sleeves." She kissed him suddenly on his bald forehead and walked off, Willy and I following, threading our way through the noisy, smoky, vulgar room.

Chapter 17

Home had vanished. I rarely thought of it now except in a vague way as that to which I owed my fading sense of guilt; so one might remember a debt, incurred years ago, which he had forgotten to pay.

Resentment is a mask. For it was resentment, more than anything else, which dimmed my recollections of home, dulled the edge of my natural feeling for the family and created the illusion that a long time separated me from it, whereas only weeks had passed. Though I could discover in myself no intention to return, I resented the fact that my father had made no effort to win me back. His leaving me thus to my own devices indicated his assurance that I would return, in good time, all the more vanquished for having voluntarily submitted to my defeat. Thus he was even willing to undergo whatever suffering my absence caused him for the sake of that greater righteousness which would be his when I came back in response to the summons he had refused to make. And so resentment drove out lonesomeness, and the more I felt myself in my family's power, the more powerless I was to prevent the transfiguration and denial of my true feelings for home.

Perhaps I longed to return; perhaps I strove each day, through some maneuver of which I remained unaware, to bring my reconciliation nearer. I would find, despite all my efforts to believe the contrary, that I was not really engrossed in the life at Minna's. Proximity had robbed it of its charm. And yet I would turn away from the insight which proximity made available to me, fearing that if I once did admit to myself how well I had come to understand Minna I would find nothing but shabbiness in the life she led. But what was that other life? In what respect was home so dear that to preserve myself in exile I had to encourage forgetfulness? The truth would dispense no favors. Had I only the courage for it I would have acknowledged that my actual longing looked neither here nor there, neither to home nor exile, but to a life foreign to both in which some beauty and freedom prevailed.

What is emptiness, what is fulness? I knew only the moments of my own experience which had carried in them the suggestion of a further brimming in time—a fulfillment of that which the moment promised—and therefore these moments were full. But the rest, the waste stretches between, the empty, futile time?

There had been moments in the life of the family—the annual exaltation of the Passover table, the gatherings and celebrations—whose joyousness (for everything fades, and in truth the family was no better at the height of its joy) was difficult to understand. Were the occasional bursts of joy but the manifestation of a poverty of spirit—true, a poverty that declared itself a blessing, that spent so freely because it had nothing to hoard, but still a poverty because joy rang so seldom in it? But perhaps the joy of privation, since we lacked fulfillment, was the only one we could know. The images of fever are the only ones that burn: and so the true life may be only a matter of hours.

Of the life I had known, all that I had ever treasured was an independent joy, independent of the circumstances that produced it, of the human beings who participated in it, independent, almost, of my own delight. And therefore, perhaps, the truth was also such: a pure thing that existed by itself, though never found alone. The task, then, was to turn away from circumstance, to unite the here and the there, this life and the other, in a single indifference for the sake of that alone which was real in us. But the rewards of such indifference could only be mystical; and as for myself, I lacked the courage.

One night I dreamed of my father. It was a simple dream, but stranger than I had ever known dreams to be. I dreamed I had become my father. I had reached his age, my hair was gray, my eyes were his shape and color, and when I looked through his eyes I saw the world, not differently, but yet altered as if it were by his own perception. I felt a melancholy that was utterly unlike my own, and yet it was mine—this was no longer the sadness that divided fathers and sons but the one that bound them. I went about with a sense of loss, of great bereavement; the world was strange, never before entered. But it was not I who was lost, rather someone else who was looking for me. When I awoke, still feeling the identity that had been established in my dream, I thought that now at last I had bridged the gulf between this life and the other, and that everything I had hitherto believed about

[241]

my father was illusion. For without knowing what else the dream signified, I knew that I was indeed his son, and that his life had been meant, at the peril of my own, to live itself out in me.

It was unfortunate for Willy that he had set himself an objective. He intended to reform Minna—nothing less. From the very beginning he had objected to her mode of life, and his continued objection—which grew stronger the more he became a part of her life, and the more he suffered from it —was wearing him down.

Minna, it must be remembered, was so long accustomed to having her own way that she had grown blind—blind to the nature of her desires and blind to the nature of others who she felt stood in her way. Willy's character was for her not so much different from her own, as incorrect. I dare say that the conflict between them rested on this basis.

I regret, however, that I never learned exactly what it was that they quarreled over. Their arguments, it seemed to me, were born at night in bed. I would hear their heated whispers and intermittent outbreaks of violence, never sustained long enough to enable me to make out their words. There would also be laughter, which I dreaded most; understanding it to be a prelude to their love-play—which in turn engendered further violence—I would steal away from their door, where I had stationed myself to overhear their quarrel, and return to my inhospitable cot.

What was the issue of so much discontent? I recalled Willy's first impression of her on that comic night when I had brought them together. She was an unhappy woman, a miserable woman who did not know how to live; falsely sophisticated, she had cut herself off from the proper sources of human satisfaction. However Willy might have come to modify his judgment, it would only have been to reinforce it.

For one, I knew Willy disliked her apparent indifference, her willingness to accept all things more or less as they occurred. Her acceptance of everything was, to his mind, a reflection of her doubt of everything. "I have no stake in the matter"—this was the position to which she invariably returned, once her emotional involvement in an event was dissipated. For all the hysteria she was subject to, nothing really seemed to move her; and it baffled him.

It was because she was yielding that he found her most unyielding. She accommodated herself, where he should have wanted her to struggle. And yet so much at cross purposes were they, that their arguments could not even claim a common term. What did he want? Minna demanded. Will, spontaneity, he insisted, he wanted spontaneity. To which Minna replied that she was the most spontaneous of women, and if he did not see her as such, it was either because he had killed it in her or else was so lacking in the quality himself that he could not detect its presence in others.

Minna, for all her apparent acquiescence, was also trying to reform Willy. Her method was different; she worked in detachment, withdrawing when she wanted most to influence him. Her reproaches were unspoken (when directed against an essential matter—minor irritations always found voice), as she tried to control him by silent disapproval. (This trait was so pronounced in my father that she may have learned it from him, many years ago.) Thus, if Willy were speaking in a vein Minna particularly disliked, soon enough it would become clear to him that her way of listening constituted a criticism. He would stop and wait for her to say something. "Go ahead, I'm listening," she would seem to say, and yet say nothing. She would sigh or shrug her shoulders in in-

[243]

dication of boredom, and perhaps undertake to correct his pronunciation—or, if the point he was making required some response, would reply—"There you go again," or, "You're very impressive, really. You must remember to use that line again."

From the look he would give her, one might think she was denying the very living man in him. She would accredit his effort like a schoolteacher, but never the true sense, the passion of what he was trying to say. Such subtle abuses, she knew, were the ones that made him suffer most keenly. Sometimes she would even pat his cheek and smile and kiss him lightly to show that she was untouched, and that all his effort must fail to touch her.

All of which inspired, I am sure, his greatest fear—that the pattern he had seen to obtain between her and Mason also awaited him. He would shudder as if in sensing that a common fate lay in store for all the men whom Minna attracted.

I wondered at her cruelty. Was it meant to protect something in herself? Was she cruel to Willy out of jealousy, admitting thereby what she could not admit openly—that he was sincere, committed, passionate, emotionally a superior being? Did she perhaps know that what he wanted—a release of pent-up and denied feeling, the liberty of spirit which she had never yet enjoyed in love—did she know that it was this which she was unable to give? Or did she perhaps flatter herself to think that she really possessed such powers, really was as he wanted her—but, so contrary and vain was her nature, did the very fact that he insisted, demanding what she thought she could give, force her to perjure herself and make herself appear other than she thought she was? Perhaps some subtle, perplexing, uncontrollable spite worked between men and women, putting a curse on desire: the truth is between them, within their grasp, and they need only join to have it—and yet they reject and destroy the very possibility of truth. It is neither struggle—for they do not join at all—nor peace that they find. It seemed to me that men and women were made to hate each other.

Minna seemed unable to recognize the nature of their conflict, the fact of their natural antagonism. I was convinced that she was indulging herself, playing with the antagonism as a much younger, inexperienced girl might play with it, not realizing what constituted human difference. She teased Willy, ran at him and stepped away, drew him on to greater and greater effort, insisting that he woo her, flatter her, fight for her. "It is because you think so well of me," she seemed to be saying, "because you think I am capable of so much that I am obliged to deny you. Not that you are wrong—I am what you think I am—but I wish you were mistaken. Then I would undertake to prove you wrong. But as it is, there is nothing I can do. Suffer if you must. The best thing would be to stop taking me so seriously—but don't you dare! So stop taking yourself so seriously!" And yet there were times when she seemed willing, at the limit of her patience, to admit that he was wrong and that she was not what he thought she was or wanted her to be—far from it. And then she would resent him all the more, as if, knowing she could never meet his expectations, she hated him for putting forth his demands and felt that his very desire to elevate her was a judgment and a condemnation. How, under such circumstances, could the spontaneous exist?

Had she spoken truthfully, had she been capable of insight, Minna would perhaps have said, "We are at cross purposes, and yet our wills do not, and never shall, come into conflict. They are sealed off from each other—frozen, paralyzed, call it what you like, but not alive. Yes, yours, too, for all that you bluster and storm, and carry on, always

[245]

lighting a fire under yourself. I am content with it—that is, deeply, deeply discontent, but I do not want it otherwise. Leave me if you must. You cannot arouse that desire to struggle in me—that desire without which there is nothing. No, Willy, it will never be."

And Willy's blindness consisted in this—that he refused to observe or to learn. He tried again and again to strike fire, draw a response, and each time he failed, he blamed her and punished himself. He became irritable and gradually began to assume poses of dejection as if, finding he had no value in her eyes, he had deliberately set about to become valueless to himself.

Their conflict drifted in its aimlessness until it was necessary that it take on direction. At once Mason became the symbol of their antagonism, as it was only natural that he should.

I am listening at my post in the kitchen and looking in from time to time, more boldly toward the end.

"Why is he always hanging around?"

"Does it bother you?"

"I can't stand him. He's a degenerate."

"A degenerate, is that so? I should say he's a man of extraordinary character."

"That's according to your standards."

"I know your standards are much higher than mine—so high, they can't even be reached by standing on a chair and using a ten-foot pole."

"You can reach yours by standing on your head."

"Your attempt to be clever isn't coming off so well," said Minna, unaware that her own effort had miscarried. "Do you realize how childish you are? You're like a high-school boy trying to show off how smart he is. Once you get—"

"All right, let's drop it. I asked you a civil question, why—"

"Once you get an idea you ride it like a mule. Fred's a 'degenerate'—the idea! All you mean by that is that he's more clever than you. He makes an effort to be charming, he isn't such a sulky boor—"

"Now look—"

"I can't stand your stupidity!" she exclaimed, wrinkling her nose in anger as if she were about to sneeze. "What right have *you* got to insult people? Fred is so very much beyond you—why, at least he's intelligent! He knows what he's doing, he—oh, it's just like you, it's just the kind of mind you've got to think that every sensitive and intelligent person—why you can't even begin to understand him!"

"I understand him well enough," said Willy, rather smugly. "Far better than you think. And I'll tell you one thing, I've no use for a man who'll run after a woman no matter what—"

"Well, listen to him!" she declared, tossing her head and setting her arms akimbo.

"Now look, shut up for a minute—just take a case like this. Here's a man running after a woman. She won't have the least part of him, but he doesn't care—"

"I suppose you think you know whom you're talking about?"

"Never mind who I'm talking about. Just keep still." He went on in a more patient tone, as if to point an elementary moral. "This man meets this woman and the first thing he does is take a fancy to her. Oh, he's sure of himself, all right. She's his, he's going to have her, there isn't a doubt in his head. So what does he do? He calls on her, he brings her candy or flowers—he takes her out once or twice, and so on, while he puts in time. The way he figures it—depending on the woman of course—that should just about do the trick. And he's right, too—that's all it takes. The whole business is settled from the start. She decides it right away, even if she doesn't know it. What you would probably call 'courtship' is nothing but a formality. It doesn't lead to a thing—it leads away. It leads away from the moment at the start of the game when the woman decided that she would have him; it's a waste of time that goes on for a while—even if it's only a matter of hours—so she can lead him on, see what he's got, find out how much he really wants it—and, just in case she hasn't made up her mind, it gives her a chance to decide. But if he figured right, if he knew what he was doing, and most important, if he knew his woman, a man can count that he's in.

"All right, just a minute, I'm not done. There happen cases, however, where it's wrong from the start. Do you know what I mean? The poor fish gets a crush on the woman and she can't stand him. The more he wants her, the more obvious it is—or you might say, the more he tried to keep it from becoming obvious, because he knows the cards are stacked against him and hard luck makes a gentleman out of him—all the more she finds him repulsive. Sometimes she can't even believe that he's repulsive to her. She looks at him. He's not handsome, but he's not ugly, either; he's kind to her, and of course he wants something, but he'd be kind even if he didn't want a thing. He's got a good heart, what's more, he's popular, say even he's got money and is well dressed, or a man about town—you know, established, more connections than a switchboard. In other words, he's the very sort of man she'd fall in love with. Only she doesn't love him. The fact is, he nauseates her. Well, this man—"

"You're talking, I suppose, about the art of love," said

Minna, who had been wanting to interrupt him for some time, during which her observation had grown stale.

"I guess you can call it that. Am I boring you?"

"Oh no, I find it fascinating. Ovid had nothing on you."

"Thanks. I don't care if you're not listening—"

"But I am—"

"This man, now, doesn't give up easily, even if he knows he's licked. You see, he knows women are contrary, so he thinks, oh she's just being contrary, and he sticks to it, hoping he'll get a break. And the funny thing is, sometimes he does get a break. The woman also knows that women are contrary, so she begins to suspect herself, and before long she's come around to thinking that maybe the only reason she can't stand him is that she really does want him. Well, the only way she can find out is to see for herself—and she does—and then she knows for a fact that she doesn't want any part of him. And she's so disgusted with him and with herself—she thinks of all the time and money she's let him throw away on her—that she hates herself, and hates him all the more for making her hateful. But by then she can be honest with him, so she tells him everything, tells him he nauseates her—a sweet woman of course will try to soften the blow—and then there isn't a thing the poor sucker can do but hang himself. At the very least, take it on the lam like a sport.

"But no, our type of man sticks around. Fact is, he's only just begun. Now, you see, they can be *friends*." Willy sneered. "Now they can confide in each other. Now he can discover she's neurotic—she's afraid of sex, she's frigid, she's incapable of loving, she's this, that, and the other thing. He can even talk her into it. She feels that she's done him such an injury, especially when he's shown that he's so big-hearted and understanding, that she lets him. She swallows

[249]

his line even though she knows better—and sometimes she even forgets what she knows. Ah, now he's in, at last! He can come around now every day and pry into all her affairs. And of course he can 'help' her—help cheer her up, help her 'adjust' herself—to what? To being saddled with him. All he ever wanted was her body, but he winds up owning a bigger piece of her soul than he'd ever have got in the normal way. That's why I think such a man is a degenerate. I'm talking about Mason, of course."

"And so you're also talking about me?"

"Correct."

"Just one question," said Minna, with her most patent effort at sarcasm, "how did you figure it all out by yourself?"

He did not reply.

"It's a remarkable performance. But would you mind if I corrected you in a few trivial details? The picture you've drawn isn't exactly one of degeneration. Fred's self-support-ing, after all. At most you might say he's a bit of a masochist, but even there you'd be presuming. And as for the flattering portrait you've drawn for me—really, that's just too much! You should know better at least where I'm concerned. Would you care to try again?"

She paused in her sarcasm, preparing to get angry. "The nerve!" she exclaimed. "Where did you get all that nerve! I never—"

"You can deny it if you like," said Willy, unperturbed, "but that's what it looks like to me. Furthermore—"

"Deny it? I should say! You're wrong, you're absolutely wrong, do you hear me? You're lying!" she cried.

"I couldn't possibly have been lying, unless I didn't really believe what I said. But I do believe it. Furthermore, the sort of thing I've been talking about couldn't exist without the woman's taking an active part in it. You must be getting

[250]

something out of it, too. The kind of pleasure it gives him to feel hopeless, to feel—I can just see it. A man as sloppy as he would naturally have a very romantic notion of himself, something so old-fashioned, you'd hardly believe it could happen today. It gives him pleasure to feel he's devoted his whole life to something he can't have. He feels he's ruined himself nobly—all for love, you know. Love! It's the most selfish, the most self-indulgent, unloving thing a man could let himself in for. And the woman gets the same kind of kick out of it. Maybe she's too guilty to be honest with herself, so she feels it's one of those great burdens, and yet, as a true friend, she bears it willingly. It's all such noble sacrifice. She gives him the benefit of her understanding, her friendship, her gratitude. She does believe he has laid down his whole life for her. And of course she appreciates it—let me tell you she appreciates it! If someone should try to break up this beautiful friendship—that is, put the poor fool out of his misery, straighten him out with that kick in the pants that he needs—why, she'd cry murder! She wouldn't allow it on your life! Break up such a wonderful friendship? Such a tender, sympathetic relationship? Let him out of her clutches for a moment? Fine chance!"

Minna had regained her self-possession and no longer seemed to resent his words. Far from continuing to regard his monologue as the supreme presumption, the threat she had originally considered it to be, she was now indulging him, smiling and nodding, egging him on with her compliance. She had apparently conceived the indisputable refutation, and was pleased to have drawn him out so far.

"Another thing I'll tell you," said Willy with undiminished exuberance. "Why does he settle for such a bad bargain?" He slapped his hand down on his thigh in answer to his question. "Because it's really what he wants! That's the point!" he cried, spurred on by her change in attitude which he obviously took to mean acknowledgment of the truth of his insight. "He doesn't want a woman. What he wants is a good excuse for not having one. That's the whole truth of the matter." He nodded his head several times in severe indictment, while a smile of self-approbation spread on his lips. "Of course I don't know him as well as you do. But that's one thing I *do* know about him, even if it shocks you to realize it. And that's what I mean by calling him a degenerate."

It was at this point that Minna, very calmly, without a trace of resentment, but with some anticipation of the shock that she knew her announcement must produce, smiled at Willy, as if to give him his last opportunity to discover his foolishness for himself, and said, "Just one little bit of information. It might interest you to know that Fred and I have been married for the last six years."

Chapter 18

Willy insisted that Minna get a divorce. Which she flatly refused to do.

To this day, I am sure, she is still married to Mason. But I have seen neither of them in years. Willy has also disappeared, though I hear from him once a year—he sends me Christmas cards. He does not, however, write the return address on the envelope and I learn his whereabouts only from the postmark. He has been in Denver, Salt Lake City, Portland, Los Angeles—I forget the other cities, all of them in the West. I do not know why he has chosen to communicate with me in this manner. Perhaps to show that the memory of Minna does not rankle; perhaps to show that it does. I have noticed that the cards he has sent me form a progression of taste. The first were cheap and sentimental, the sort one might buy in a candy store. The more recent ones, as if to show that he was taking account of my growth in judgment, have all been more expensive and in better taste. The anxiety, I cannot help thinking, of an exposed man.

If I appear to anticipate the end of the story it is because, so far as actual events are concerned, the story was at an end. It had reached its natural close and only the blindness, the imperfection, the intensity of their emotions carried it forward in the short time that remained to a belated, anticlimactic and in all truth, a shabby conclusion. Willy insisted that Minna divorce Mason and Minna refused.

I do not doubt that Willy, in spite of the shock it gave him, was pleased to learn that Minna and Mason were married. It put a handle to the impalpable, giving him a convenient means of turning her character to whatever purpose of disapproval he might choose. This was the concrete symptom after so much vague diagnosis, the cause and effect and appropriate name of the disease whose nature he had been groping to determine—and the proof, should he have wanted it, of his own health. He had been right, in his own words, right as rain: he had had the scent all along in his nostrils and had tracked it down, by God!

"Tracked what down?" Minna wanted to know, drawing up, alarmed, to defend herself.

"That marriage of yours. If that's what you call it. I was right, by God!"

While I should have wanted to know why she was not living with Mason, why she kept her marriage secret (was she ashamed of it?), what the circumstances were that kept

[253]

them either together or apart, however one chose to regard it, to Willy's mind the fact of the marriage explained everything. This, now, finally, was Minna, clearly defined—Mason's wife.

But it was not yet the end—and it seemed that the nearer they came to the breaking point, the further they really were from attaining it. Willy's satisfaction in turning defeat into victory soon faded away and he was left in need of further obstacles to prove himself against. Thus it was that he refused to accept the obvious fact that she would not hear of divorcing Mason, and devoted himself to obtaining precisely that end. But the end represented sheer enterprise, conflict alone—for as it was clear to everyone but himself, he had not the least intention of succeeding Mason as her husband.

It surprises me only that something so idle as Willy's need to be in conflict with Minna should have resulted in so much industry. It was a disinterested mania burning, like a fever, for its own sake, the object it once might have sought to achieve long since having been consumed.

In a few days Willy's appearance had grown careless all over again. He very quickly touched the point of sloppiness that I had first known in him and rapidly sank beneath it. He let days go by without changing his shirt, days without shaving, without stirring out of the house. He had given up accompanying Minna to work, along with the pretense of looking for a job; he lay in bed in the heat and ordered me away from him, insisted that I go back home where I belonged. When Minna returned from work, he sprang at her, eager to quarrel and at once began to insult her and "her husband," as he now called Mason, preferring to avoid his name. Minna ignored his provocations, no longer took him seriously. As far as she was concerned, it was clear that she expected him to leave—and yet, so carefully did she control her coldness and indifference that she refrained from saying a word to this effect. He would leave when he pleased, when he realized that it was all over between them. And so when she came home from work she was always sure to greet him cheerfully, as if nothing whatsoever had happened.

He no longer washed the dishes left standing from the night before. But as soon as Minna began to wash them, before preparing supper, he would rush into the kitchen and profusely apologize for his negligence. Whatever the purpose of such behavior, it did him no good. Minna remained noncommittal, and therefore drove him to even greater extremes. For a time, he would be boisterous and would shout and sing, slam doors and stomp about the house, setting the floors atremble; and then sulk, brood, frown, groan, mutter sullenly, and once again do his utmost to insult her. Or, though he had been lying in bed all day, a half hour before she returned he would spring up, make the bed, wash the dishes, straighten the house, put something on to cook, shave and barely have time to come out of the shower, powdered and wearing a clean shirt, before she came in. He would strut for awhile, hoping to win her acknowledgment of his effort to please her—and would fail and go back to slovenliness and again refuse to get out of bed, and spend entire days in his pajamas, unwashed and unshaved and not eating, and grow dirtier by the hour, cursing her. But Minna refused to criticize, knowing that criticism was a trap. She accepted all the extremes he was capable of attaining, just as calmly and indifferently as she accepted (or ignored) his more normal conduct. And yet—and how well he must have known it! —her indifference was but the measure of her general contempt for the emotions, and the more resigned she was to his petulance, the more contemptuous she was of it.

The momentum of Willy's original impulse carried him along, and, unaware of the depth to which he had sunk, he may have believed that he was still seeing it through. It is impossible to observe the exact moment when the desire to be loved, like love itself, changes into its opposite. The need to win response persists long after the possibility of its realization, and even hatred, which comes last in the downward course, may appear to be an emotion which, once gained, would signal a victory. He had come to win her love, and now lingered, in his wrinkled pajamas, for her hatred. Above all he hated her because she refused even to hate him. Such were the reasons for the delay in the final break.

The last occasion of malice that I can recall was a party which Minna gave on a Sunday afternoon. She had not spoken a word of it to us and we did not learn that a party was under way until the guests began to arrive. The purpose of the gathering became clear when the guests, carrying bundles under their arms, went one by one into the bathroom and emerged dressed in pajamas. It was a "spontaneous pajama party—the idea just hit me—" these were Minna's words. But she could not resist introducing Willy, who was already in costume, to her guests as "the inspired reviver of an old custom—such quaint old-fashioned fun—I owe it all to him."

I had never met her friends before; but from the difficulty she had in recalling the names of some of them, it was obvious that they were by no means intimate acquaintances. Yet she embraced them all, crying, "I'm so glad you've come! Make yourself right at home!" and flitted from one to another in unbounded hospitality, never once embarrassed. "I've been so bored!" she repeated in a shrill voice, "I was just over-ripe for a blowout!" Bottles of whisky appeared and food—better and more plentiful than we had been eating all these days—and the party was soon on its way to becoming a success.

There is no point in describing it all. I had seen the same thing so many times already, at home and elsewhere, that I was not intrigued by the event. At the beginning, disgusted by the obvious means which Minna, at the end of her patience, was employing to put Willy to shame, I kept to myself as well as I could in the small apartment and crept out on the back porch whenever it was unoccupied.

Mason of course had come—and was sporting the loudest pair of pajamas in the crowd. The manner in which he made jibes at Willy confirmed my belief as to the purpose of the party. His courage was now worked up to proportions that could only be considered heroic in the light of his natural cowardice. His apologetic and disarming cough was gone and he had abandoned the attitude of helplessness with which he had been accustomed to shield his spite. He seemed to have changed outwardly in accordance with the altered status he had acquired in our eyes.

But even without Mason's help, Willy would not have been slow to understand. He saw the party, I am sure, as an effort of Minna's to surround herself with all that he found repugnant in her life; better yet as an act, miscalculated, out of place and much too late in time to confront him with the assertion of her liberty. He seemed, on the whole, to be amused by it, taking it as additional evidence that she was at the mercy of her own pretensions and he was pleased to see that she had forced herself into a ridiculous position. For she had surrounded herself with people whom, one might well say, she inwardly despised and could not bear to touch in order to show him that he could not touch her.

I dare say Willy was right. Minna's enjoyment was strained

[257]

and unnatural; the necessity of standing by her friends soon proved too much for her and several times I saw her look anxiously at Mason, as if imploring his help. They were in all truth a dreary lot. I had not yet entirely lost my awe of what I imagined to be Minna's circle, but I had been exposed to Willy's influence so long that while I was meeting her friends for the first time, I was already suspicious and prepared to disapprove of them. I would find myself watching one with great interest—say the bearded young man who spoke in a false Russian accent—only to remember what I had learned and draw away from him promptly. So also with a woman who had been drinking heavily and now went about trying to convince the others that it was too warm to wear both parts of a pajama suit. One woman especially played upon my divided sensibilities, a stout redhead who had lost one of her earrings. She amused herself by hugging me whenever she came upon me—drowning me in the moist, ungainly flesh of her bosom—and insisting that since I was the only one present who was not wearing pajamas, I should at once find me a pair or else strip to my underwear. A gray-haired man, observing how young I was, decided that I must be a genius and demanded to know my accomplishments. Another contended that far from being a genius I was most probably a glandular case, every bit as old as he was, and now that he thought of it, he was fairly certain that he had once seen me in a side-show in Milwaukee, while a woman, giggling hideously at references I could not quite understand, attempted to smear my mouth with lipstick. But on the whole my presence was taken for granted and my sweating and blushing and fits of shame were gratuitous. I was free to indulge myself either in secret enjoyment, or in conscious contempt, the learned response.

Willy, having seen that the party was well out of Minna's

control, that the guests rejected her many invitations to ridicule him, and that she was quickly coming to regret the entire affair, settled down to the task of going wild and drank far more than anyone else, smacking his lips as if to show how well he thrived on the poison of her intent. All the day's malice had soon shifted to his keep. He selected the youngest and most attractive girl in the crowd and flirted with her and kissed her repeatedly in Minna's presence. He was the first to respond to the entreaties of the overheated woman and removed the top of his pajamas, thereby gaining general admiration for his tattoo marks. Then he took to calling Mason a horned toad and sang "cuckoo" at him and set his hands on his head to represent a pair of antlers.

His moment of greatest triumph, shortly before I left the party, driven out by an atmosphere of gathering violence, was when he announced, utterly drunk, "the complete truth about these two," as he called it, revealing with exaggerated indignation that the relationship between Minna and Mason, so tenuous, queer, and oblique, was none other than marriage. Not that anyone was shocked to learn this or in any way passed judgment upon it, but the marriage at once became the topic of conversation and her guests flocked about Minna, wanting to know when it had occurred and why she had kept it a secret. It need not have been more than a trivial embarrassment, but Minna appeared completely crushed—as much perhaps by the ruining of her party as by the discovery of her secret—and her embarrassment was in no way relieved when Mason stepped onto a chair and exclaimed, "We will now receive your belated congratulations. This way, please!"

Chapter 19

I boarded a streetcar and rode, it did not surprise me to discover, in the direction of home. At once the old neighborhood smiled at me. Street signs, the color of a brick house here and there, occasionally a tree, claimed me, asserting an established friendship. It was enough to hear the names of the streets called out by the conductor, "Rockwell," "California," "Albany," "Kedzie," to feel my history, and my place in it, restored. I rode past our own stop, seeing our block, and our house at the end of it, swing by. I got off at the entrance to the park and made my way in, at once seeing the lagoon, and the gilt dome of the refectory at the edge of it, and these, together with the unchanged landscape of the trees and the sweep of lawn down to the tennis courts, took up their accustomed position in the simple and instantaneous traffic of identity between the world and the self.

I went the way I had always gone, over the stubby hill to the water, then over the bridge and the playing field to the gardens, hoping I would not meet anyone I knew. The park was in late summer, burned brown in the center of the field, the grass green and unscorched, carefully trimmed along the water, the trees heavy, and bearing the full heat without thirst. The boats were out as usual; there was a cluster of children around the drinking fountain, and of buggies along the walk, among them a few governesses and a majority of mothers. I made my way over to the fountain, waited for a child to remove her hands from the basin, and stooped low, not to be recognized, and drank long, looking at the wet stones; the water had a pleasant but iron taste.

Rising over the trees in the center of the park were the glass roof and upper walls of the conservatory. Some of the panes were out, and the tops of the plants were thrust forth, a green within green. I went toward the conservatory, discerning, as I came closer, the blades, and the brown coarse hair of palms and tendrils of ivy through the open panes, and the more shadowy and indistinct forms through the glass. High points of sun, like a battery of searchlights, sent out their rays from the angle of the roof. Nearby, on a knoll, but made almost inaccessible by thicket of bramble bushes, rose the bronze statue of the medieval warrior, weathered to an acid shade of green. He stood, helmet thrown back and his head and shoulders rearing above the thorny branches, an unknown figure with a wild broad beard, running down in metal rivulets upon his breast; the carving on the rock pedestal which told who he was, had long since been overgrown and obliterated. But he, too, was a figure of peace and a guardian of my history and passing by on the way to the conservatory I threw him a wink, as it was the family's custom to do.

Perhaps the effect was as artificial as the cause, and it was as much a matter of deliberation for me to feel awe among the great tropical plants as was their very presence here in the city, under glass, thousands of miles to the north. But my sense of awe, even if I had come prepared for it as I had many times in the past, was nevertheless as compelling as it should have been in the proper jungles of the equator, and again it seemed to me that I stood flush with the force common to all existence, and again it seemed to threaten me in my right to call my existence my own. For these trees, or palms, or plants—I did not know what to call them—had so much stronger and more ponderous a grasp of life than I, that they were rather some huge mineral creation of color and heat, compared with which my life was ailing and cold, and even at its fullest, but a form of death.

There were other rooms, each at its own temperature and

with its own design, devoted to varieties of flowers and shrubs, the more human and reconcilable species. But I preferred to sit in the tropics on a stone bench, damp with the steaming atmosphere, down through which hung aerial roots and streamers of moss. At the far corner of the room ran a waterfall dropping some ten feet from a ledge of brick into a pool where lilies floated. This, too, was in keeping with the prevailing unnaturalness of the scene, but my participation in it was not thereby diminished. I shut my eyes and I could hear the water hissing, maintaining a steady rhythm in the general downpour while a few drops fell at the edge of the pool with a sound and cadence of their own. I tried to pick out the individual drops and make them register separately and instantaneously their brief existence, and in doing so, I felt again what it meant to be overpowered and alone. For it seemed to me that I could sit here in eternity and the fact would never change—the single thing was endlessly varied, always fresh and distinct, and yet life took no account of it and ran on, blotting it out. So, too, with the green that spawned beyond my closed eyes, the scum of moss, the leaves of the trees, the spiked palms. I could imagine each plant in the glass garden, each stem and twig and flake of bark, unique and complete in itself, yet meaningless and momentary and without true existence; and I felt that this world exerted a threat against me.

I opened my eyes. So vividly had I pictured the scene, that the sight of it restored nothing to its reality. It lay before me, loomed over me, swarmed around me, oppressive with time.

What was there to fear? I merely felt that all this green was alive. A common life ran through all of us, but it was precisely that which was fearful. For if it was the same life, it was also the same blindness, the same unconscious growing and reaching for the sun and the same meaningless nonbeing, counting for nothing. The truth was spoken by the hiss of the water, malevolent, untiring, dashing itself down. We would all die ignored.

There was no way out unless one bore forever the vision of the jungle, of life's vast, meaningless profusion, and fought against it; fought against it by never sparing a moment of the true life and the true human beauty, greener than the trees, which broke so rarely into the darkness. Such moments I had known, perhaps at home, perhaps in childhood; perhaps, too, they sprang into being only when one became aware of their absence, so that one could never know the truth but could merely protest against falsehood. And yet, it seemed to me, sitting alone and in fear, that I had always had some human assurance, though it may have been no more than the love of the family which was given almost in spite of itself, unconsciously and without direction. Or, had it always been present, a large and obvious thing that only I had overlooked? Perhaps my fear pointed to my own failure and not to the blindness and hostility that I imagined to be the condition of life. But no matter, for either way, love was a meaning into which I would always have to inquire. What was it? Wherein did the failure lie? I only knew that I was afraid and that fear demanded it. For without love, without the signal that one flashed to the other's existence, we died alone, our protest vain and unheard. I told myself I would go out, I would inquire, I would learn, I would see where I had been wrong, I would cease being afraid. I would emerge from the jungle in which my life had been spent, choked and over-run with wild growth. . . .

Even so, I remained in the park until long after sundown.

Chapter 20

Although he had been asleep and therefore might very well have been at a loss, my father showed neither shock nor surprise. He stood at the door while I mounted the stairs, stepped aside as I entered and closed the door behind me. His eyes were blinking, but perhaps only with sleep. He was barefoot and wearing a bathrobe, striped like an awning. His hair, which he combed every night before retiring, was still neat.

My stepmother, however, shrieked, rushed out of the bedroom, her robe coming apart, and fairly lifted me off my feet in a hug—and as quickly let me down. She looked at my father as if expecting him to indicate the proper manner of receiving me. He provided no clue, but stood to a side, shaking his head.

"So you're back." He did not know what else to say. Because he was my father he felt he should speak, judge me, pass immediate sentence, condemning or forgiving. This he felt he should do, just as I expected him to do it. But his emotion was the same as mine. In my embarrassment I avoided him, keeping my eyes averted to the floor, and while I still expected him to speak to me, it seemed to me that he, too, was staring at the floor. I saw him turn and leave and go to the front room. There, I knew, he would stand at the window, looking out.

My stepmother compressed her lips, wrinkled her chin like a peach pit, cupped her palm around it and rested her elbow in the palm of her other hand, an elaborate gesture which she employed only when, rarely, for lack of knowing what to express, she let the gesture express itself. But she soon recovered, whisked me into the kitchen, turned on the light and simulating a whisper, but loudly enough for my father to hear, began unburdening herself. "A fine son you are, shame on you! Can't you find something to say to your father? Go in right now and talk to him. Go on!"

I remained silent, avoiding her, and looking about the kitchen which had lost none of its brilliance during my absence. The checkered dish towels hung on their racks, the sink was gleaming, the jars of spice on the shelves above it had their old clean and sturdy air.

"What's the matter? Don't you know what to say? You can go in and say you're sorry. You can ask him to forgive you. Fine tricks! After making him suffer so much, all you can think of doing is to stand around with your hands in your pockets. Take your hands out of your pockets!"

She seldom ordered me about. It was usually "Please do this," or "Would you mind very much doing that?" I had forgotten the meaning of her politeness, and now that she had given a command, which I promptly obeyed, it recurred to me that her customary deference was a form of submission. She was only my stepmother, and did not want to presume. Even if I had been unaware of doing so, I had always exploited her deference. Old guilts were reopened before me, old habits whose significance I had ignored for years, were struck afresh with my re-entrance into the house, and I realized that to redeem my life with my father and with her I should have to begin, deep within myself, as if I were to question the uses to which I put the very air I breathed. For if I had wondered what love was while living with Minna and Willy, I now saw looming before me the more disquieting, if simpler, mystery—what was the relation between parent and child, what was a father, a mother?

"Don't be so proud and stubborn. If you realize you've done wrong, own up to it. And don't be afraid. For my part,

I'm glad you're back—and so is your father. Would he throw his own son out of the house?

"Although, I don't mind telling you, maybe you would deserve it, young man." She knotted the belt of her robe, which had come undone. She, too, was barefoot; her bunions seemed to have grown larger. "After all, what you did is unheard of, simply unbelievable! Imagine, planning it! Doing it on purpose! Inviting that woman—ptoo!—making her come when the whole family is together, so she can open her dirty drunken mouth, so all those terrible things can come pouring out like pitch! And she not even fit to stand in the same room with your father. Oh, let me tell you, you deserve it!"

I tried to interrupt her, to explain that I had not been responsible, but my stepmother, having discarded her politeness, having, in fact, become my mother, would not hear me.

"What makes it so bad is just that—that you planned it. You little sneak, you! Snot nose! You pissher! When I married your father you still used to wet your pants. You came home from second grade once with your pants full. You should do a thing like that? You should make plans, you, mister? Pretend and make off like you didn't know a thing—and even take an interest in the house, all of a sudden! That's what beats me. You should run to the delicatessen and the butcher and make telephone calls and help me clean the walls—ah, I'll never undertake such a job again!—and all the time you should be planning your little surprise! What did you do it for? Well, I ask you. Did you think it would be fun? Did you want your poor father—"

"But I didn't, I didn't, I'm telling you! I had no idea she would—"

"Ah, what the man suffered. That his own son should play such a trick on him! But what do you know? You've got

[266]

as much brains as a cat. Do you know what it means to be a father?"

She would not listen to me. I no longer tried to interrupt her. She was right, as usual, absolutely right in the impulse if not the content of her words. I did not know what it meant to be a father.

"Believe me, if you were a son of mine! . . ." She had reached the peak of her anger, had taken me by the sleeve and begun to shake me, her face, meanwhile, having turned bright red and her lips nearly white. There were tears in her eyes, but they were not only tears of exhausted rage; for in the rising of her anger I had felt her achieving an intensity of emotion far beyond the demands of the moment, an emotion unnecessarily large, overweighing the need of reproving me and of expressing sympathy for my father. She was no longer speaking merely as his loyal wife, but, for the first time, was striving to satisfy herself, and in doing so had grasped at the passion hitherto unavailable to her—the intensity of personal suffering of which she had always felt herself deprived because she was not a mother. While she was shouting and shaking me I sensed the rush of her love, and my own answered her as I wanted to embrace her, to become her son, feeling that not only she, but I, too, had been deprived.

"Well, what are you standing around for?" She had spent herself. "Go wash up and eat something. You're hungry, aren't you? You should see what you look like—feh, skin and bones. She wouldn't even feed you right, that aunt of yours. Ti, ti, ti, ti—" here she wrinkled up her nose, folded her arms, and shook her head from side to side in mimicry of Minna. (That Minna never made such gestures was quite immaterial to her.) "Wait, just a minute. It wouldn't hurt you to take a tub either."

"Right now? But it's late—"

"Never mind it's late. You're dirty, you smell—I bet you didn't take one in all this time. Aie, such pigs! Go ahead, go live with your piggish aunt and eat pigs and roll around in the mud and look green and skinny like a stick. I'll give you a pig that you'll have something to remember!"

Having said which, she went off to the bathroom, and I soon heard the water running in the tub.

My father looked in on me several times while I was eating, but each time went back into the front room. This was evidently to remind me that we should have a talk when I had finished; and yet it was not his eagerness for the talk, but rather his anxiety over it that impelled him to come to the kitchen. When he appeared at the door I would begin to bolt my food, as if to let him know that I would soon be with him; but I would immediately check myself for fear he would see how hungry I was. It was difficult to eat, although the food was excellent; in fact, after Minna's suppers, the brown gravy that drowned the vegetables, winked with eyelets of fat, seemed to convey the very essence, the warmth and the familiarity, of home. I trembled, anticipating the scene with my father. It was not until I had seen him again that I fully remembered my guilt; for it was then that I realized that the impulse which had made me return home— an impulse that seemed to me so praiseworthy, that I was sure he would consider it to my credit—would be entirely discounted. He had every right to take my homecoming for granted, since from his position it was the very smallest debt that I owed him, and not until it had been paid could one consider the actual issue of right and wrong. Thus my homecoming, which I imagined would wipe out my guilt, was the very thing that established it. And so I no longer knew quite where I stood, and even my hunger was complex and compromising, for insofar as I had wronged my father my appetite was gluttony, and yet not to eat would further have demonstrated my ingratitude.

I finished supper and waited for my father to appear at the door again, meanwhile looking about the kitchen and noticing, one might think for the first time, the minor details of the room, the chip in the black porcelain knob of the kitchen door, the grain of the linoleum, the rough silver paint on the radiator, as if by absorbing myself in the security of the inanimate I might safely enter into the sense of home. "I'd like to have a word with you," said my father. I rose, scraping the chair on the floor, and followed him into my room.

We took up our accustomed positions: he on the bed and I in the chair at my desk. Even now I was in some measure denying him—the bed was lower than the chair and not as comfortable to sit on, and I had not waited for him to be seated first. But he shook his head in melancholy irony when I offered to let him have my chair. He seemed to be saying, "That's the least of my grievances."

Except that we were both wearing pajamas—I had dressed for bed right after my bath—the scene was as usual, the light at my desk, my father sitting in partial shadow. He would lose feature and personality and, no longer himself, would become mere and absolute father, an image at the periphery, never clearly seen. I, sitting in the light, would owe both my discomfort and my advantage to him. The light of my desk lamp would be shining in my eyes, for I would have turned it to prevent its falling into his. And yet he would be sitting in the outer darkness of the life he had created and furnished for me.

"Well, what do you have to say for yourself?" There was

harshness and finality in his voice, as if, intending to shut out all criticism, he were telling me that there was only one account to be given—mine—and that he was in no way involved.

"I've nothing to say."

"Nothing at all? So. Very nice."

This was the end of the first interchange, and a most satisfactory one insofar as it was to my interest to defend myself against my father. But I could not overcome a sense of disappointment in myself for having done so, and I realized that it was only the fact that I wanted to yield to him which made me fight against him. I shifted nervously in my chair, and further lowered the shade of the lamp, casting the light more directly into my eyes—but setting him in an even deeper shadow.

Father—either unwilling or incapable—still did not seize the advantage over me. By my stubbornness—which was at bottom no more than fear of honesty—I had laid myself open to reproach, and now I was so full of the sense of my guilt, that my father, with the very least assertion of his judgment, could have brought it pouring out of me. But the moment of weakness passed. For father did not press his advantage, but preferred rather to pity me. My embarrassment grew as he forced me to recognize his restraint. Why had he chosen to pity me? Was it that he abhorred weakness so much that he would on no account make use of it in others? This only made me the weaker.

At last he asked, "Why did you go away?"

"I was afraid," I replied at once, making an effort to be honest.

"You were afraid? Of what?"

I realized that I wanted him to pity me. Why did he allow me to evade him? "I was afraid," I repeated.

[270]

"Afraid!" he cried, finally with that sternness I had been fearing yet longing to encounter. "A big boy like you!" But there was a note of bitterness and mockery in his voice; he was still not allowing himself to use his full force. "What were you afraid of?"

"You would have thought I told her to come, that I had done it on purpose!" I cried. But the moment I had made my confession it no longer was a confession, having become an empty and meaningless thing, a further evasion, even if a sign of the truth. All the same, once I had confessed, I resented having had to do so. For I should have preferred to have him accuse me of conspiring with Minna; then, though I had not done so, the charge, while false, would at least have been honest. But by attributing it to him, as a false suspicion, I had suppressed the possibility, if not the element, of truth that I felt it to contain. Had he forced me to accuse myself?

If I had ever feared him, it was because he was my moral superior, capable of an honesty so much greater than mine that I would always appear mean-spirited and unworthy of him. But now, believing he had deliberately turned my own devices against me and forced me to accuse myself, I suspected that our relationship had changed entirely in the few weeks I had been away, and that he could no longer afford his original honesty. He was a weaker man, no longer the impartial, disinterested, yet intimate judge who, if he restrained himself, did so only out of an inherent modesty in the recognition of his righteousness and the employment of his strength. Now, rather, he had cause to defend himself—he had begun to fear me for the same reasons that I had long feared him.

"No, my boy. Why do you bring that up? That never entered my mind. I thought no such thing."

[271]

"I was sure you did," I insisted, convinced now that he was lying either to spare me, or, more likely, to spare himself. "I was sure you were blaming me for it. You knew I'd been going to see her—you must have known she had found out about the party through me. And then when I left the house with her, that must have proved it to you!"

"But I tell you I had no such idea," he replied, somewhat disconcerted by my aggressiveness, which must have made him realize that I was eager to cover myself with guilt. He held back, speaking softly and trying to fathom my purpose. "I only felt very hurt that you left home—and that you went to live with her. I never held you responsible for what she did."

"But ma does!" I kept pressing the point. "She blames it all on me. She says I planned it, that I wanted it to happen. She doesn't even say that Minna made me do it, but that I figured it all out by myself. Didn't you hear her hollering at me?"

"I wasn't listening," he replied. But he had caught the implication—that my stepmother would never advance an opinion unless it reflected his mind. All my uneasiness had been transferred to him, and I now appeared the accuser.

He got up from the bed and walked about the room, stopping before the bookcase and looking at my books. He always seemed to regard them as strange and remote objects, symbols of myself, and thus related to him—it was with his money that I had bought them—and yet as alien and hostile as I myself had become. My father ran his hand along a row of the books, which were standing neatly aligned on the shelf, as if he meant thereby to say, "You haven't been at them for a long time."

"To tell you the truth . . . I've forgotten about the whole thing." He came toward me but stopped outside the circle of light. "All I know is that you're back. It was wrong of you to leave, so wrong—you have no idea what it did to me! ... But now that you've come back, all I want is that you should . . . This is your home!" he cried, shaking his extended finger and emphasizing the words, not, however, with the anger I had expected him to direct against me, but in protest against the impalpable that had drawn me away from him. "This is your home and your family, and you're going to live here! If it's not good enough for you, I want to know the reason why and I'll make it good! Here you stay until you're old enough to go out into the world to establish your own home. I didn't bring you into the world to—to—to become a bum, do you hear me?—and if I've got the means to provide you with a home, there should be no reason on earth why it's not good enough for you!"

While he was speaking to me, his expression had lost some of its customary acuteness. From what I could see in the dim outer light, he had ceased to stare at me and was no longer intent on penetrating the disguise of my emotions. He had turned harder in his love, and was berating me now for my ultimate denial; and yet he had a look, not so much of anger, pride, or sorrow as of distraction, as if the suffering he had borne prevented his passing far enough beyond his own emotion to understand mine. For though he may have come upon my true failure as a son, still he could not see that I remained unrelenting in the very face of his discovery. In all truth, what did it matter to me, or how should it touch me, that he had bared, along with his sternest and therefore most actual love, that vision of himself, the father as provider and homemaker, that justified the hardships of his life and made them ideal necessities? Although I had heard him proclaim his creed of fatherhood many times—so often that the present occasion, despite his emotion, impressed me as

[273]

nothing more than a recitation—I was still in no way dedicated to preserving his illusions. The truth was that I lived my own life and would continue to do so, without a thought for the gratifications necessary to his.

But this, he would never understand, did not bar me from loving him. He failed to see the direction my impulses took. Though he knew me to be selfish, and upbraided me for it, he could not grasp how deeply my selfishness depended on him and involved him, so that, while I was leading my own life, nothing I did was truly independent of his, if only because, to find pleasure in selfishness—I could not bear to be alone—I clung to him, needing the knowledge and the assurance of his nearness. My love was my guilt.

It was for this reason, though I understood my motive but dimly, that I refused to let him wave aside the subject of Minna, and returned to it, insistently telling a lie in which, however, I realized there was more truth than in any other statement I had ever made before my father. "But pa, it's a fact!" I cried. "I really did plan it! I did want to go and live with Minna. As long as I've known her I've wanted to. I arranged the whole thing with her because—because of the way you treated her!"

I sprang out of my chair and stood before him, both defying him and urging him to believe me. "It is so! I'm telling you the truth!" I shouted, taking him by the sleeve of his pajamas (how rarely there had been physical contact between us!) and feeling there need be no further proof of my sincerity than the fact that I had hurt him.

He looked at me sadly, as if to say, "Can't you understand that I don't demand an explanation? It is I who have to explain!" I realized then—without being aware of it, I had feared this most of all—that our guilt was doubled and shared, and I felt so much the greater a need to affirm my own.

But he pushed my arm away and saying, "I don't want to hear about her," quickly left the room.

My stepmother must have been standing at a discreet distance from the door—near enough to placate her curiosity, yet too far to hear what was said; and evidently she believed it had all ended happily, say with the exchange of my humble apology for my father's warm-hearted forgiveness, for I soon heard her feet padding by my door, then the creak of the telephone chair as she sat down upon it, and the sound of a nickel and my grandfather's number spoken to the operator.

My father and I both ran to the phone to stop her. "What are you calling for?" he cried. "You don't have to call anyone."

She indicated the coin box by way of saying that the nickel had already been dropped. Father yielded to this, as to a piece of superior wisdom. Stepmother, smiling broadly, winking at us and failing to understand our reluctance, announced, "Morris, he is here!"

I heard my grandfather's exclamation come shrilly through the receiver, then a series of hacking sounds, as of laughter, or coughing, or words rapidly shouted, if not all three. Stepmother, the receiver stuck to her ear, sat facing the wall, immensely enjoying his oration. She did not turn to look at us; this was what her heart needed.

"Here, he wants to talk to you," she said, beaming, and giving me the phone. She stopped short when she saw that we were frowning. "What's the matter? Isn't it—"

I took the phone from her and resigning myself, said hello to the old man.

"Oh—ho—ha—this is you? How do you do?" His voice set the metal plate of the receiver rattling. "How do you do, a

[275]

fine how do you do! So you're home again? No more running around like a bandit? You've come home, you bandit you? Aie-ya! Do you know what I would do to you?" He was all questions, but would not wait for me to answer. "Schmeissen! Schmeissen!" he cried. "A spanking and another spanking, a good one. You haven't had a spanking in years. You need a spanking, but good! Here, I'm coming over and I'll give you one! I'll give you a spanking that you won't be able to see straight. You won't be able to catch your breath for weeks! Here, take off your pants, come on, unbutton—and now your underwear, don't be ashamed. Now lie down, lie down you devil, spread out, that's it, aie-ya—one!—ha!—two!—ah!— three!—oo-vah! That's the way, that's it, that does it, but good you bandit! One-two-three—now you'll know! Now you'll have something to remember!—"

My father took the phone away and replaced the receiver, gently, as if to avoid hurting the old man's feelings.

"What's matter? Harry, I'm sorry. Was it too late to call?" cried my stepmother in consternation, unable to believe that her good will had miscarried, or that the affair had not come to a happy close.

"I'll talk to you later, Bessie," said my father, and putting his hand on my shoulder, led me back into my room.

"Boy, there is something I should tell you," he began. "Maybe you know already. . . ." It was difficult for him to speak; he paused, hoping, perhaps, that it would not be necessary. "Do you know what really happened between your aunt and me?" he sighed.

"Yes, I know," I replied, myself anxious to avert his discomfiture; but added, at once, "I mean, I don't really know. . . . I'm not sure, I mean." For I would hardly have prevented him from debasing himself if I indicated that I already knew what he had to confess.

He sensed my embarrassment. "You'll understand better when you grow up. . . . I just want to clear away any misunderstanding you may have now. . . ."

He stood near me; his expression, I was sure, was the same as my own when I feared him—when I stood ashamed in his presence. My father looked at me pleadingly, rather bewildered by the transformation that was taking place, the necessity he felt himself under to confess. He was still hoping, perhaps unconsciously, that I would stop him.

"Please, you don't have to tell me. Please, I really don't want to know about Minna." But I was aware of my deceit, persisting even to this moment. For while I honestly wanted to spare him the embarrassment, I nevertheless wanted him to commit himself, and, accordingly, I was not preventing him from talking.

"You heard what she said," went on father, "that night at the party. . . ." He paused, on the verge of an absolute commitment, still balancing alternatives. "Well, maybe she exaggerated a little," he smiled self-consciously, as if to make the truth seem less than the truth; "she was drunk, she wanted to make trouble . . .

"I don't know why I'm telling you this. But I don't want you to think that I'm hiding anything from you." He had taken fresh courage; I felt myself shrinking from our intimacy. "I know we've both hidden a lot from each other. It isn't right, Bernard. . . . It shouldn't be like that. We should have absolute trust in each other. You shouldn't ever be afraid to come to me. If there's anything you need, if there's anything you want to say, or to confide in me . . . We should be absolutely open with each other."

"No, please, pa, don't talk about her." I did not want to

hear more. I was trembling inwardly and there were tears in my eyes. I knew now that I had reached the point of honesty with him. And yet in that very moment I could feel the beginning of a sense of disappointment—he had, after all, avoided talking about Minna.

"All right," replied my father, as if only to please me, "I won't say any more." He moved away and sat back on the bed. He was silent for a moment, and I saw that he was breathing very slowly; it seemed to me that he was carefully expelling—and concealing—a sigh of relief. "But tell me," he brought out suddenly, "how does she live? Does she have a decent life?"

"Yes . . . she has," I faltered, my disappointment growing in me. "She wasn't really drunk that night . . . just excited."

He smiled. "It's all right, I understand. You know, you seem to have changed, you seem to understand certain things better. . . ." He yawned briefly; I saw by his wrist watch that it was after midnight. The house and the neighborhood were quiet. In the pauses of our talk there were now empty stretches of time. I felt that he wanted to end the conversation. "Well, tell me, do you still plan to see her? I want you to know I have no objection. . . ."

"No. I won't see her any more," I answered, resenting his generosity.

"Not on my account," insisted father. "Don't say that because you think I want you to."

"I'm saying it because *I* want to. I won't see her any more."

"Well, and Willy? Is she going to marry him?"

"No. They're breaking up."

"Ah-ha!" he cried, slapping his thigh in satisfaction. "I could have told you that in the first place. I knew that man would never settle down."

The vestige of an old loyalty to Minna had not permitted

[278]

me to mention her marriage to Mason. I was shocked to see how lightly my father had let himself off and regained his pride, adding the final self-esteem of a boast. And I had wanted to throw off my pride, even as he had appeared to be discarding his. It was too late now.

"Well, don't be so down-hearted," said my father, rising and running his hand over my head. The caress seemed an expression of gratitude for the lightness of his ordeal. "Cheer up and let's forget about it. . . . Of course, this won't go any farther. . . . I mean, we won't talk about it to anyone. . . ."

I showed my disappointment.

"What's the matter?" he asked, drawing himself up against any further encroachment on his pride.

Was this my father, the man who never spared himself, who shamed the world by the struggle he conducted with his conscience? "But I don't understand!" I objected. "How can you—"

"Ah, child, enough," he interrupted me with a final pat on the head. "We've had enough of this. I think you need a good night's rest. You look all worn out." And turning back at the door he remarked with a smile—was it mockery, or paternal pride in the exploits of a son?—"And no wonder, the way you've been running around. Now get to bed. You'll have plenty of time to knock around later!"

And was this what it all came to? I lay in bed, unable to sleep, regretting my homecoming and my interview with my father, which had established nothing. I might as well never have left, or never come back.

Was this childishness? Was it this which my father, and apparently the whole world with him, considered childish? I had wanted to make an absolute commitment of the truth I had discovered about myself. Our lives contain a secret, hidden from us. It is no more than the recognition of our failing; but to find it is all of courage, and to speak of it, the whole of truth. If this was an error of childishness, I was proud to be a child.

I felt myself suspended over the unmade declaration, the postponed scene of final understanding. I had been ready to follow my father into the peril of intimacy where we speak clearly and know one another all too well. I had been prepared to reveal all that I had grasped about myself, to confess all my guilt, my inability to be honest and clear.

Now, I thought, it was too late. I had put off declaring myself, only to have my father deprive me of my last opportunity. From now on I was bound to accept him without question—and if without fear, also without the knowledge that there lay some truth between us into which we both might enter. My only hope had been to confess that I did not love him, to admit I had never known what love was or what it meant to love, and by that confession to create it. Now it was too late. Now there would only be life as it came and the excuses one made to himself for accepting it.

This book is printed to last
on acid-free paper.